red
and the
the Wolf

VIVIENNE SAVAGE

Also By Vivienne Savage

DAWN OF THE DRAGONS

Loved by the Dragon

Smitten

Crush

THE WILD OPERATIVES

The Right to Bear Arms

Let Us Prey

The Purr-fect Soldier

Old Dog, New Tricks

THE WOLVES OF SAN ANTONIO

Training the Alpha

IMPRACTICAL MAGIC

Impractical Magic: A Halloween Prequel

Better Than Hex (Coming Soon)

MYTHOLOGICAL LOVERS

Making Waves

ADULT FAIRY TALES

Beauty and the Beast

Coming Soon

Goldilocks and the Bear

A Note from the Author

FAIRY TALES CAN be amazing things. After pouring my heart out into *Red and the Wolf*, I wondered how many people would expect the same old predictable story about *Little Red Riding Hood*. Wanting to do more than retell the same old story, I decided to make it a flipped fairy tale. This means that while the main elements of a wolf, girl in a red cloak, and grandmother remain prevalent themes in the story, the role of some characters may be reversed.

Although it is different, I do hope you'll enjoy it. It was a labor of love to bring you a story with as much epic adventure, magic, and developing romance as *Beauty and the Beast*. As the series continues, I promise to conclude each book with the happiest of definite endings like the tales you've grown up to love—with a little spice.

Prologue
14 Years Ago

FIVE LONG YEARS of battling for their lives upon curse-tainted land had driven shapeshifters and humans to merge their settlements. During that time, the people of Cairn Ocland mourned the loss of Dragon King Rua and Witch Queen Liadh, their rulers murdered by an enemy kingdom. The remaining heir, Prince Alistair, locked himself away within the castle a year later.

Then the Scourge arrived.

Oclanders called it an infestation at first, a plague infecting the very soul of their country as well as the animals within it. Despite the grim reality of the evil spirits lurking in the forests, Conall loved his homeland.

And so had his mother, until precious moments ago when a corrupted monstrosity cut her down in the city's residential square while dozens of human townsfolk hid inside their homes. No one had raised a finger in aid, each willing to bear witness to a good woman's death. What made their lives so much more important that they could not fight alongside their shapeshifter brethren?

His father demanded to know the same thing. Bradoc of Clan TalWolthe, the mighty and supreme alpha of every wolf pack across Cairn Ocland, trembled with rage as he addressed the small circle of city councilmen surrounding the campfire. The firelight glowed orange upon his massive frame, highlighting his chiseled jaw and hawkish nose.

"You could have helped her!" Bradoc roared. "You have bows and swords, yet you stand there quivering like petrified rabbits waiting to be eaten. All of you! What excuse do you have for watching as my mate was murdered to protect you, Matlock?"

"If Moira was no match for it, what makes you think we could? Have any of us her speed or strength? We would have been slaughtered!" Elder Matlock said.

Bradoc narrowed his eyes at the pudgy, balding man across from him. "How many of us must die so you can live? Look at all of you, five men for every one we have. Yet we fight."

"It's your place to guard us!" someone yelled from the crowd.

"Our place?" Bradoc repeated in a whisper. His voice raised, and his bearded face darkened to purple. "Our place? We are not your dogs! We are not your slave beasts! And now, now we are no longer your neighbors. See how well you fare without Clan TalWolthe at your beck and call."

In all his life, Conall had never seen his father in such a rage. He watched the exchange, a mute observer to the argument between the wolves and the human leader.

That was it. The humans gave no apologies or remorse for their cowardice. His mother would never come back, her unappreciated sacrifice given for nothing.

Matlock wiped his sweaty brow with a silken kerchief. "You can't possibly be serious, Bradoc. How will your wolves survive without us? You need us as much as we need you.

Calbronnoch is the last remaining city that hasn't fallen to the Scourge, and you'd be a fool to take your people away."

"We are just the same as you. We hunt. We farm. *We* will survive without you, but can *you* survive without us?" Bradoc sneered. "I doubt it. The true men among you died with our king and queen."

"You can't do this!" Elder Matlock cried.

"We'll all be slaughtered in our beds!"

"Please, don't leave us. I beg you!" another elder pleaded while wringing her hands. "Who will protect us with you gone?"

"Learn to protect yourselves."

Even as humans pleaded and begged forgiveness, the mighty alpha's stern expression never softened. He turned his back on the humans and strode across the courtyard. Each alpha of the seven individual packs followed, creating a procession from the meeting fire. As the immutable clan leader, Bradoc had earned their loyalty.

Conall moved close to his father's side and walked tall beside him. As tall as any ten-year-old child could walk following the death of his mother.

"What will happen if we leave them, Da'?"

"They'll learn to fight their own battles, or they will die. Whatever course they take, it's no longer our concern. We will never again be their shield. So hurry, and take only what you can carry on your back. I want every wolf pack gone before sunrise."

Chapter 1

A FRIGID BREEZE WHISPERED between the forest branches, tossing the brunette waves of hair spilling from beneath Sorcha's green hood.

The unusual weather had put her entire clan on edge and disrupted the natural cycle of death and regrowth. Snow littered every inch of the ground, and woodland animals lurked on the forest floor and scampered through the thinned branches while the world around them lingered in a suspended state of winter.

"What I wouldn't give to see a few flowers in bloom," Sorcha's mother said. "Do you suppose it'll be green to the east, Aengus?"

Her father shook his head. "Doubtful. This weather's not natural, I tell you. It just isn't natural." The older man's red brows drew closely together as he studied the skies. "Winter should be long over and spring upon us now."

"Nothing's been natural for years," Sorcha muttered. "The lifting of the curse hasn't changed that. Too many creatures were tainted."

"And people," her mother murmured.

A shiver snaked down Sorcha's spine at the memory of the last ghoul they'd encountered. That unfortunate soul had once been human before dark magic twisted it into an evil spirit.

Fortunately, putting down aberrations was what Clan Dunrathi did best.

Years ago, during the war between Cairn Ocland and Dalborough, they had lost more than their beloved rulers. They had lost their land to an insidious curse woven by their invader's court wizard. It tainted the ground, the curse spreading cancerous growths throughout the forests and countryside and turning harmless creatures into flesh-eating monsters known as the Scourge.

It seemed like only yesterday when Dragon King Alistair slew the wizard and shattered the curse to restore peace to their kingdom. Unfortunately, the damage had been done. While some areas of Cairn Ocland flourished green and vibrant beneath the sun, the curse clung tenaciously to the forests and outer edges of the kingdom.

The worst of the creatures went to ground, sensing their days were numbered.

Those were the creatures Sorcha's clan hunted, seeking them in caves and desolate farms. They searched the deep marshes and dark places for signs of the sickness rebounding.

"Look! I can see the castle from here!" Sorcha called.

The castle dominated the mountain peak, spires stretching to the sky like golden fingers reaching toward the heavens. Sorcha stared up at it, caught by the breathtaking beauty. Late afternoon sunlight gleamed burnished red on the gilded turrets and winked against glass panes.

"C'mon, we'll be there before dark falls if we press hard," her father said. He spurred his horse forward and led the way.

"You heard him, laddies. Let's get going." Sorcha flicked

the reins to the two large draft horses hitched to their wagon. They nickered and started after her father's stallion. The wheels creaked as they moved across the uneven ground, but eventually they reached a wide swath of smooth dirt road lined with large boulders. They ascended the mountain in record time, and Sorcha got her first good look at the heart of their kingdom.

Dozens of lanterns illuminated the winding road, each hung from an iron post. Sorcha stood on the seat as they passed one, leaning close to peer at the glowing stones inside the decorative holders. Each fist-sized stone glowed pale blue and emitted subtle warmth.

"Get down from there," Egan hissed. Her twin brother glared at her from his buckskin gelding.

"I was just looking. You'd think I was nicking the damned things." She dropped back down to the bench.

"Don't mess with a dragon's belongings," Egan said in a curt tone as he rode by to join her parents in the lead. She stuck her tongue out once his back was to her.

They passed a flourishing orchard with an impressive variety of trees, but she only recognized apple among their vast number. A large fountain came into view on the other side of the trees, and water streamed from a pail held by the stately figure depicted by the granite statue.

Every foot of the grounds appeared more exquisite than the last.

"On foot from here," her father called out. He dismounted first then helped her mother down, even kissing her cheek once his wife was on level ground. "There you are, beautiful."

Her mother reddened and stole a kiss in return.

After twenty years of marriage, they still giggled and blushed at each another like newlyweds. It was the kind of relationship Sorcha wanted one day—true love and happiness, a man who treated her as an equal and a beloved bride.

Sorcha sighed and climbed down from the wagon to stretch out her stiff limbs.

Once they had secured the horses, Aengus and Margaret Dunrathi led the way through the tall gates into the courtyard. Sorcha followed their example by walking tall and proud beside her twin, resisting the urge to look around and gape like a child. Egan nudged her and nodded toward the castle.

Queen Anastasia waited by the castle doors, and Sorcha had to wonder if she'd witnessed their approach through her fabled spyglass. Rumors claimed the queen owned an immense telescope at the top of her highest tower, and with it, she saw the ills of the world below.

Sorcha both envied and admired their ruler. Her glorious red hair resembled fire beneath the setting sun, glittering in a cascade of loose waves and beaded braids. She wore the colors of her husband's clan—bold forest green tartan draped over shoulders bared by a sleeveless gold dress.

Although they were mere commoners, the queen greeted them with a courteous bow. "Welcome to Castle TalDrach."

Powerful wingbeats blew back Sorcha's hood and tossed her hair into her face. A majestic dragon, covered from the tip of his tail to the end of his snout in glittering ruby scales, settled down behind the queen.

Sorcha stared. She'd never met either ruler before, though she knew of other hunters who had fought alongside them during the reclamation of Cairn Ocland. She froze, speechless and unable to utter a greeting until Egan elbowed her.

She dipped into the lowest curtsy she could muster in the presence of their royalty, but her knees trembled at the sight of the dragon, and she feared tumbling over onto the stone path.

"Please rise. There's no need for that," the king said. His chuckle stirred the air around them, blowing warm heat.

Though she'd met many shapeshifters over the years, beings ranging from wolves to massive snow lynxes, she'd never seen anything so majestic or powerful as a dragon. Her mother claimed King Alistair to be one of the last.

"It is my honor to meet you both again," the king spoke in a deep, rumbling voice. "I appreciate the timely visit, Aengus. It's been too long."

"Aye, it has, my king. I fondly recall our hunt on your fourteenth birthday. No one since has taken down a wyvern as cleanly as you."

King Alistair grinned, revealing over a dozen teeth longer than sabers. They gleamed in the lantern light. "Welcome but unnecessary flattery, my friend. Now, who are these two in your company?"

Her father set a hand on her left shoulder, the other on her brother's right. "Our children, Sorcha and Egan. They were but tots when we last met."

Despite the many tales her father had told over the campfire, she had never quite believed his claims, thinking them exaggerations meant to entertain and inspire hope. She must have been small indeed to not remember meeting a young man able to shift into a dragon.

"You have both certainly grown. I can remember a time when you wouldn't quite reach my knee."

The queen touched a hand against her husband's massive arm and gazed up at him. "They don't reach your knee now, my love."

King Alistair shifted, shrinking down to the form of an attractive human within seconds. He stood taller than her father, and red hair reached his broad shoulders, making him and his wife a matched pair. "Apologies. It's been a long day, and I forget if she doesn't remind me."

Sorcha had never seen a man so handsome or perfect to the eye. As he was her king and quite taken, she quickly averted her gaze to her booted feet.

"Come, you must be eager for rest and a hot drink around the hearth," the queen said. "Your horses will be well tended to, I assure you."

"Thank you, Your Highness," Sorcha's mother said.

Both monarchs led them into the castle to an upper-level guest residence. They walked over lush carpets and passed beautiful paintings of Cairn Ocland's highlands and green countryside. Above them, multiple chandeliers shone with vibrant crystals, each one glittering brighter than the stars in the night sky.

At the rear of a great hall with carpeted floors, they encountered a curving staircase leading to the upper levels. Of the many doors, only three hung open to reveal the lavish interior.

The queen gestured to the open doors. "A room for each of you to recover your strength and rest as needed. Supper shall be served in an hour in the royal residence, and you're quite welcome to freshen up and join us if you'd like."

"You'll find bathing accommodations within each room,"

King Alistair said. He tugged his wife close with an arm around her waist. "As well as clothing inside the wardrobes. Take whatever you need and enjoy the hospitality of our home."

"We would be delighted to join you for dinner," her mother said for all of them. "Thank you."

Once the monarchs were gone, Margaret eyed both of her children. "We don't want to keep them waiting, so the both of you should be ready and presentable for royal company within a half hour."

"Of course, Mum," Egan said.

Sorcha nodded. "It'll only be a moment."

Once she'd stepped into her room and shut the door behind her, all common sense and good intentions evaporated. She stood awestruck and mute, unable to comprehend the elegance surrounding her.

For the first time in all her life, Sorcha had a room all to herself and no idea what to do while there. Normally when on the road, the four of them piled into a single inn room to save money. The rest of the time, they made camp around the wagon, crowding inside during the cold season.

She inspected the wardrobe first, delighted by the colorful garments within. Dresses hung beside soft leather pants and silken tunics. From there she skipped to the luxurious bathing chamber, where she marveled over the tub. It was deeper than anything she'd ever seen before, with piping to bring in water.

By the time her mother knocked to check in on her, she'd washed and dressed, donning fitted leather pants and a matching bodice. She admired her reflection in a handsome floor-length mirror framed with black wood, turning left and right to appreciate the cut of the garments.

It was if she'd chosen it out of a dressmaker's shop herself and had it tailored to her size.

"Honestly, Sorcha, couldn't you wear a dress for once?"

"I tried one onbut felt naked. No, thank you. Besides, who has time to fiddle with all those laces and tiny buttons?"

Her mother chuckled. "In another time, you would have run around in such things, buttons and all."

Sorcha leaned over and kissed her weathered cheek. "Maybe so, but this is the time we live in, and I'm content."

Her brother emerged resembling a dashing gentleman for once, though she was surprised to see their family's deep blue and purple patterned tartans clothing him and her father. She knew the king and queen had expected them, but what she didn't understand was how they'd had time to acquire Clan Dunrathi colors, or if they normally held such an assortment.

"The wardrobes must be charmed and enchanted. It is a magical castle after all, if all the rumors and tales are true. The entire thing was blessed by the hand of a fairy princess," her mother whispered.

"That explains it. Nothing short of magic could make a handsome man of my brother," Sorcha said.

"I'm plenty handsome," Egan muttered.

A radiant blonde woman clothed in clan green and gold awaited them at the end of the corridor. "Greetings to all of Clan Dunrathi." She dipped into a low curtsy. "I am Victoria, cousin of the queen. Ana asked if I would escort you to dinner."

"You have our gratitude, Lady Victoria," Aengus said. His eyes lingered long enough for Sorcha's mother to elbow his ribs, but he snapped out of it. "My wife Margaret and our twins, Sorcha and Egan."

"The pleasure is all mine, my lady," Egan said. His low bow struck Sorcha as absurd.

With a bright smile on her face, Victoria led the family up a flight of stairs to the upper level where the king and queen resided in their royal suites. The atmosphere changed from regal and elegant to… a sensation of home she never experienced without visiting her grandmother's cottage.

How she envied them. The life of a hunter was never easy, requiring sacrifices made each day they were on the trail. But she longed for a home and wanted to be like the settlers, farmers, and villagers who reclaimed their lost land.

She passed a child's doll and stepped over a few other toys before a long-legged hound sprang past them in the hall. Then a little one squealed.

"He'll come back," Anastasia consoled the crying child.

"But I wanna play with him now."

They entered a smaller receiving room warmed by a roaring hearth, the fireplace surrounded by many furnishings designed to seat several people at once. Knitted blankets covered the back of the settee, and a thick quilt in beautiful shades of green and earthy brown had been tossed over a heavy armchair across from it.

Unlike her father, Sorcha had never set eyes on the previous Cairn Ocland rulers, but she recognized them by description in one of the two portraits hung above the hearth. King Alistair and his father resembled one another closely, but his mother's dark hair fell around her shoulders like an oil slick. In the next picture, the current king and queen posed with their toddler and a newborn infant.

Sorcha glanced at the round dining table to see both

smiling monarchs sitting beside one another. Alistair stood and greeted them as if they were equals, but Anastasia remained seated while nursing the same copper-haired infant from the recent family portrait.

"I'm so glad you could join us," the queen called. "Please, come sit. You must be starving from your long journey to the mountains. Supper shall be served soon enough."

It felt so personal a welcome, more than Sorcha had expected from their country's royalty.

Once the king returned to his chair, the couple's eldest child, no older than four, scrambled onto his lap and hugged his neck.

"Daddy, I want dessert."

"You've eaten dessert, and it's now time for your bed, little one."

"I don't want to."

Alistair chuckled. "But you must, Elspeth. How will you rule as a just and fair queen like your mother if you don't rest to grow strong?"

"Awww."

"It's true," Victoria added. "Come on, wee lass. I'll read you a story."

The little girl's sulk vanished, replaced by an eager smile as Victoria took her by the hand and led her away.

Once the child was gone, a trio of servants entered with a cart bearing several silver platters with covered dishes. They set the table at once, poured heavy flagons of mead, and left as quietly as they entered.

Sorcha's mouth watered at the sight of grilled fish on a bed of vegetables, slices of rare roast beef, and fluffy rolls glazed in honey. The rich aroma assaulted her at once. One by one, they took servings from each of the delectable dishes.

Every flavor exploded against her tongue, a symphony of exquisite spices and unfamiliar delights she'd never tasted. By the end, Sorcha had filled her belly too much to easily remain upright in the chair.

"More mead?" King Alistair asked her.

"No, no, Your Majesty. I couldn't possibly."

"As grateful as we are for your benevolence, I'm certain there were more pressing matters on your mind when you sent our invitation to meet you." Aengus grinned.

"I've a favor to ask of you."

"Anything, Your Highness."

King Alistair gave him a tight smile. "You might not be so willing once you've heard what I ask, Aengus."

"Just the same, let us hear it."

"Very well. The Shadow Glen on our southwestern border remains the final holdout of Rangvald's curse. It will take the effort of many to rid our country of these abominations, but our people are still scattered. It took me all this time to find you in the northern woods."

Aengus grinned. "To be fair, we are good at hiding, Your Grace."

"That you are, but you're also good at finding, which is why I ask your help to locate the remaining clans. We will need every hunter we can find if we wish to retake the Shadow Glen."

"Why not raze it to the ground?" Egan asked.

Sorcha kicked him under the table. "Hasn't the curse taken enough from us, brother? Those woods are as much a part of Ocland as this castle or the lowlands. They're part of our great kingdom."

"Precisely that," the king said. He grimaced. "But in a desperate moment, I did try, and we've discovered even dragon's breath is no match for the dark magic there. Slaying Rangvald was only the first step to cleanse our land of his filth. According to my wife, curses are tenacious things."

"But that isn't all," the queen added. "I sense there is something else in the glen, something more powerful than Rangvald himself. When I tried to gaze through my spyglass, I found much of the kingdom shrouded from me by a haze of shadows."

"With all due respect," Sorcha's mother said, "you have an army, Your Grace."

"This is true, but while our armies slept under a fairy curse, the clans tackled the wilderness and learned to survive. My men are by no means soft or weak, but they are ill-trained, even now after five years, to take on what the hunters have seen. We need you more than ever, my friends."

"Some have ventured into the southern territories," Sorcha said. "A few years after the curse was cast, many clans decided Cairn Ocland was lost."

The king bowed his head. "Yes. I failed my people then, and I know that. It's time to set things to rights. Time to bring our people home and restore this kingdom to what it once was."

Her father nodded. "We'll do it. I know many will be happy to assist with spreading your word."

"Thank you, Aengus. When we have enough people to safely forge ahead, we will cut through to the heart of the

Shadow Glen and purge the remaining evil."

Following shared drinks around the hearth, Sorcha had excused herself to her bedchamber while her father remained to reminisce with the king. Someone had lit the fire in her room, so she was greeted by cozy warmth and the shimmer of flames reflected against the stained-glass window

Part of her hated knowing they would be leaving by morning, and part of her couldn't imagine living in such luxury. Not that it would ever become a problem. Her family had no home of their own.

Before she could make progress with unfastening her bodice, a knock interrupted her plans. She eyed the door, expecting her brother to be up to some mischief and wanting to drag her along. Instead, she found the queen and startled back a step.

"Your Majesty?"

"Hello," Queen Anastasia replied, a warm smile on her face. She didn't appear any older than Sorcha, but shifters and their bondmates aged differently. "May we speak for a moment?"

What had she done? Had she broken some high-society rule or kingdom law? Had she stared at the handsome monarch too long during dinner when the alcohol clouded her mind?

Sorcha thought to herself this would be the moment of her death, struck dead by lightning for daring to appreciate the attractive qualities of a witch's husband. She quelled the shaking of her hands and nodded, mute. She shut the door after Queen Anastasia strode inside then turned to face their powerful ruler. The regal woman stood straight and tall, blue eyes glittering within a flawless, oval face.

"How m-may I serve, Your Highness?"

"Do you fear me?"

In all her life, she'd never been alone with a spellcaster, especially one with the power to take on an enemy kingdom's entire army. "I'd be lying, and foolish if I said no. You're not only my queen but a sorceress. You could turn me inside out with a word. Or into a frog with a gesture of your pinky."

Laughter bubbled out of the queen, and it was musical. Almost magical in itself. The stories claimed her to be part fae, and having spoken with her up close, Sorcha was positive she'd heard the truth.

"Dear, you need not be afraid of me. I've come as a friend, an interested friend, you might say."

Her brows shot up. "I'm not sure I understand, Your Grace."

"Call me Anastasia."

"Anastasia," Sorcha repeated, testing the word on her tongue.

"Splendid. Over these past few years, I've had the opportunity to read through the journals and notes left behind by my husband's mother. She used to trade with your grandmother for rare herbs."

"I had no idea, though it doesn't surprise me. Granny collects all manner of herbs and roots during our travels. Well, she used to anyway. She doesn't leave home often anymore."

"I wondered if you might take something to her for me, for a trade if she's able."

Sorcha dipped her chin. "I imagine we'll be returning to

check on her after the king's task is completed."

"Ah, yes, about that." Anastasia spread her hands out. "The herbs I require are for a ritual, which I hope will aid us in cleansing the Shadow Glen. I thought, perhaps, you might handle my task while the rest of your family sees to my husband's request."

"You mean go on my own?"

Anastasia's smile broadened. "It's fair weather for a ride to the east, isn't it?"

"I suppose so."

"How long has it been since you've seen her?"

"Close to three months. We normally take wine and cake to her once a month, but the season has been busy."

"Then it must be time to pay a visit to her again soon, wouldn't you say?"

As tempting as it would be to take on a solo task for their queen, Sorcha doubted her father would allow her to split from their group. He'd create an excuse as always for them to remain together or blather about the dangers of the road. She frowned. Wasn't she a member of Dunrathi too? Couldn't she fight as well as any other hunter?

"I'll do it," she agreed, giving it no further consideration.

"Excellent." The queen reached within her robes and removed a folded square of red fabric, its bold color brighter than blood. She shook it out, and before Sorcha's eyes, it opened to reveal an immense scarlet cloak lined in lush silk. "Then this is for you. May it keep you warm and during your travels."

"My queen, I couldn't take th—"

"You can and you shall. You're on an official errand for

me, and all shall know it." She leaned forward and winked. "Besides, maybe that will discourage any brigands from waylaying you. No one wants to anger a dragon. Or a sorceress."

"But TalDrach colors are green and gold."

"The colors of our royal messengers are red, however."

"Thank you." She took the crimson cloak and held it against her chest. "I'll wear it proudly, Your Gr—Anastasia."

"Lovely. I'll let you get your rest and speak with you again in the morning. Breakfast is served at eight, and lunch by noon. As I said to your mother, you're all welcome to join us for either."

With a gracious bow to her guest, Queen Anastasia stepped into the hall, leaving Sorcha to marvel at her luck.

The king didn't join them for breakfast, but Anastasia met them at the table with her two little ones and chatted animatedly about the provinces and where she'd spied the different shifter groups.

"It's been hard to find them, let me tell you," the queen said between bites of food.

"They keep to themselves, Your Grace, and don't like dealing with humankind. The wolves especially," Egan said.

Anastasia sighed softly. "Alistair tells me it was once different."

"It was," Sorcha's mother agreed. "But without a ruler, the shifter clans grew distant and looked after their own skin, and we can hardly blame them. Times were difficult for all."

A servant stepped into the room and hurried to Anastasia. He leaned close and whispered in her ear, and a vivid smile spread across her serene features. "The groom has prepared your wagon, hitched your beasts, and provisioned each of you with travel rations. But please," she said as she rose from the table, "take as much time as you need to refresh yourselves prior to your undertaking. If you'll excuse me, I must seek my husband."

The door shut seconds later, and Sorcha sprang her news. "Mother, Father, I'm not going with you."

"Don't be ridiculous, Sorcha." Egan scowled at her. "What are you going to do? Stay here and stuff yourself like a gluttonous pig?"

She met her twin's gaze with a cool stare. "Far from it. The queen requires a rider and has personally asked me to serve as her messenger."

Her parents exchanged startled looks.

"What do you mean, Sorcha?" her mother asked.

"Did you know Granny once worked with the old witch queen? Well, I've been asked to get some special herbs for Queen Anastasia. Things to help with the Shadow Glen. Look, she's given me a messenger cloak." She pulled the scarlet silk from her bag and shook it out.

Her mother placed a hand on her husband's arm. "Aengus, a task from the queen. We cannot deny that."

His frown didn't budge. "I don't like the idea of you going alone. Take your brother then. Your mother and I will make do on our own if we must."

The panic clawed through her insides at once, twisting her belly into knots. It was her adventure, and she had no desire to share the honor with her twin. This mission was one thing she wanted for herself.

"No. Egan will be more useful to your mission. Especially since he has a connection to the lynxes in the Blyden Mountains. I, on the other hand, will be doing nothing but returning home to deliver a package for Queen Anastasia."

"It's no place for a young woman to travel alone."

"I agree with Father. It's simply too dangerous."

"Egan!"

"What? I'm only telling the truth," her twin argued. "You'll be eviscerated and left for dead by some awful creature. We both know you can't shoot the broad side of a red-painted barn."

"My aim is just fine! Better than yours, if I recall. Who was it who nearly allowed himself to be gored by a wild boar?"

Hot patches of color appeared on Egan's cheeks. "I'd run out of bolts!"

"Hardly an excuse," Sorcha retorted.

"Enough. Your brother will accompany you. That's final."

Her heart dipped into her stomach, hopes of independence and freedom abolished.

Her mother rose and slammed her hand against the table. The loud thump made her father flinch. "If you wouldn't do it to Egan, you won't do it to her. She's twenty-two now, a grown woman capable with all of her weapons. More importantly, she's passed her trials and needs no approval from either you or me to take off on her own."

"Margaret—"

"She will go and do as she pleases. If our queen has faith in her, why shouldn't we?"

"I'm old enough to go on my own, and the roads are safe now," Sorcha said.

Her father's mouth stretched into a disapproving line.

"Fine. *Safer.*" She raised her chin and refused to break eye contact. "Would you prefer to upset the queen? The king?"

"Certainly not."

"Then let me do this, Father. I want to."

He stared at her for another minute. Each time he opened his mouth to speak, he closed it again without a word. The staring contest ended with a resigned sigh from her father. "So be it."

Chapter 2

CONTRARY TO HER father's fears, Sorcha encountered no dangers, beasts, or abominations. She rose by day and made camp by night, rolling out a blanket beneath the stars beside a campfire then rousing early with the dawn.

The crimson cloak troubled her at first, and then she grew accustomed to it. As a hunter, she preferred muddy brown, olive green, and other bleak colors intended to blend with her environment. The brilliant red color left her feeling exposed, but so far, no harm had come, and other travelers had greeted her courteously. In fact, they'd practically groveled at her feet, recognizing her as a member of the royal court.

Giddiness raced through her each time an encounter ended with kind words. A young couple with a trio of tots ranging from two to seven invited her into their home for the night when she cut through one of the newly established villages. Later she crossed paths with another pair of hunters from Clan Kolbroch.

Citizens of Cairn Ocland were usually kind to one another—especially the hunters who protected them—but the presence of her red cloak inspired admiration.

Sunlight slanted in through the barren branches over her head, spearing narrow beams of golden light through the green glow. Put on edge by the lack of birdsong, her nape prickled, and the sensation of being watched crept over her.

Years of traveling alongside her parents told her tranquil and serene no longer had any place in their forests.

Growing warier by the second but just as stubborn, Sorcha straightened in the saddle. She placed a hand on the hilt of her sword then let her gaze dart over the surrounding woodland. A green flicker met her vision, the eye shine of a tremendous creature.

The wolf had to be one of the most beautiful she'd ever laid eyes on. His russet coat gleamed in the muted light, and his bright blue eyes followed her. Only a werewolf could be so large, and with prey animals being in short supply, a normal wolf might have mistaken her and Eachann as food.

Sorcha loosened her grip on her sword. The shifter's presence explained the silence in the woods. While the werewolves of Cairn Ocland didn't often deal with the humans, she also knew his presence didn't present a threat. Her father had taught her they were noble creatures with long memories, lethal once crossed but loyal to only their own people.

Without slowing her pace, she acknowledged him with a moment of eye contact and coaxed Eachann to continue. All the while her gelding trotted down the road, she imagined a handsome man hidden beneath the fur. Would his hair blaze with the same golden highlights beneath the sun?

"If ever there was a fetching sight to my eyes, it would be you." A deep masculine voice pulled her away from her thoughts.

Sorcha schooled her features to hide her smile before twisting in her saddle. Coming in fast behind her, a black stallion of muscular proportions bore a rider of equally

Red & the Wolf

impressive stature. They were both broad-shouldered beasts with enormous girth, one adorned with brown studded leather molded from animal hides, the other in matching protective barding.

"It's rude to sneak up on people, Ferghus, or have you been in the woods so long your manners have been forgotten?" she teased.

"If I've taken you by surprise, then you shouldn't ride these paths alone, dear friend."

She pressed her lips together and stared down her nose at the grinning man. "I heard your damnable horse three miles back, as much noise as he's making. I only thought I should let you know it was a poor attempt."

His stallion danced into place beside Eachann, snorting steam and shaking his hunter's braids. The horse raised his massive hooves high with each step, as if strutting in lieu of the rider on his back.

And Ferghus did strut, the cocky bastard. Despite it, she adored him no less.

Much as she would adore a brother, contrary to her friend's desires to court her and seek her hand in marriage. If ever there were a more unsuitable suitor, it would be Ferghus. He'd pursued her for most of their adult lives, even asking her father's blessing as if they were one of those heathen kingdoms where men sold their daughters into marriage.

Aengus Dunrathi had left the decision in her hands while making it no secret he'd prefer for her to give Ferghus a chance. Egan, on the other hand, had threatened to disown her as a sister if she accepted.

"Perhaps you'd like for me to accompany you. You're

returning to Frosweik, aye?"

Sorcha rolled her eyes. "No thanks. I'm quite capable of making it to my grandmother's house on my own. I know the roads and require no nursemaid to monitor my actions, thank you very much. Did Father send you?"

Ferghus's deep belly laugh resonated in the air with genuine amusement and warmth. "No, and he didn't need to send me. The moment I heard you'd passed through Narth wearing the queen's red, I knew I had to come lend you my aid. The roads are dangerous, and there's a blizzard coming. You need me alongside you and should be *wanting* me there, lass."

"There is no such thing coming."

He leaned closer and plucked at the hem of her cloak. "That's not what the woodkin say."

"And what, pray tell, do the woodkin say?"

"There's a storm brewing. It'll be the fiercest one since the winter of Rangvald's curse. Of course, you and your brother were just wee bairns then so it would surprise me not if you're unable to remember. Now, what can I do to help you?"

Sorcha pressed her lips together and nudged her horse into a trot. "I'm fine alone. And you're hardly much older than Egan and me."

Ferghus stared at her from beneath his thick and bushy brows. "This is your answer then?"

Was it? A silent study of Ferghus took in the finer qualities of his appearance from his stoic features to his ash brown hair. He wore it shoulder length but drawn into a neat tail while on the hunting trail. His unshaven face sported a red beard, which was a bright contrast to eyes grayer than the dismal sky.

More than once, she'd wondered if marriage to Ferghus

could be a pleasant, modest life. Sorcha had always known she'd have to one day part from her mother and father's hunting party, or better yet, that they'd be absorbed into another group.

Would it be so bad to join Clan Dunrathi and Clan Corwell in marriage? There were worse men to choose than a hunter as loyal as her friend, who was skilled with a blade, bow, and knife. And when he wanted to be, Ferghus was downright charming, though those moments were tempered by his vanity.

As a child, he'd been the first of the hunter children to stand up for her when she fell behind in her training. He'd sparred hours with her after until she matched them in skill. Of all the other hunters born to their generation, she trusted Ferghus most.

But she didn't love him—not the love required for a marriage at least. As much as she cared for her friend, he didn't stir her heart or her desires. "It is, just as it always has been, no," she said in a gentle voice.

The smile faded from his face, replaced by a frown. He looked away.

They traveled alongside one another for a few paces, neither speaking nor making eye contact. He averted his gaze from her entirely and focused on the path ahead.

To their rear, a wolf howled, and she wondered if it was her handsome red and ivory beast. Ferghus glanced over his shoulder and scowled.

"Fine then," he spoke when they reached the bend. "But you should take care on the road. The wolves are riled, venturing closer and closer to our camps. They won't be scared off by your red cloak. If you ever need me when we cross paths again... Well, I'll be there for you with no strings attached, Sorcha. I wish the best for you."

He spurred his stallion and raced past her, pounding down the road. His loud exit scattered a flock of ravens, and as they circled overhead like a dark omen, Sorcha wondered if their friendship would survive her refusal.

Conall lowered his nose to the damp earth and breathed in the scent of moist leaves, black soil, and evil. He'd been tracking his quarry for days, barely stopping for rest until his body gave out and forced him to hunt for food. He slept infrequently, determined to press on until the little voice of reason demanded him to stop.

A flicker of white light darted past his right shoulder. "How are you going to kill *anything* when you haven't eaten in two days?" the fairy's tiny voice asked.

The wolf raised his head and sat back on his haunches. He frowned at the fairy as much as his wolven muzzle would allow then shifted to his human form. A wolf one second, a man in the next, he ran his fingers through his auburn hair and remained sitting on the ground.

"I ate a rabbit yesterday, Tink."

Tinker Bell flashed crimson with indignation. "One whole rabbit for a big bad wolf like you? You stupid ass. If an aberration doesn't kill you, starvation will."

He rolled his eyes and pushed up off the ground. "All right, *Mother*."

Shifters, like Conall, with command over their abilities, always transformed with their clothing and belongings intact.

They didn't appear in his wolf form unless he willed it, but they always returned with his human body. The unexplainable act of magic came as natural as breathing.

"I take it you're bringing up food because you saw something."

"I did. There are quail in the bushes," she announced proudly. The weightless woodkin landed on his shoulder and muted her glow to a dull sparkle.

In no mood to devour his meal as an animal, he shot a pair of quail with his bow instead and cooked them over a fire. Tink had her own ideas of how hard he should push himself to catch the elusive aberration hunting his clan's wolves.

And as the alpha, it was up to him to protect them, even at the risk of his own safety. He couldn't remember the last time he'd had a full night's rest, but if he fell in battle, he'd prefer if it wasn't due to exhaustion.

"You should have brought others," she chided

Conall grunted. "There weren't enough of the others. They'll be needed there to protect their families if the beast loops back around to our territory."

He was among the strongest of the shifters in Clan TalWolthe, but even he didn't know what kind of creature he'd tracked from the boundaries of their land. And since it left no survivors to describe its appearance, the beast's entire existence had been shrouded in mystery.

Despite the worries on his mind, his lids felt heavy. His eyes fluttered open again as he battled against the weight falling over his limbs. Exhaustion crashed over him like a tidal wave, and his head fell back against the tree behind him.

"Sleep. I'll keep watch." She fluttered up from her perch

VIVIENNE SAVAGE

on his shoulder, winking between shades of tranquil blue and green.

"Did you...did you fairydust...me?" His words slurred, and then he slipped down onto his side, the ground cushioned only by dead leaves.

"Maybe," she replied, drawing out the word.

"Gonna...gonna swat you when I get up."

"You do that." A cool touch alighted against his cheek. "Sleep well, Conall."

He awakened hours later with the dawn sun upon his face, beams of light filtering through the half-barren branches above where tenacious orange and gold leaves clung.

Spring should have been fully upon them, but ice crystals blanketed the ground in a fine sheen of glittering white. He gazed up at a dormant forest in shades of gray and a little fairy resting on his chest.

"Feel better?" she asked.

He grunted, too proud to admit she was right. Tink's glow shifted to vibrant orange, accompanied by chiming laughter gentler than bells.

"You need a bath."

"Aye, well, that isn't happening any time soon. Haven't seen a creek deep enough to submerge even my ankles."

"A village lies nearby."

A human village. "No," he snapped. "I won't be going into the village, and that is that."

The little woodkin huffed and flew from his chest. "Fine. Where to now?"

"We continue following the trail. The beast will kill again."

"More reason to head toward the village," she argued. "It's

a good place to strike."

"Except this beast hasn't killed any humans," he spat. "There's a bear clan to the east. I'll check there."

The dull sound of hooves on dirt caught his attention. He shifted and maneuvered behind a tree. Tink fluttered down to his head, taking her preferred perch behind his left ear. He listened with head cocked to the side as the hoofbeats of a single, unhurried rider neared them. Eventually, the horse came into view around the bend.

Without a doubt, she had to be the most beautiful woman to ever cross his path. Her hair fell dark as a raven's wing, the ink-black color of the night sky. She rode upon a chestnut gelding and wore red.

And he knew what red meant. While he had little to do with Clan TalDrach and had only met King Alistair once in passing, he knew the favored color of the queen.

The royal messenger followed the eastern path at a sedate pace, and only once did they make eye contact. In the stark and barren forest awaiting the touch of spring, his red and ivory coat provided no camouflage.

"Aren't you in a hurry?" Tinker Bell whispered.

He ignored her and shook the fairy off.

As much as Conall loved his companion, she'd run off enough potential mates. Not that the unfamiliar royal messenger was compatible with him. Humans and shifters never mixed well these days, their lifestyles too different and the animosity between them too great. He suppressed the possessive surge of desire, the force of it striking him with all the intensity of a fist to the gut.

Tink tugged one of his ears. "Hello, hello! You have a job

to do, Conall."

A low growl rumbled in his chest, but the little woodkin was right. He didn't have time to pursue pretty women. Turning away, he put the red-cloaked rider from his mind and headed back into the tree line with his nose to the ground. Dirt and old pine needles shifted beneath his massive paws.

A rotten stench clung to the lowest branches of a nearby pine. Closer inspection revealed a tuft of multicolored fur caught against a spined pinecone. Whatever his quarry was, it wasn't mindful of its surroundings.

He almost missed the second scent on the breeze, a sour note under the rot. Tink bristled in warning at the same moment a twig snapped behind him.

Conall twisted around and snarled out a challenge at the creature charging from the forest. Malformed, bony growths protruded from the animal's spine and resembled disfigured wings. The peryton reared to its hind legs, and Conall easily avoided its sickle-shaped front hooves before either could cleave into his body.

While many creatures had been able to fight off the corruption, the weakest of them fell to the darkness and arose as something new and different. It may have once been a deer, but only the antlered head resembled the peaceful, herbivorous creature it originated from.

And it wanted his flesh.

Conall snarled in defiance and loosed his magic with a howl, channeling a single powerful gust that forced the peryton back a few steps and blew snow into its eyes.

Tink darted into the peryton's face, a buzzing red blur it couldn't avoid or catch. Playing the part of the distraction, she threw out ember-hot sparks and gave Conall the advantage he needed against the antlered aberration.

He dove in against the creature's side and sprung back as quickly. Back and forth he went, never stopping, snapping at the fell deer's hindquarters. With Tink's help, they drove the creature over a dried creek bed, where its hooves had no balance or grip on the rocks.

The moment it tumbled over, he lunged and seized it by the neck, biting down and plunging his teeth into the unprotected throat. It gurgled and thrashed as the hot taste of its life flooded his mouth, as abhorrent and disgusting as ever.

Once the body ceased twitching, Conall stepped away from it. He found a nearby stream to wash the monster's blood from his face, chest, and paws, thankful the corruption didn't spread by contact.

That would have been too evil and would have devastated the shifters who often learned to fight with tooth and claw before they were taught to ever raise a weapon.

No, the sickness plaguing Cairn Ocland was an illness of the soul, and while their monarchs had cured the disease five years ago, remnants of its symptoms remained like insidious scars defacing the land.

"You should bathe while you're here," Tink suggested.

Lest she harass him for the rest of their journey, he took her advice, stripped, and waded into the water. The cold temperature raised goosebumps over his skin.

Tink waited on a rock. "Aren't you glad you listened to me?"

"Think of how much gladder I'd be if you weren't an obnoxious gnat," he retorted, too noble to shiver in the frigid spring.

She laughed, her ever-present glow shifting from yellow to pink then back again.

Conall's scowl faded into a grin. "Put yourself to some good use and do something with my clothes."

"Very well," the nature spirit agreed.

Tink washed his tunic and tartan while he scrubbed in the frigid water. By the time he emerged a few minutes later, the little woodsprite had pulled both garments from the chilly creek, wrung them out, and draped them upon a branch to dry with magic.

He shook dry in wolf form before donning clothes scented with a liberal dose of fairydust. He sighed at her without voicing a word of complaint, deciding there were worse smells to carry on his person than the essence of nature itself.

After donning freshened clothes, he set out on all fours again and passed the eastern road for a second glimpse of the red rider. Although he'd hoped for a chance to make her acquaintance, he stopped in his tracks. She wasn't alone and had been joined by another huntsman. Typical.

Any thought he had of engaging her in conversation on the trail vanished, though it was probably for the best.

After all, humans and shifters belonged to different worlds, and too many years had passed since they broke ties.

Chapter 3

As Sorcha approached her grandmother's house, the still and silent forest raised fine hairs on the back of her neck. A few miles back there had been bird song at least, and she'd seen fat squirrels scampering through the trees.

Now there was nothing. Dry leaves and dead grass crunched beneath her booted feet, but as she came around to the front of the cottage, she saw the door hanging askew on its hinges. The wooden panel had been shattered, splinters of it lying on the porch.

Her palms grew sweaty as she ascended the wooden stairs.

They'd been asking her grandmother to move into the village for years to rejoin the others, but of course, old Granny had a dozen reasons to refuse their requests. Her husband had built her little cottage in the woods when they were young, newly married sweethearts. They'd raised their children in the home, and she'd die there before she abandoned it to the wilderness.

Had Granny's prediction come true?

With her heart in her throat, Sorcha stepped through the door and into a nightmare. Grisly puddles of fresh blood pooled over the wooden floorboards, splashes of it against the unfinished blanket on the floor beside the hearth. The last embers still glowed cheery spots of red warmth against the ashen remnants.

A table had been overturned, spilling a bowl of winter fruits across the floor. Several laysplit open or mashed into the floorboards, revealing the fleshy white interior. Her grandmother's rocker had been reduced to wooden fragments beside the hearth.

And amidst the wreckage stood the werewolf from the trail. Years of living in the forest had given Sorcha a keen eye for discerning between werewolves, their ordinary counterparts, or the mindless beasts tainted by Rangvald's curse. He stood twice as tall as a normal wolf, roughly the size of a small pony. His winter coat had already grown full and lush, making him seem much larger.

Blood still stained his muzzle, but he bore no signs of the corruption affecting other creatures in the wilds. Clear eyes, no bone spurs or spikes, no black saliva dripping from his maw.

Yet he had harmed Granny.

Although she'd yet to locate her grandmother's corpse, the likelihood of her surviving the loss of so much blood struck Sorcha as improbable.

Blinded by rage, she rushed forward with her sword drawn. The beast was bigger, but the narrow confines of the house were to her advantage. As her opponent tried to back away, she lunged and sliced her blade through the air. The razor-sharp edge drew a thin line of blood down the wolf's black nose.

Snarling and snapping, he evaded the next stroke from her sword, proving faster on his feet and more agile than she expected of so large a creature. She swung out with an arc meant to remove his head, but he lunged beneath it and rolled to the side. Then he darted and took the feet out from beneath her.

Sorcha screamed as she fell, but she wasn't helpless yet. She fired a bolt from her wristbow when the werewolf attempted to pin her, desperate to protect her throat from its massive teeth. If she allowed him to get her by the neck, if she lost her focus for even an instant, she'd share the same fate as her grandmother.

She couldn't allow that to happen, couldn't allow her father to be proven right.

Missing him, the bolt hit the ceiling instead. As the wolf flinched back, she struck at the opportune moment and landed the hard wedge of her boot heel into his nose. He reeled from the direct hit, granting her precious seconds to roll to her feet before he recovered.

The werewolf shifted, trading his large, furry shape for that of an equally large man. Sorcha had all of two seconds to process the change and take in his features before he was on her again. He yanked the sword from her grasp, and it clattered across the blood-speckled floor. Without her primary weapon, she kicked his chest.

"Murderer!"

"I—"

"You ate my grandmother, you monster!"

Everything within her reach became an improvised armament. Sorcha grabbed a stone candleholder and threw it at his head, followed by a chunk of wood halfway carved into a horse.

The shifter batted aside the first but took the second to the head and growled. Without wasting a second of her advantage, Sorcha charged forward and slammed into him. They hit the floor together and rolled, but her opponent's larger size gave him the upper hand.

The wolf-turned-man slammed her against the ground, hard enough to make stars spark across her vision and the world above her spin.

"I didn't hurt your grandmother! This is exactly as I found the cottage when I arrived."

For a normal human woman, she was strong; she'd dedicated all her adult life to battling creatures larger than her. She writhed beneath her opponent and broke his hold, bucking him up then bringing a knee between their bodies. In a matter of seconds, she maneuvered the same leg over his arm, twisted, and rolled the limb between her thighs in a crushing lock.

"Blasted woman!" he swore. She wrenched the joint, dislocating it in one sharp jerk before he could get a handle on the situation with his greater strength.

"I found you wallowing in her blood!"

"I tracked another beast to this location and it led me here. All you saw was me trying to identify the victim! I swear to you, lass, I had nothing to do with whatever happened."

"What good is your word to me?" She sneered and pulled on his arm again until he flinched.

"I swear it on my title as alpha, I caused you and yours no harm, nor do I plan to."

"Alpha? Who are you?"

"Conall of Clan TalWolthe."

Sorcha released the leglock, shoving him away before scrambling to her feet and recovering her sword from the ground. "My grandmother was here only hours ago, and now she's dead. There are still embers in the hearth."

The big shifter climbed to his feet as well, although his left arm hung lower than the right. "Have you found a body?"

"No, but—"

"Then she isn't dead."

She gestured with her sword, thrusting the tip toward the blood-stained rug. "Isn't dead? How could anyone survive after bleeding so much?"

"This is pig's blood."

"What?"

"This is pig's blood," he repeated. "I do believe the signs of battle are genuine, but whoever did this stinks of pig. And they've also taken your grandmother."

"Why would anyone splash pig's blood around after a kidnapping?"

"Perhaps for the exact reaction they received. You were ready to skewer me on sight." His eyes dropped to her sword before raising to her face again and holding eye contact.

"Of course, I did. I came in and found a wolf in my grandmother's bloodied house. What else was I to think?"

"Someone in your village would have pointed the finger at the shifters in time," he growled. "You know as well as I do that no normal wolf could make this mess. And no werewolf would have a reason to mangle a human woman's body. Why would we? We've got plenty prey of our own to devour in the woodlands. There's no reason for murder. We have no taste for human flesh."

  VIVIENNE SAVAGE

"I…" Given a moment to cool her head, his words made sense to her. "That doesn't explain why I found you in my granny's home. Why are you here?"

Conall touched his nose and wiped away the dried blood. The thin, superficial wound from her sword had already healed, leaving flawless skin in its place. "The same beast that took your grandmother slaughtered three of my kinsmen. I've tracked it for days, lass."

"Poorly, it would seem." The werewolf's eyes flashed, and she instantly regretted her quip. "I'm sorry. Fear for my family is no excuse for disrespect. Name's Sorcha, I should have said as much when you introduced yourself."

He stared at her a moment then inclined his head. "Forgiven, Sorcha."

"Thank you. Now, if you'll excuse me, I need to either find my grandmother or avenge her."

"You'll never manage it without my help."

"I'm a Dunrathi. We're the finest trackers to be found."

Conall leaned forward into her personal space, fearless despite what she'd done to his arm. He towered above her, with at least a foot of height between them. "Can you say with absolute certainty that you can kill a beast capable of murdering three werewolves?" He spoke in a low voice. "Two of them were together. My newly wedded cousin and his mate. Strong wolves who had every reason to fight for their lives."

Her confidence faltered and she hesitated. "What manner of beast is it?"

"No one knows. It's… nothing natural. No werebeast I've ever met. It smells of familiar things and darkness."

"Like pig?"

Conall shook his head. "Not merely the pig's blood, but of many other things as well, yet nothing recognizable at the same time."

"We should warn the villagers."

"Warn them of what?" he asked. "That yet another aberration roams their woods? Tell me what they don't know."

She drew in a deep breath and released it on a huff. "Fine. Then we should get going before this beast gets any more of a lead on us. It can't have gotten far in a few hours' time."

"Fine. Tink? Any insight on this beast?"

Sorcha startled back as a little ball of yellow light shot out from the rafters above them, zipping through the air in a dizzying aerial display. The little woodkin fairy finally settled down on Conall's shoulder and emitted a gentle, tinkling noise.

She blinked, surprised by the creature's emergence. "You travel with a sprite?"

Conall tensed his shoulders, jaw tightening. "And what of it?"

"Nothing. It's only... I've never seen them travel with anyone for any length of time."

Sprites were the hallmark of good people, preferring the company of the kind-hearted and the generous most of all. Sorcha moistened her lips and studied him, then she finally stepped forward and touched his shoulder. "Let me help you with your arm."

"Care to finish the job?"

She smiled and shook her head. "Surely you aren't going to whine over a simple dislocation. I could have broken it, you know."

"Yes, I believe you could have." Without protesting

further, he turned to give her access to the injured arm.

While she'd seen the occasional shifter before, she'd never met one as large as Conall. His thick biceps easily surpassed the width of her thighs, and she wondered how the hell he hadn't overpowered her.

Had he let her win, or had he underestimated her entirely?

Probably a combination of both, she thought with no small amount of pleasure that she'd taken a clan alpha by surprise. She relocated the arm with a sharp pull and set the bone into place again. He didn't flinch or grunt, giving no indication he felt it at all.

"There. You'll heal soon, won't you?"

"Aye." He rolled his shoulder. "We shouldn't tarry, lass. Your gran's life may depend on it."

Chapter 4

CONALL HADN'T WANTED to mutilate or harm her as a wolf, yet she'd gotten the upper hand over him the moment he shifted.

He shook off the wound she'd inflicted to his pride and studied his unexpected companion as she mounted her horse alongside him.

She'd handled herself against him as well as any female werewolf, if not more vicious and desperate to win. Experiencing a surge of respect, he remained quiet and considered the task ahead of him. It would have been foolish to allow her to go alone. All the combat prowess in the world hadn't helped his kin, and they'd had special abilities granted by their shifter nature. Without those, Sorcha would be as good as dead.

Twice, while they'd fought, he could have ripped her arm off if he'd wanted, and the beast that had taken her grandmother wouldn't be so kind, wouldn't allow her to seize an opening. It would slaughter her as ruthlessly as it had killed every other living creature it encountered.

Sorcha took the lead, nudging her horse toward the trail Conall would have suggested if he remained in his human body. The gelding didn't shy from his wolf body, so he traveled alongside them both, focusing on the broken branches and trampled ground. Their quarry left an obvious trail speckled with drops of blood.

It had been bleeding when it fled the old woman's home.

Sorcha glanced down at the splatter of red on the rotting orange leaves. "She wounded it, didn't she?"

He nodded, no longer impressed *or* surprised by the girl's sharp eyes. She hadn't lied after all about her skill in the wilds.

"There are no animals here, have you noticed?" she continued. "The birds are all gone still."

The bloody trail ended a mile into the woods and forced Conall to sniff out their quarry's direction. The sharp tang of blood muddled with the pungent bite of crushed pine needles and the crisp scent of snow in the breeze.

Tink had warned him for days about the storm brewing in the north.

He shifted but remained crouched on the ground near a trampled clump of ferns. The blood might have stopped, but whatever beast they tracked hadn't covered its tracks well.

"Whatever it is, it isn't mindless. I have my doubts we're searching for an aberration at all," Conall said as he ran his fingers through the damp ground where the leaves had been turned over to conceal passage over them. Nearby, thick gouges in the trunk of a tree reminded him of the claw marks left by a climbing animal. "It took to the trees here, see? It left claw marks on the trunk."

"Whatever it is, it has my grandmother. I won't stop until I get her back or bring her home for us to mourn."

"I believe you, but we'd be foolish to plow ahead blind. Besides," Conall lifted his face to the sky and drew in a deep breath through his nose. "We need to take shelter."

"But we have hours of daylight left."

"A storm is coming. We'll have snow within the hour."

Sorcha turned to the left and right, studying each cardinal direction in turn with her brows raised. "You're the second person to tell me that today, but there isn't a hint of snow or a storm on the horizon."

Conall stared at her in disbelief before barking out a low chuckle. "Do you doubt my senses, Red?"

Scarlet surged to her face within seconds and spread a rosy blanket of heat across her cheeks. "Well, no. I'm merely saying that snow seems unlikely when there isn't a cloud in the sky or hint of frost in the air."

He grinned. "If I say it's going to storm, then it's going to storm, lass. And from the looks of it, it'll be more than a few flakes melting against the forest floor. We're in for one hell of a blizzard."

"But our tracks!"

"Don't you worry so much about our tracks. If we're forced to slow, you can rest assured that our quarry will also seek shelter."

"But our tracks," she repeated. "How will we find them and remain on its trail?"

"I thought the Dunrathi were the best trackers in all the land. Surely a wee bit of snow won't change that. Tink, search the area for us, would you? We'll need a roof over our heads for the night. Anything will do."

"Will do!" the little woodsprite cried before darting off into the sky.

Conall was forever grateful for his companion. Not a day went by that he didn't wonder how he'd become so fortunate to have her as a friend.

It hadn't been long after his father's death when he found her in a poacher's trap on the forest floor of the southern woods. Hunters from the kingdom of Liang often ventured over to capture the gentle woodkin. Then the fairies were sold on the open market for their wings and any other valuable parts of their tiny bodies.

He'd freed the sprite and expected that to be the end of things, but she'd started to follow him. Despite numerous attempts to shoo her back to her forest, Tink stuck by his side. Eventually he'd given up and accepted the companionship. Over the years, she had proven to be loyal, if territorial. Few women were open to accept courting—even from an alpha like him—when a spoiled fae took to playing pranks on them the moment they had his attention.

And if one naughty fae was all it took to dissuade them, then the haughty bitches weren't worth his time in the first place.

"Look at her silly cloak," Tink said when she reappeared on his shoulder. "I spotted her from far above, even through the trees."

Conall lowered his voice. "They're royal colors. You've seen the couriers sporting them before."

Tink blew a raspberry.

"If you were to spend less time behaving as a wee baby and more time finding us shelter, we'd be indoors by now," Conall pointed out.

"I found a place," she said in a defensive tone. "Two miles ahead where the forest meets the hills."

"What's she saying?" Sorcha asked.

"She says shelter isn't far ahead. We'll want to veer eastward," he replied.

Within the hour, Tink guided them to a small abandoned cottage set back in the hills near a creek. Rotting wood littered the ground outside, the remnants of what had once been equipment used to sift for gems and minerals in the water.

"It may be a little cramped, but there's enough room inside for your animal to join us."

Before they could enter, gentle fluffs of white fell from the sky around them. Gradually, the snowfall picked up speed until heavier clumps drifted to the ground and covered the barren soil. He shot his companion a smug look and headed inside.

The single room cottage had seen better days. Thick layers of dust covered every surface and cobwebs stretched across the room's corners. Broken pieces of a forgotten bassinet lay next to piles of furs and blankets, both positioned by the cold hearth.

Although the dwelling had long since been picked clean by scavengers seeking valuables or weapons, Conall wondered where the inhabitants had gone. Was it the corruption or another foe who chased them from their bridal home with a newborn?

While Sorcha coaxed her horse inside, he secured the window shutters and looked for something to bar the door.

"What are you doing?" he asked when Sorcha stacked wood in the hearth.

"If it's going to snow, we'll need a small fire."

He grunted and batted her sticks aside. While she gaped at him, he arranged several broken bricks into a tidy pile.

"Tink, if you would please."

His friend drifted down and sprinkled the stones with dust. She snapped her little fingers, and the stones glowed red hot.

"We don't want to give away our location with fire and smoke," Conall explained. "There are other dangers in these woods, and I'd prefer not to court them while in pursuit of our enemy."

"I've never seen magic used like that." She moved over and held her hands out. "It's as warm as coals."

"Good for heat, less so for light." He blew dust from two wax candles on a small table and asked Tink to light them. She flit over and sparked red-orange over the wicks until they caught flame.

"Useful companion, your Tinker Bell. Do the woodkin often work with shifters?"

"Why wouldn't they?" he asked.

"No reason, I suppose. I guess I assumed they would find your company intolerable."

His frown deepened. "Why? Because we don't assist the humans? Because we're beasts?"

Sorcha bristled and lifted her chin. "I never said such a thing. It's been my experience that shifters are more violent than the gentler woodkin, is all. It has nothing to do with your ability to take a wild shape and more to do with your temperament."

Conall narrowed his eyes and studied her. Tink circled over his head, shining pink in amusement.

"Have you dealt with many shifters?"

"A few. My father would always speak with the elders

when we traveled through were territory."

"What do you know of my kind?"

"Very little," Sorcha admitted. "We tell nothing of your history now, so you're all a mystery to me. I know all of you aren't able to transform with your clothing and that it takes a powerful were to do it."

"It does," he confirmed. "Did you know there were once a dozen shifter clans?"

Her eyes grew large as she leaned forward to hold her hands above the enchanted stones. "No one's ever mentioned it. We know of only nine."

"It is said our ancestors were twelve mortal men praying to nature for guidance during a time of great turmoil and sorrow in Cairn Ocland. They had prayed to the old gods, to the deities of Creag Morden, and even pleaded to the fae. None listened until one eve the stars took pity and answered instead."

"The stars?"

"Aye, lass. The stars themselves twinkled an answer to their prayers, each constellation above us giving its own gift. It began with the dragons, and Clan TalDrach was born. Then next came the wolves of Clan TalWolthe, followed by the Clan Ardal's bears, until each of the original clan leaders had been blessed by the skies. Along with our wild shapes, each of us in turn received the gift of an element. The dragons their fire, the bears their stonecraft, and us wolves given the gift of air and wind."

"I've never heard this story before, though I did hear you wolves have a penchant for blowing things down."

He grinned. "Aye, we do. Most of our stories aren't written

in paper or chronicled in stone. We pass history by word of mouth to our wee ones...but that also means some things are forgotten. We lost many of our best storytellers during the darkest days of the Scourge when the abominations first crawled from the soil and tainted the woodlands."

"What darkness was so bad that the stars themselves gifted your people?" she asked.

"A fairy."

"A fairy," she repeated. Both of her dark brows raised high.

"Do you not know your history at all, lass?"

"I know that Dalborough invaded our kingdom, slew our rulers, and cursed our lands. That's the world I grew up in. What came before hasn't been of much interest."

"I've been raised in the same world, but even we make time for stories. Especially one as important as the tale of Maeval the Black."

"If it's ever been told to me, I've forgotten. Would you tell me the story as you know it?"

Tink landed on his red and silver tartan-covered knee, blinking in a wild spectacle of giddy colors. "It seems you're both in agreement. A story it shall be then."

The wind rattled against the shutters and loose shingles on the roof. Outside the dingy glass, the world was lost in a white curtain.

"It was a long time ago, before the first shifter ever walked the highlands. An awful fairy queen by the name of Maeval lived in a black fortress beyond the tallest peak of Mount Kinros. Those who defied her were made an example, and soon she became so powerful none dared to cross her—not even the white fae who took us Oclanders as their godchildren."

"She sounds formidable."

"Indeed she was. Many feared the dark fairy, and for good reason. She was an eater of children. and each full moon, she forced the people of Cairn Ocland to deliver their first daughters as sacrifices, and then she would devour them. The people fought back at first, but were never capable of defeating her, and to punish those who refused, she would slaughter the entire village."

Sorcha's widening eyes reflected the flickering light from the two candles nearby. "So that's when your elders pled to the stars?"

"Aye. Led by Dagryn TalDrach, the leaders of the twelve great clans appealed to any force of magic willing to listen. Each founder and their living descendants were changed, and with their new gifts, they initiated a siege against Maeval's fortress and rid Cairn Ocland of her forever. Our stories say Dagryn himself speared her through the heart with his claw and was made king."

"A shame no one cares to reward our pleas of late," she said in a quiet voice. "Even with the wizard dead and the curse broken, the land is still rife with abominations and pockets of twisted magic."

He snorted but said nothing. The humans had squandered their chance. Yet, looking at Sorcha, he was grudgingly forced to admit that she handled herself admirably in a fight. His shoulder still twinged and wouldn't be healed until morning at the earliest.

"How long will the blizzard last?"

"It will be over by dawn if we're lucky, but Tink expects it to last longer."

Conall stood and left the blankets to blow out the candles on the table. The loss of them pitched the little cottage into darkness lit only by the scarlet glow in the hearth. "You take the furs. I've got one of my own." Without giving her the chance to argue, he dropped down on all fours and shook out his coat.

"Goodnight, Conall."

She adjusted the furs and tucked her crimson cloak around herself, then laid down. Conall waited until she was quiet and still before settling nearby with his face toward the door.

Over the course of the night, a cold chill permeated the small cottage. Chinks in the roof and walls let in the frigid air. Comforted by the mountain of warm fur beneath her cheek, Sorcha stretched over the blankets.

Then realized the warm pile of animal skins was moving. Breathing.

Sorcha raised her head at the same time the wolf did, his muzzle leveled toward her face. Even with his humanity cloaked by the form of an animal, she saw his brows shoot up in his furry face. She jerked upright into a sitting position.

"I am...so sorry," she babbled. "I had no idea, and I would never use you like a pillow like that. Please accept my apologies."

The transformation happened in an instant, the wolf gone and replaced by a man in the time it took for her to blink. It never failed to amaze her since the cautionary tales she'd heard as a child mentioned painful shifts and a gruesome moment when the shifters were both human and animal in looks.

"Sorry for what, lass? It was only a wee bit of cuddling. Surely nothing you haven't done before, aye?" He stretched out and folded his hands behind his head, penning her in between his body and the wall.

His hard, incredibly enticing body, was clothed in only a loose shirt and a heavy knee-length tartan. When he bent one of his knees, the fabric tumbled down to mid-thigh and exposed the perfect musculature.

She swallowed. "I am not in the habit of cuddling with strange men."

He hadn't moved away, and the warmth of him continued, his flesh radiating the same heat she'd enjoyed from his furry body.

"Strange, am I?"

"I barely know a thing about you."

"What do you want to know?" He edged closer.

"Doesn't your clan and mate wonder where you've gone off to?"

"Don't have a mate yet."

Why did that little tidbit bring a skip to her pulse?

"I thought all clan leaders had mates."

"They do, when they're ready to find one. I haven't looked for long. Did you think we just grabbed some poor she-wolf and claimed her in the name of the pack?"

She blinked and furrowed her brows. "I don't know, really. I thought the two strongest wolves tended to get together."

"The best mate is the one who makes your heart sing and inner wolf howl as if she were the heavens itself. You don't find that by claiming the first to come along. Besides, there's more

  VIVIENNE SAVAGE

than one kind of strength. There's physical strength," he said while setting his hand on her leg, "and then there's strength of will and character."

Why is his hand on my thigh?

Better yet, why did she like it? His touch was almost scalding through the leather, and when he stroked downward toward her knee, she shivered in delight, suddenly aware of how cold the rest of her body had become.

"Conall?"

He leaned closer. "Aye?"

Tinker Bell zipped down from the rafters and buzzed around Conall's face. The tiny woodkin flashed from red to orange. Her tinkling voice sounded like chimes, and Sorcha regretted lacking the natural aptitude for the language. Her brother understood the tiny creatures with ease.

"What?" He blinked at her.

"What is she saying?" Sorcha asked uneasily when the chimes rose in volume and intensity.

"Nothing important. The usual fae things." His hand fell away from her leg, and he rolled to his feet. Tinker Bell landed on his shoulder and Sorcha had the oddest feeling the little sprite was laughing at her. "The snow has stopped falling. We should go if we want to catch up with our quarry."

"Right."

Lacking time to hunt for a suitable breakfast, Sorcha shared her dried travel rations with Conall. Once he'd knocked the edge off his hunger, his lead returned them to the end of the trail. Frost glittered against the cold trunks and icicles shone from barren branches.

Between his keen nose and Sorcha's trained eye, they

pieced together a trail and followed it through the frigid woods. Fresh claw marks on a tree trunk guided them to the west, and then Conall picked up the creature's odd scent veering toward the north. Wherever it went, some evidence of its passage remained, whether it was a tuft of white fur clinging to the branches, or prints against the snow.

Sorcha crouched to study the tracks. "It walks on four legs at times."

"Or two at others," Conall said. "It dragged something large through this path."

"A bear, do you think?"

"Not like any I've ever tracked. The smell is wrong, for one, and the prints do not match. These forepaws remind me of a wolf. See the spread of the toes against the snow?" He gestured to the outline behind them, the shallow indentations of his own paws identical to the marks left in the snow. "But the width is too great, and if we sought a wolf, it would be a great beast easily twice my size."

She studied him and considered his great bulk. "You're far from small. I find it hard to believe such a monster could exist for so long in the woods without notice."

"And yet it does exist and has thrived beneath the noses of your people."

"And yours," she fired back. "This monster struck your clansmen first."

Conall's expression changed, becoming as neutral and hard as stone. "Aye."

Within seconds of the words departing her lips, remorse tightened an unyielding fist around her heart. "I'm sorry, Co—"

Resuming his lupine form, the alpha bounded onto the trail ahead of her and forged through the taller snow drifts. She followed in his wake until he slowed and a growl alerted her to something ahead. She crouched beside him and studied the cavern entrance he'd discovered.

With tracks leading to and from the entrance of a cave rising from the frozen soil, she couldn't determine if they were alone.

Had the beast left already?

The wolf's hackles raised, fur the color of rich cinnamon standing along his back. He snarled and stared into the open mouth of the cave. Petrified of what they would find, Sorcha placed a hand on the hilt of her sword and trailed behind him.

"Your grandmother was brought this way, and she's alone. The beast must have taken her to its den and abandoned her." Conall whispered after taking on his human guise again. She'd paused by his flanks, so when he changed to a man again, their stances remained close enough for her hip to brush his thigh.

Terror and excitement tightened a vice around Sorcha's chest. "Then this is our chance to save her before that beast comes back."

"Agreed, but we must go with caution."

Conall took the lead, and for once she didn't argue, trusting his enhanced senses above her human vision in the dark cavern. Tink glowed a dim orange on his shoulder.

Proceeding forward, they discovered a yawning pit in the middle of the floor. Her companion crouched beside it and tilted his head down to peer into the hole.

"Tink, would you mind?"

The wood sprite zipped to the bottom, trailing dust

behind her. Her golden glow intensified until the warmth of her light illuminated the pale features of Emilia Dunrathi, Sorcha's only surviving grandparent and a legend among every human clan for her herbal remedies.

"Grandmother?"

"Sorcha?"

"Hold on, I'll get you out of there. Are you hurt?"

"Not enough to keep me down, girl. Now be quick before that abomination comes back."

With a rope from her pack, Sorcha created a loop for a makeshift harness. Conall pulled her grandmother to safety within moments.

Once free from the pit, Sorcha dropped the rope and pulled her grandmother into her arms.

"I thought you'd been killed."

Emilia's brittle laugh sounded weaker than Sorcha remembered. "It takes a lot to kill me, as you know, my dear."

"What was it?"

Her grandmother glanced at the pit. "I don't know, but we shouldn't hang about to find out, now should we? Or did you fancy a stay in the pit yourself?"

Sorcha's cheeks warmed. "Of course. We can talk about it once we're away. I—"

Rocks skittered and clattered against the ground at the cavern entrance. Sorcha put herself in front of her grandmother and unsheathed her sword, ready to face the returning beast.

Chapter 5

CONALL GROWLED AS Red drew her blade. Without regard for his safety, he dove forward toward the opening of the cave in his wolven form with his jaws open. He collided with an unprepared human outfitted in leather armor. His heavier weight took the man down to the ground, and an axe tumbled from his enemy's hand to the snow. Prepared to end his opponent's life, Conall closed his teeth around a throat protected only by a leather gorget.

The polished leather collar wouldn't stand against a werewolf's fangs.

"Ferghus? Conall, wait!"

Before he could crush his opponent's windpipe, Conall raised his head and gazed into Sorcha's bewildered face. He shifted, replacing his dangerous teeth with a fist poised above the other man's cringing face. "You know him?"

"Aye. He's a... member of one of the hunting clans. And a family friend. A slightly irritating one who follows when he shouldn't," she added with a tired smile, "but a friend nonetheless."

"Slightly irritating? Then maybe it'll be no loss to any of you if I snap his neck," Conall offered.

Sorcha sighed. "As pleasant as that would be, I'll have to decline, as I would miss him dearly. Let him go," she said, saving the hunter from Conall's wrath.

Conall released him and straightened.

"Is this what I receive for my concern, Sorcha?" Ferghus demanded. "After crossing paths with you on the western road, I thought to confirm you had arrived safely, as I know Aengus would want me to do," he said. "When I saw the blood, I feared the worst and followed the trail here as quickly as Brute would bring me."

"You're a good lad, Ferghus," Emilia said as she limped over. "I'm certain Sorcha would have sought your help if she hadn't been assisted already."

"Aye, you weren't needed," Conall said. He brushed debris from his kilt and moved to Sorcha's side.

Ferghus stared at him. "Who in the blazing hells are you, anyway?"

"Conall TalWolthe, clan alpha."

Ferghus's sneer deepened into a scowl. "What's this, Sorcha? Consorting with beasts now instead of hunting them?"

Sorcha sighed. "Show a little respect, Ferghus. He helped me track Granny." She rummaged through the travel bag lashed to Eachann's saddle and removed a plain green cloak to draw over her grandmother's shoulders.

"My apologies, Sorcha. Emilia." Ferghus bowed his head to each woman and ignored Conall entirely.

"Accepted. Now enough of this, I've got to get my gran home to a warm cottage and soft bed."

Emilia chuckled weakly at the pair and drew the woolen cloak tighter around her frail body. A cough rattled in her chest. "Agreed."

Conall was glad to put the cavern behind them. It stank of

old blood and magic and stranger things he couldn't name. He moved up closer to Sorcha and spoke in a low voice. "I'll escort you to your granny's home." When he glanced at Ferghus, he saw the man had already helped Emilia into Eachann's saddle.

"But your beast, you'll lose days of tracking."

"Better to see you back safely first, then return here. This creature, as far as I'm aware, has never attacked a human before until now. Maybe I missed something at your grandmother's cabin." And he didn't want to leave her alone in Ferghus's company when the wolf in him desperately hungered for the chance to stake his own claim over Sorcha.

Tink huffed but said nothing.

"Ferghus, be a dear won't you, and ride ahead of us to the village. Make sure no one else was hurt or killed by the beast," Emilia said.

"You're certain, Emilia?"

"Yes, yes. Go on, now, or I'll tell your mum you've been disobeying your elders."

Ferghus bowed his head and turned his stallion away before dashing onto the trail. He was out of sight within moments, leaving only the huge prints of his magnificent horse behind.

It didn't take nearly as long to return to the outskirts of Frosweik as it did to find the cave. With Sorcha and Emilia riding together, they took a direct route from the beast's lair back to the cottage.

Leaving nothing to chance, Conall investigated the small home before the women entered, inhaling a combination of old scents and fresh air wafting through the shattered door.

"Thank you, young man," Emilia said. The feeble old lady

didn't match his expectations, her spine curved and bones fragile in appearance. On trembling legs, she stepped into her home with her granddaughter's aid.

Conall waited outside while Sorcha tended her grandmother's injuries and settled her in bed. Later, she emerged from the cottage after securing a set of heavy drapes above the doorframe with nails.

"That's the best I can do until I find a carpenter in the village."

He eyed her handiwork. "Hang a second set, Red, or the chill will freeze you both."

"I'll see what we have."

"Good. Now, how is she?"

"Tired from her ordeal, but some rest and a hot meal will do her good. I'll scrub out the blood while she's asleep and set the house to rights again. Tidy what I can and dispose of what I can't."

"Has she said anything about what took her?"

"Only that it was huge with patches of white and black fur. She said she didn't really get a good look but named it as a wolf."

"Whatever it is, it's no wolf."

"As I said, she didn't get a good look." Sorcha gave him a small smile. "I suppose this is where we part ways then. I won't forget what you did, Conall. If ever there is a chance to speak highly of Clan TalWolthe, I'll sing nothing but your highest praises. Thank you."

"Sending me off so soon?"

"I figured you'd be itching to get back on the trail and avenge your kinsmen."

He stepped forward and Sorcha moved back. "You could come with me, lass. Your grandmother is safely returned to her home. A few of your kinsmen in the village will no doubt watch this cottage, aye? Come with me."

"Excuse me?"

"Think of it. On the trail of some new and terrible beastie. There's glory to be had in killing such a monster." He took another step, maneuvering her against a tree. Conall placed both of his hands against the trunk behind her, effectively pinning her against it.

"I don't hunt for glory."

"Neither do I, which is why you should come along. We'll be putting down a threat to both of our clans." Waiting for her reaction, he stretched his body along hers and pressed closer.

"That's far from necessary when you're clearly quite capable of tracking your own aberrations." Despite her protest, she didn't push him away. Considering the way she'd manhandled him in her grandmother's cabin, he had no doubt that she could have not only wiggled free, but broken him again if she wanted to escape.

"I think you liked traveling with me. Admit it."

"You're awfully sure of yourself."

He grinned down at her. "It's called confidence, lass, and I know when I'm right."

"Smug is more like it," she muttered. "Are you going to let me go?"

"Ask me nicely."

"I want you to—"

He kissed her. Unable to stand another moment without knowing the taste of her mouth, he tipped her chin up and claimed her lips, seizing her in a kiss until the tension of her body melted away. She yielded, and then her fingers were on his broad shoulders, curling against them to hold him closer instead of pushing him away.

Conall savored every second, every quiet breath, every heave of her chest.

Then he tried to calculate how long it would take to unfasten her leathers.

The moment he reached between them, she bit his lower lip. Her hand left his shoulder, and before he could blink, her palm cracked against his face. Conall staggered back and stared at her.

"What was that for?" He rubbed his stinging cheek.

"You kissed me."

He scowled at her. "That I did, and you kissed me back."

"A momentary weakness."

"You bit me."

"I did."

It was a very she-wolf thing to do. He swiped his mouth and glanced down at the back of his hand. She'd drawn blood. Only a little, but enough to leave a smear on his skin.

She definitely had the spirit of a wolf.

"Next time you want to cuddle and kiss, lass, I'll remember this moment. You'll have to beg me."

"There won't be a next time," she replied, raising her chin.

"There will be," he said with confidence. "Though I'll say goodbye for now, since you object to my company." He gave her a bow. "Be safe, Red, and keep an eye on your granny so you don't lose her again."

At another time, in another place, he would have courted

her with animal skins and fresh meat for her family. He would have hunted for her and her granny that evening and done whatever was necessary to prove he could provide.

But Conall lacked the time. No matter how much he desired Red, or how much the inner wolf inside him demanded for him to remain, he'd be foolish to turn aside his quest to pursue a human girl. With that in mind, he lowered to four paws and raced away into the forest.

Chasing the beautiful huntress could wait for another time. Vengeance for Clan TalWolthe came first.

Chapter 6

SORCHA WAITED UNTIL Conall was out of sight before she sagged back against the tree. What a kiss. He had quite literally stolen her breath away, made her toes curl, and every other pretty cliché she knew of from her favorite books.

Once her heart slowed to a normal rhythm, she headed back to the house and busied herself with tidying while her grandmother slept. The blood was easy to clean, but the smashed memories of a lifetime in the house could never be replaced—much like her grandmother. She picked up the broken shards of a pot and smiled sadly at the small handprints painted on the sides. She and Egan had made it together when they were only six years old.

Perhaps the artisan in the village could put the pieces together again.

"Sorcha?"

"I'm here." She wiped a hand across her damp cheeks and crossed to the bedroom door. "Is everything all right?"

"A little spooked, I suppose," her grandmother said after a dry chuckle. "Is everything okay out there?"

"We'll have to replace the door, but I can go into town tomorrow and fetch Master Corwin."

"No rush, dear. After so long a journey to find me, you deserve rest."

Her grandmother coughed again, a dry, racking sound that rattled in her lungs. Sorcha frowned at the sound of it.

"Would you like a bath, Granny? I can get water boiling."

"Oh perhaps later," the old woman said, shivering. "The wind cut straight through me while that beast had me in its clutches. I feel as if I'll never be warm again. Perhaps you'd come join me in bed, lass, and warm these old bones?"

Sorcha had never seen her grandmother so pale and blue from cold before, nor had she seen her in poor health. She'd been a robust woman with a sturdy frame. The ordeal had weakened her. "Surely, you must be starved."

"Very much."

"I'll put together a hot meal for you first."

Sorcha tucked her grandmother into bed with an extra blanket and hurried into the kitchen to heat a kettle for tea. She lit a fire in the oven and oiled a pan to fry eggs.

Within moments, the smoky aroma of sausage filled the cottage. She scraped the eggs onto a plate and steeped tea blended with lavender and chamomile, her grandmother's favorite. As Gran loathed dining in bed, she set the plate on the table then stoked the fire.

Damn. They needed more logs. Dreading the cold, she donned Anastasia's red cloak and stepped into her boots. Heavy steps thundered over the wooden porch, announcing a visitor's arrival before Sorcha reached the makeshift door.

Conall threw back the curtain and stepped inside.

Her heart sped at the sight of him. The memory of his kiss remained fresh on her lips. "What are *you* doing here?"

Had he come back to finish what he started? Part of her had almost hoped he would make promises of courtship; then he'd wandered away instead, leaving her to wonder if it had had only been a game of seduction to him.

"Conall?"

His nostrils flared, and he took in a long breath. "Something didn't sit right with me."

"If this is your way of trying to get another kiss—"

"Nae, lass, you've made yourself quite clear. These lips would sooner drink poison before touching you again. I told you, you'd have to beg the next time."

Her spine stiffened and her belly lurched toward her knees. "Fine. I certainly won't be begging for you to manhandle me again, so you can kindly see yourself away. Perhaps you didn't notice, but Gran needs rest and privacy. She's not well, and I can't have you storming about in her home."

Conall crossed his arms. "That's just it, isn't it? When you spoke of your grandmother, you described a strong and stubborn woman, wise with herbs and familiar with the forest."

"Because she is."

"Then why does she reek of death and hobble like a feeble crone? The beast had her for two days—hardly enough time to make her this pathetic wretch. This isn't your granny, Red."

"It threw her into a pit, you ginger galoot! It—"

"Do we have a guest?" Her grandmother appeared at the open bedroom door, a shawl around her shoulders.

Sorcha halted and stared at her grandmother, lips twisting into a frown as she noticed the abnormal pallor to her skin. "He was just leaving, Granny."

"Good. We don't need his kind around here. Best you leave, sonny boy. I won't have you sniffing around my granddaughter."

"You heard her, Conall. Please go." After leading her grandmother to her favorite chair, she stretched a heavy blanket over the elderly woman's lap.

"This is a mistake," Conall said, a hard edge to his voice.

"Tell the beast to begone," Granny snapped. Her tone and words were so unlike her that Sorcha stared. Emilia Dunrathi was as well known for her temperament and charity as she was for her talent with a potions pot.

Could Conall be right? *No*, she told herself. *She's been through an ordeal, taken by a shifter set on eating her. Of course she'd be frightened of Conall.*

Sorcha touched her palm to her grandmother's cool cheek and gazed down at her pale features. The color had never returned to her wrinkled face, and a few wisps of graying hair escaped from her bonnet beside her ears.

Her ears—long, tapered ears with delicate points poking from beneath her pink and white bonnet. "Grandmother, what long ears you have."

"The better to hear you with, my dear. You'll see, when you're as old as I am."

The longer she studied her grandmother, the stranger her features became, like an odd caricature of the granny she'd known since infancy. "Your eyes are so large."

"The better to see you with, my dear. Please send him away and let's go to bed. The cold has settled in these old bones."

"Red." Conall's voice was harsh and desperate. Pleading. "Something's wrong. Get away from that thing. It isn't your grandmother."

Grandmother gazed up at Sorcha and smiled, though

there was no love behind the expression. "Your wolf friend doesn't know of what he speaks."

"But, Granny, your teeth…" A quiet buzzing filled her head. She squinted and leaned forward, gaze focused on the canines poking out from her grandmother's mouth. "They're so big."

"The better to eat you with, my dear!"

Emilia's sudden lunge knocked Sorcha off balance. Her footing faltered and she tumbled to the floor, bottom first, with her grandmother hunched over her. Except, it wasn't her grandmother any more. Its eyes burned yellow and saliva dripped from its crooked fangs.

The red cloak blazed around her, flaring bright with mystical energy. The changeling bounced against it and fell back with a scream. Blisters arose on its skin everywhere it had touched her.

Then Conall stepped forward, drew his sword from his back, and skewered the creature through the shoulder with one stroke. He planted the tip of the enormous weapon into the wooden wall behind it, pinning the changeling in place.

"Why are you here?" he demanded.

Screaming, it pushed at the blade, but he twisted it in deeper. Its meager strength couldn't compare to extraordinary shifter might.

"Answer me!"

"I can't, I can't! I'll be dead!"

"You'll be dead if you don't answer," he snarled.

Sour bile rose in Sorcha's throat when the changeling shed the rest of its disguise. It was squat with a bulbous head and gangly limbs. Its indistinguishable features blurred together like a melted wax figure. How had she ever mistaken it for her grandmother?

"She...she sent me. Set me on the red rider. The red rider must be slain. She demands it!"

Conall twisted the blade. "Who is she?"

It howled and fervently shook its head. "I won't tell. Can't tell."

"Then you're of no use to us."

"Conall—"

The sword withdrew then plunged forward, slaying the creature. Numbed by the ordeal, Sorcha sat in a chair while Conall dragged the changeling from the house, and she was still there when his heavy steps crossed over the threshold again minutes later.

"The carrion birds will have a grand feast," he announced, but when she said nothing, he moved over and touched her shoulder. "Red? Are you all right, lass? Did it hurt you?"

"I failed my grandmother. The creature's killed her, hasn't it? It killed her and took her skin."

Crouching before her to meet her eye level, Conall took her face between his palms. "No, you failed no one and did all you could. Besides, we've no reason to suspect Emilia is dead."

"It looked like her. It wore her skin!"

"There's a fine difference between a changeling and a skinwalker, lass. The former is left behind when a dark fairy spirits a mortal away. That was certainly a changeling. It had no form of its own."

Sorcha tensed. "The Shadow Glen."

"What?" His forehead wrinkled and his brows drew together.

"Anastasia—Queen Anastasia said something was in the Shadow Glen. Something dark and powerful that was interfering with her magic. That's why my family isn't with me. They're gathering the clans so the king and queen can retake the glen."

"Sorcha, the only dark fairy with that sort of power died centuries ago. Remember the story I told you? Maeval is long dead."

"Regardless of when she died, I need to tell the queen. I'll have to ride to Benthwaite, but... I need to find my grandmother, too. She's still out there."

"Send a letter to the queen with your thoughts and tell her what happened here. Then join me in tracking the beast. It's our best lead in finding your grandmother."

His logical reasoning gave her pause. She swiped her eyes with the back of her wrists and gazed up at his face.

"What made you return?"

Conall shrugged. "Is it so hard to believe that even the shifter clans know of your grandmother? Emilia the Brave they called her during the early days of the war with Dalborough. They say she and your grandfather rode side by side into battle, and wherever a man from our side fell, she was there to mend his wounds and raise him to his feet again. That thing, that was no war hero. Changelings are devious creatures, as are the dark fairies who sire them, and they can imitate many things. Your looks. Your smell. But never your heart and your demeanor."

"But you'd never met her before."

"But I know *you*, and how you speak of her."

From anyone else, she would have believed it was a line to

gain her favor. From Conall, it sounded true. Upon deciding there was nothing to gain by questioning his motivations further, she hurried to the nearby table and penned a concise letter to the queen. Within the missive, she detailed the events of the past two days and her plans to track the monster to recover her grandmother. Once the ink had dried, she rolled it up and tucked it into her pack.

"I'm ready. The town healer keeps pigeons and carrier ravens. We can make it there before nightfall if we hurry."

"Aye. Good plan."

With her riding Eachann and Conall traveling on four legs, they made it long before dusk—not that she would have allowed the darkness to hinder her mission.

Prior to the war with Dalborough, villagers had spread across the valley. Thousands had died during the ongoing battles, and even more in the aftermath once the curse destroyed their farms and ravaged the wild game. Nothing could be grown in the soil, chickens laid rotting eggs, and the few survivors gradually starved.

Then the aberrations came, and the people had flocked together into a more fortified position. They tore down the outlying cottages and used the stone and timber to build a wall. New homes were built close together around the forge and town square. It wasn't ideal, but it had kept them safe over the years.

Emilia had been one of the few to refuse to abandon her home, and Sorcha's parents had chosen life on the road for their family over the cramped squalor.

The guards standing watch by the gate recognized her and let them pass without question, though both men gave

Conall distrusting glances. Strangers didn't come by often.

Sorcha led the way through the narrow streets to the heart of town, where everything was quiet. Children didn't play outside and mothers didn't gather at the well to trade gossip.

"I know," she said after looking at Conall's face. His tense jaw and disapproving frown spoke for him. "It's depressing, but it's all they have."

"I was going to suggest you stable your horse here, but now I fear they'll eat it."

"Why would I stable Eachann?"

"Because, lass, where we'll be heading, a horse will be a hindrance. A fine specimen he may be, but a stallion cannot climb ravine walls or travel through the underways. He'll be left behind and unguarded in territory where fell things crawl in the dark."

They stopped in front of a squat building with a blue painted door. Sorcha patted Eachann's neck and dropped the reins. "But *I'll* slow us down. I cannot keep up with your four legs."

Without waiting for her permission, Conall lifted her down from the saddle. His warm hands lingered at her waist even after he set her on her feet. "You'll ride me, if you have the need."

The low, husky words made her entire body clench. Heat and desire curled in her lower belly, invoking sensual visions of their bodies pressed together in an intimate embrace.

No. She was not going to let one flirtatious wolf get her off track—even if his kisses were divine. Even if he'd swooped in to the rescue when she needed him most, displaying loyalty she hadn't encountered in anyone beyond her clan, except for Ferghus.

She stepped back from his hold without resistance and bumped into the door. A smug smile spread across Conall's face, and although she wanted to slap it off, she spun on a heel and stalked inside, shutting the door in his face.

"Sorcha, is that you m'lass?"

"It is, Master Larwell."

The white-haired elder who rose from a seat by the hearth chuckled and gestured her closer. "Injure yourself again? I remember the day I had to set your arm. You barely came up to my knee, but you were so stubborn you wouldn't let a tear fall. Egan cried for you."

"You have a long memory." She had been ten and Egan had challenged her to a tree climbing contest. She had nearly won, until a brittle branch snapped beneath her weight. "But I haven't come for healing. I require your fastest bird."

"Certainly. Where am I to send it?"

"To Benthwaite. I have an urgent message for the queen."

Chapter 7

CONALL REFUSED TO stay overnight in the town, and Sorcha couldn't blame him. After sending a missive addressed to Queen Anastasia by carrier pigeon, she found a family willing to stable Eachann among the herd.

She'd never left her four-legged friend alone in other hands. After sharing an apple with him, she kissed his velvet nose and they parted ways.

"We'll be slow on foot," she muttered.

"Slower if we're forced to go around the mountains," Conall countered. "We'll cover ground faster if we travel as the creature moves by crossing over and beneath obstacles a horse cannot, as I've already said. Besides, you'll be heartbroken if some ogre carries him away while we're preoccupied."

"So the alternative is to offer yourself as my beast of burden?"

He shrugged. "I'll never complain about having an attractive lady on top of me."

Sorcha stared at him, but he merely grinned back at her in return. Suppressing the urge to slap the werewolf's smug face, she scowled and turned away. She was no cheap tart to roll with him in the hay, no matter how attractive she found him. No matter how many times her mind returned to the wild taste of him against her lips, or how much she wanted to slide her palms over his bare chest.

Taking the high road, she sniffed and started forward on foot. Conall's amused laughter followed.

Contrary to her initial impression of him, he quieted and grew serious during their evening travel across the woodlands. With the cave as their destination and the loss of Eachann, they made slow progress once night fell and eventually set camp.

Conall required no bedroll and carried minimal supplies, claiming a true man learned to live off the land. Sorcha rolled her eyes at him and crawled beneath the blankets with her sword close at hand. He then settled opposite the campfire to sleep in his wolf form, one of his pointed ears occasionally stirring whenever a forest sound made her jump.

But no matter how tense she remained and prepared to leap to her feet to do battle, no monster appeared to drag her or Conall away in the dead of night. The skies remained still, the forest peaceful.

They reached the cavern by the following afternoon, damp from an endless drizzle over the course of the day. Sorcha might have been miserable, but at least the snow dumped by the blizzard was washing away. The relentless rain had stopped an hour ago, and she was grateful for the break.

In his wolf form, her companion scouted the area then returned in a human body to relay his observations. "We can camp here safely. As for our quarry..." He crouched near an indentation on the ground, the distinct four-toed imprint of a wolf's hind paw captured in the mud. "It hasn't been back since we found the changeling."

"Do we need to worry about scavengers?"

Conall shook his head. "I'd think not. When there's a creature like this, the scent frightens away even the most formidable of predators.

Sorcha joined him and followed the muddy paw print to another track. "It's headed east."

"The bears call the eastern forests their home. When I first started tracking this thing, I believed that's where it was headed. Perhaps your grandmother was a detour and now it's resumed its original course."

Anxiety turned her belly into a turbulent mess. How could she ever claim to be as great a hunter as Ferghus if she couldn't recover her own relative from disaster? She sighed and leaned against the tree behind her.

"If you'd like, I'll catch dinner if you can ready water for stew," Conall offered. "A hot meal would serve us both well."

"Agreed."

While the wolf loped away, Sorcha prepared camp in a clump of trees away from the cavern entrance. She couldn't bring herself to take shelter within the horrible place. Finding enough dry wood for a fire proved the most difficult part of her task, but soon enough a small blaze crackled beneath the dismal sky. After digging out a pot from her pack, she headed back toward a narrow creek they had crossed and filled it.

Something glimmered against the murky creek bottom. Sorcha drew back with haste when the gleam intensified but remained at the water's edge against her better judgment. With a hand on the hilt of her sword, she leaned forward for a better look.

Three feet of the creek glowed with an eldritch green light, and when the brightness dimmed from a blinding sheen,

VIVIENNE SAVAGE

she blinked down at the image of her queen reflected in the tranquil surface.

"Anastasia?"

"I've found you at last. Your letter worried me, and I sought to contact you the only way I knew how—with magic." The queen's youthful features belied her reputation as an accomplished sorceress. Her image shone in the water with the clarity of a mirror, revealing Anastasia's figure from the waist up and a library backdrop to her rear. "I'm sorry about Emilia. Are *you* well?"

"As well as can be expected."

"If you and your companion are correct and a dark fairy has taken her, the odds remain in our favor that your grandmother still lives. Do not lose hope for that."

The words brought bittersweet relief, but little comfort. "I won't, but the presence of a changeling bothers me all the same. Could there be more? How do I know them for what they are?"

"I don't know," Anastasia admitted. "I've never encountered one before. And if your fears about an ancient dark fae are even close to being truth, then we'll need to act swiftly and gather more help."

"I spoke with one of the elders in Frosweik before we left and told them of your plan to clear the Shadow Glen. I'm not sure if anyone will go, but…"

"Thank you, Sorcha. No one will blame them for remaining to keep their own homes protected, but I appreciate the effort all the same. Now, tell me more of this beast."

"There's not much to tell. I haven't seen it yet. Conall says it smells unnatural, even for an aberration. I—"

"Red? What are you doing?"

She twisted at the waist, gaze darting toward Conall's voice. He stepped from the trees with a brace of coneys in one hand and his sword in the other.

"It's fine. Queen Anastasia contacted us."

Her words didn't ease the suspicion on his face. He dropped the trio of dead rabbits and approached with his weapon at the ready. Sorcha couldn't help but giggle at the sight of the stalking warrior, wondering what he'd do to banish the supposed threat. Slash the water?

The corner of Anastasia's mouth raised. "You must be Conall TalWolthe. It's a pleasure to finally meet you, though I wish it were under better circumstances."

"How do we know this isn't some dark fairy trick?"

"Conall!" Sorcha hissed.

"No," the queen said without losing her serene smile. "He's right to be cautious. While I have no way to prove myself to him, I can tell you that my final words to Sorcha were 'Be true to yourself and your heart. Let love be the compass to guide you through all deeds.' Will that suffice?"

"She's right," Sorcha confirmed. "She whispered that to me right before I set off. Only she would know that."

Satisfied, Conall put his sword away. "We're tracking the beast into bear territory. I have a feeling,since it's slain three werewolves, Clan Ardal may be next."

Anastasia pursed her lips. "Then I have another task for you, Sorcha."

"But—"

The queen raised a hand. "Finding Emilia is your top priority, of course, but as you pass through shifter territories, I would ask you to speak to them on my behalf. Ask them to aid us. Can you do this?"

Sorcha dipped her head. "Of course."

"Excellent. Should you require anything or have news to share with us, send another bird at your first convenience. In the meantime, I'll scour my library for this Maeval, or anything like her. For the good of the kingdom, we must discover whether she's returned from the dead."

Conall's brows drew together, leaving deep lines in his brow. "Is it possible for a fae to return from the dead?"

"This is what I shall determine," Anastasia replied. "I leave it to you both to find out the rest."

Travelling with Conall proved to be more comfortable than Sorcha expected. The wolf kept his flirtations light and showed a humorous side to his otherwise stoic demeanor. His spritely companion, on the other hand, seemed less eager about their partnership.

The morning after their first camp beneath the stars, Sorcha had awakened to find twigs tied into her hair. This time, she'd awakened to discover her boot and corset laces had been twisted into knots. She and Conall spent an hour undoing the damage.

"It's all in good fun," Conall told her. "She means nothing by it."

Sorcha slanted her skeptical gaze toward the green glow settled on Conall's shoulder.

The fae tinkled.

"Tell her to keep away from my damned things. I mean

it."

"I have, but do you know how difficult it can be to control a sprite? They have minds of their own, same as you and me."

As they forged through a field of tall grass, the golden-brown stalks brushed against her waist and the matted tangles of dead grass squished beneath their feet. How long would it be until places like this flourished again with life?

Sorcha squinted into the distance at a farm that had seen better days. She might have thought it abandoned like most of the other settlements in Cairn Ocland if not for the clothesline strung between two trees. Fresh clothing dangled from it.

"Someone still lives there!" she cried. "We can ask them if they've seen a strange creature or heard anything unusual."

"Brave of them to strike out so far from the walled towns." Admiration filled Conall's voice.

Sorcha sniffed. "All of us aren't cowards."

"I never said that you are."

"Of course, only implied it."

"Perhaps it's all that I know of your kind!" he snapped back.

Quieted by his outburst, she stood back and watched him stalk ahead. Something about the change in his demeanor seemed personal. What had happened to Conall TalWolthe for him to hold humans in such disdain?

Drawing closer to the struggling farm revealed a wooden corral surrounding a patch of dusty, barren ground. Chickens clucked around in the dirt and pecked desperately for grubs and worms.

Three horses and a single cow shared the fenced pasture. The two mares had the look and build of plow animals, with dull but well-tended coats. The third shone by comparison, his coal-black mane braided in a familiar fashion.

"I know this horse," Sorcha said. She gestured toward the stallion in the field. "That's Brute. I've never seen him parted from Ferghus before!"

"Greetings!" A burly man with a gray-streaked beard waved to them from the opening to the adjacent barn. "What can I do for a royal messenger?"

"I mean no trouble, but I know that horse in your field. Has something happened to his rider?" Her pulse sped as a hundred different scenarios rushed through her imagination. With the beast on the loose, no one was safe, especially her braggart of a friend.

The farmer smiled. "Worry not for your friend, young lass. A huntsman asked if he could stable this fine steed with us for a short while. Told us he's on the trail of a wicked creature and would prefer his stallion to be safe."

Relief eased the tension in her chest. "Thank the stars. Did he pass through here recently?"

"Aye, only yesterday. You missed him by a day."

Conall grunted. "We're tracking the same beast. Have you seen anything strange in these parts?"

"Seen, no. Heard, yes. As I told the other fellow, there was a mighty racket the night before he arrived. A bloodcurdling scream echoed over the fields. It reminded me of a deer I shot in my youth, when my aim was poor and one arrow wasn't enough. It's a sound you never forget."

Sorcha blinked. "A deer's scream? I didn't know they could scream."

"They do, but this echoed across the fields and spooked

the animals. Terrified my wife and children."

"I can imagine." Sorcha gazed out across the fields and pursed her lips. The sound could have come from anywhere.

"You're welcome to join us for supper. We haven't much but potatoes and leeks, but what's ours is yours."

"The offer is appreciated, but we must continue moving." Sorcha's gaze drifted out to the field again. Brute stood at the pasture fence, snorting and flaring his nostrils. Desperate for her attention, he pranced alongside the wooden perimeter and stamped. "Thank you for caring for Brute."

"The well is sweet, if you'd like to fill your skins at least."

"Thank you," Conall said.

Leaving the farmer to return to his work, they collected a few of the tubers he'd offered then refilled at the well. The sweet water reminded Sorcha of days long past and the years of her early childhood prior to the curse.

Rangvald's reign of evil had truly ended. Although too stubborn to fade from all of Cairn Ocland, it was vanquished from most of the land. She watched an enormous buzzard coast by overhead and smiled. Carrion birds were always a good sign. Aberrations left nothing, not even bones when they crossed paths with a carcass.

"What are you smiling about?" Conall asked.

"Nothing."

"I know what nothing looks like, and it certainly isn't that."

"I was thinking of how much the land has changed since King Alistair destroyed the black wizard. It almost reminds me of how Cairn Ocland once was."

Conall snorted and raised her bag to his shoulder. In the

absence of Eachann, they'd decided to share the burden of carrying the supplies. "Are you even old enough to remember how it once was?"

"I'm not a child, Conall."

Eyes bright with interest, the werewolf turned to study her at length. His gaze dragged over her from head to toe, lingering over her hips, which weren't as curvy as she wanted. After a pause at her slim waist, his attention lingered on her breasts, sufficiently flattened by the studded leather corset. "What are you then? Fifteen?"

Sorcha's spine stiffened and her voice rose. "Fifteen? You think I'm fifteen?"

"What, you're not? Surely you're not a day over sixteen, being as it's only your first adventure. By the time *I* was sixteen, I'd been on several."

A flash of hot fury swept over her. "I'm twenty-two, you furry twat. Soon to be twenty-three."

"Ah, I see," Conall said after exhaling a long-held breath. "Old and used up before your prime then. No wonder we've had to travel so slowly."

A smile flit across his features, and had she blinked, she would have missed the subtle raise at the corner of his mouth.

The insufferable ass was teasing her.

"You're impossible!" Before she could swat him in retribution, he danced away beyond her reach and dropped to all fours, pack and belongings melding with him in a seamless transition of magic. "And a cheat!"

The wolf grinned at her and bounded ahead. Without the burden of her supplies, she dashed after him, laughing when he paused long enough for her to capture his tail. If she closed her eyes, she could imagine it as strands of plush, scarlet silk beneath her fingers.

Tink joined in their game of tag along the way. While it was childish, it became a necessary distraction that urged the trio ahead down the roads. It broke the monotony of their eastern journey.

Above them, buzzards circled below the gray clouds. She smelled an incoming rain on the wind, the sweet fragrance of a distant rainstorm.

It seemed like months ago that a blizzard had swept through Cairn Ocland and piled a thigh-deep blanket of snow over the land.

Where had winter gone? Sorcha shivered.

Before she could pose her question to Conall, he shifted into his human shape and glanced skyward. "We're close to something. I can smell it, and so can they. It must be large for there to be so many all at once. Do you want to see if it's the farmer's mysterious screamer?"

"I suppose so. It shouldn't be far."

Sorcha's human nose detected nothing but the odor of damp, rotting leaves and mold beneath their feet. Trusting him, she trailed alongside the werewolf until they reached a descending slope with a deep, angled drop into a mossy ravine.

Upon reaching the edge, she peered at the bottom, only to stop dead in her tracks, and threw both hands over her mouth. An ivory stag larger than any she'd ever seen lay in a crumpled heap at the bottom of the tree-speckled gorge.

A dozen buzzards picked at it, and more landed nearby to await their turn.

Their mysterious screamer was the most beautiful

creature she'd even seen, even in its death. Tears burned behind Sorcha's eyelids, and she didn't argue when Conall took her by the hand to descend to the lower forest level.

"Are you all right?" he asked in a gentle voice. Tink landed on his shoulder.

Sorcha quickly swiped her eyes with one hand. "It's nothing."

"Doesn't look like nothing," he replied, but he didn't press it or tease. He released her and crouched beside the corpse. "It fought for its life," Conall murmured. He bowed his head in sorrow while running his hands over the dappled white and gray fur. Deep slashes glistened against the remaining pelt, most of it stripped neatly away with surgical precision.

"How can you tell?"

"See the blood on her antlers? And this tip was recently broken."

"Her? I didn't think female deer had antlers."

"Most normal ones don't. But this is a white hart of Clan Cernun, and they're anything but typical deer."

"Isn't a hart a male deer?"

"It's the name taken by Clan Cernun, the ghost stags of Cairn Ocland. Though I'd thought them all long dead and hadn't realized any survived the Purge. Years have passed since one has been seen in the lowlands."

"The Purge?"

"It's what we shifters call the time shortly after Dalborough killed the TalDrach monarchs. Before leaving the highlands and cursing our kingdom, they hunted all shifters they could find. Slaughtered women and children in our villages while the men were off to war. Despite all our power, we weren't enough to battle them once our king had fallen. I was only a wee lad, barely in control of my shape."

"How is it your ancestors in the stories could defeat a fae but not an evil king?"

Conall's mouth flattened into a tight smile. "Maeval had only magic at her disposal and an army of fairy creatures, but King Frederick came with more. My father was there on the day King Rua died. He called it a nightmare given life, unlike anything he'd ever seen before. They came with their dark sorcerer and great machines belching flames and poison. One by one, the thunderbirds fell from the sky, and then they speared his sister, Princess Teagan, through the heart. The king battled to the end until a great lance tore him from the sky. He fell to the castle grounds where he self-immolated seconds afterward in a great column of flame, leaving only his ashes as all dragons do when they perish."

Although Sorcha knew the tale of Dragon King Rua and Witch Queen Liadh's defeat, she listened without interrupting. He spoke with a rich, deep baritone, his attractive voice paired with a penchant for storytelling. She could listen to him all day, and often did when the mood struck him during their journey.

How could she love one man's voice so much?

"But how did the castle remain standing once the dragons were dead?" Sorcha asked. "I don't understand why Dalborough didn't tear the castle to pieces brick by brick."

"They tried. They say the queen fell last, but not before she gave her life while weaving a powerful spell to protect all who dwelled in the castle, including Prince Alistair. Had she not stood her ground, Benthwaite Castle would be no

  Vivienne Savage

more than a pile of bricks and shattered stone. As for how my ancestors were able to defeat Maeval but failed to push off our attackers… clearly they didn't finish the job."

"It *does* sound like a nightmare."

"The things they came with, Sorcha, it wasn't natural. No human wizards should have so much power."

"Queen Anastasia does," she pointed out, raising her chin. "She's powerful beyond any skill Rangvald had."

"And part fae. And if she's so powerful, why hasn't she swept in and abolished the rest of this curse, or flown on dragon's back to slay Maeval?"

Sorcha hesitated to answer with the quip on the tip of her tongue. The truth was that she didn't know, and she could only assume Anastasia's vast power held no contest against a full-fledged fairy queen.

"I'm not disparaging our new queen, lass," he said in a gentle voice. "I'm only telling you the truth as I see it. Our queen can't do it alone, no matter the power you believe her to have—"

"Believe her to have?" Her voice rose an octave, and she stood straight, raising her chin. "I know Queen Anastasia's power. I've seen it, and so have you."

He sighed at her in the same way her father often did when she was being stubborn. "Parlor tricks to contact us in a river surface isn't power. It's—"

Conall's head snapped to the left and he sniffed the air. Breaking away from their discussion, he moved toward the brush and crouched.

"Don't think you can get out of this talk by pretending to sniff something."

"Who's pretending? There's something here."

Her brows lifted. "You can smell in your human form?"

"Aye. Not as well, but I can't talk to you when I'm in my other body. We're not all as fortunate as the dragons, although I've heard some of the griffins can speak too."

"I wouldn't know. It'd be useful if you could, though." The importance of the previous argument dwindled, forgotten in as few seconds as it took for him to smile at her. Damn him for being so handsome. For distracting her from the grisly sight that had upset them both. "What do you smell?"

The glowing sprite on his shoulder lifted into the air and darted toward a slanted tree painted with rust-colored splotches of old blood. Conall followed her, and once standing beside the trunk, he craned his neck to gaze up the steep slope beside it. Deep grooves and hoof marks left imprints against the soft soil. "The creature we're seeking pursued this white hart. She fled this way and slipped due to her injuries. Smashed her head and broke her neck during the fall."

"But she's been skinned for her pelt. Are you saying it found her corpse then skinned her?"

Conall's features darkened. "She was dead or dying, and for her sake, I hope already gone. Either way, this tells us something about our beastie. It kills for the pleasure, lass. It hunts to hurt and perhaps even for vengeance. She escaped, and it searched through the brush to find her. Look there." He pointed toward broken branches and outstretched root systems crawling over the ground. Something large had torn through them.

Dark splatters of dried blood stood out against the green. "That's the creature's blood, not hers, isn't it? It pursued her while also injured."

"Aye. She hurt it. Although my brethren put up a good fight, I doubt they injured it as deeply as this deer. Yet it still gave chase and came after her."

"Then we should get going. If it's hurt, we have a chance to end its miserable existence."

Ferghus stumbled between the trees with a hand against his side. More than a day later, the wound continued to bleed at an unrelenting, but nonthreatening rate. It would close, granting him a brief reprieve, but once he resumed the fatiguing trek across the lowlands, it would tug open again within the hour.

If not for the magical link binding his soul to the cloak, he would have bled out the previous day. Some traveler on the eastern roads would have found his corpse if stray abominations didn't pick his bones clean and run off with the pieces.

At a distance, it appeared to be an ordinary mantle, although it had been sewn from numerous furs. The fairy had promised that while he possessed the magical garment, no one could smell or see its true form unless he willed it, and that had served him well in eluding the werewolf alpha on his trail.

He hated the shifters, and he loathed them for what they'd allowed Cairn Ocland to become. In his distant memories, he recalled a beautiful land of endless green and clear blue lakes, but the reality of the current times yielded a kingdom of backward seasons and infested waters haunted by dangerous aberrations.

The farmers may have returned to sowing their crops, but only hard work could abolish the malignant beasts lurking in the wilderness. Hard work performed by hunters while shifters fled to the green and forsook their own countrymen.

The furry cowards.

They didn't deserve their powers. And the dragon on the throne didn't deserve his respect and fealty. Where had Alistair been while his people suffered? Hiding in his enchanted castle, safe and sound, with all the food he needed.

Ferghus staggered and fell to a knee as blood seeped from beneath the bandages he clutched to his ribs.

Puck appeared in a blaze of cold fire, black tendrils of smoke arising from the top of his horned head. "You know what you have to do," the imp said. "Sew the deer skin into your cloak. Make the change and use its combined power."

"I don't have the time for that."

"You'll bleed out," Puck warned.

"I'll be caught if I stop now."

His entire plan had gone to hell when Sorcha showed up to rescue her grandmother with the werewolf at her side. Had she come alone, he could have been the hero of the story, rescued her grandmother, and had Sorcha's true love.

But he had a second chance, an opportunity to fetch the true Emilia and bring her home.

"There is another way, a quicker way," Puck said. The imp cackled, stirring a sense of trepidation in Ferghus's gut.

"What? Why didn't you say so from the start?" the hunter demanded.

"You were too weak then, but now you are strong. Strong enough to wield the true power of the shroud. Eat it. Make its flesh a part of you," the imp goaded. It leaned forward, orange eyes bright in a tiny face no larger than Ferghus's thumbnail. "Consume it."

"The skin?" Ferghus eyed the bloody strips of deer hide. Thick hair covered the outside, and the thought of forcing himself to swallow it down turned his stomach. "That's disgusting."

"Any part will work, though devouring her heart would have served you much better. There's more power there, and it would have been all yours to consume."

"Give me the needle," he grunted. Puck said nothing more about eating the torn flesh.

The imp twisted around and presented his barbed tail. Accustomed to the routine, Ferghus snapped off the long stinger without any hesitation. With his own hair, he created thread by tugging a few strands from his scalp and twisting them together. Puck licked his black lips and leaned in closer to watch.

Ferghus jabbed the needle through the skin, poking it in and out the ragged square of untanned hide until it became part of his cloak. It wasn't pretty work, but he'd come to understand that it didn't need to be neat and tidy.

Maeval's magic took care of the rest, and within seconds the blood-stained deer hide melded seamlessly to the rest of the grisly garment.

"Don the shroud! You must, you must!" Puck urged him. He bounced up and down in place while clapping his soil-colored hands.

What choice did he have? Ferghus shed his clothes as quickly as his injury would allow, and wherever a piece fell,

Puck skipped to gather it into a leather sack.

Moments later, Ferghus stood nude in the dwindling sunlight. He cast the cloak over his shoulders and fastened it with a metal clasp bearing an unfamiliar rune. Gazing at it for long gave him a headache like spikes burrowing into his eyes, but it was the mark of Maeval. Pressing it into his upper chest nicked the skin and gave it the blood sacrifice required to fuel his transformation.

With crystal clarity, as if it were only yesterday, he recalled the whisper of her frigid breath against his nape when she'd given him the simple clasp.

"From blood and bone I take thy power, the deepest darkness will devour. Ripped from soul once true and bright, twisted by thine selfish spite."

Every shift hurt as much as the last. It was fire in his bones, a chisel in his joints rending his body to pieces and reshaping him anew. As Ferghus collapsed to his hands and knees, the cloak of skins and fur melded to his body in a grotesque cocoon. He gasped and rolled onto his side, paralyzed and unable to breathe.

It suffocated him, every excruciating second filling him with regret.

Why had he done it?

Why?

With Maeval's magic, he could finally free Cairn Ocland from the tainted beasts roaming its grounds and bring true justice to Dalborough.

Every part of him tingled. The magic twisted around him, soaked into his soul, and burned through his mind. Bones cracked as he was reborn. His teeth sharpened and his face elongated into a furry muzzle as claws with keen edges sprang from the tips of his fingers. Strength flooded his body, replacing the misery with euphoria.

The creature arose on two hind legs and sniffed the air. A thousand scents and sensations rushed to his sensitive nose and tickled his whiskers. He became aware of each bird in the trees overhead, the scurrying rabbit in the brush, and squirrels scampering down barren branches. A fleeting minute of pain had made him the apex predator, a better hunter than he'd been as a man.

Each sound became the distinct parts of a living symphony, and his new ears heard every note. He lowered to a crouch and touched his nose against the damp soil. He wasn't yet strong enough to take on Benthwaite, but soon the time would come.

And when the time came, vengeance over Dalborough would be his.

But first, he had to kill Conall TalWolthe.

Chapter 8

ANASTASIA DRIFTED FROM shelf to shelf in the library, removing books one at a time to flip through the pages. During the years since her arrival at the castle, she'd gained a commendable knowledge of the Oclander language.

"Will you not come to bed and rest?" Alistair called from the doorway.

Anastasia glanced over her shoulder and smiled. "Actual rest?"

"Actual rest," he confirmed, grinning. "With war on the horizon, it does neither of us any good to be ill slept and exhausted." They'd flown that day over the Shadow Glen in search of signs of Maeval's awakening. Upon finding nothing unusual, they scoured the dark forest from above then returned to the castle.

Anastasia chuckled and crossed to him. "Words of wisdom spoken like a true king." After standing on her tiptoes, she kissed his cheek. "I will come to bed soon."

"I will hold you to it. Or send Elspeth. She asked me to fetch you."

"Soon. I promise."

Once her husband had gone, Anastasia returned to her search. Years ago, when she'd been new to the castle, she'd crossed an old tome—some TalDrach record related to the old times of Maeval—but she'd had no need of it then. Knowledge of it tickled the depths of her memory, but with so many books on the shelves, she couldn't locate the mysterious book. It could be anywhere, on any of the multiple levels stretching toward the ceiling.

"Damn," she muttered.

"Burning the midnight oil, my cousin?" Victoria called from the doorway.

Although the interruptions persisted, Ana turned to regard the blonde with a smile. "Only a little."

Victoria had lived with Anastasia for five years, leaving behind their mutual family in their native kingdom of Creag Morden. By their standards, her cousin had long surpassed marrying age, now an old spinster who would never have a family.

But she was beautiful, not only outside, but within as well, and Anastasia adored Victoria with all her heart. Try as they might, she'd met no one in Ocland who gained her romantic interest, and teased that she'd live vicariously through Anastasia's passionate romance with the king.

Moving inside the library, Victoria stood beside a table and raised a brow. "Perhaps you should get to bed with your husband."

"Aren't you a little mother hen? I thought you'd be sneaking in wine and chocolates to help me with my search."

Victoria sniffed, folded her hands in front of her primly, and looked every inch the proper young noblewoman. "It's late. Your books can wait."

Ana's nape prickled. A bizarre change came over the room, the air growing heavy and thick, an oppressive weight on her shoulders. Before she could move to the stairs, light from her lantern glinted off a reflective surface among the nearby row of unaligned books.

"What's that?"

She raised the lantern, and its warm glow shone over the gold-embossed title stamped against the leather. *Fables of the Darklings*. The book sat out a few inches further than the rest of the titles on the shelf.

Had it been there moments ago? In five years, she hadn't yet grown accustomed to magic sometimes providing the objects she needed. But if the enchanted castle sensed she needed it…

Anastasia removed the book from the shelf and tucked it beneath her arm before she descended to the lower level. Each step closer to her cousin made her pulse roar in her ears like thunder.

"Here, I'll flip through it while you go to bed."

"Why are you so insistent I leave?"

"You work yourself far too hard, and for such a trifling nuisance." Victoria fluttered her fingers toward the window. "One forest is hardly worth all this effort and the loss of your beauty sleep. And poor Elspeth, the little one wants more of your attention, but you're hardly there to give it. Always flying somewhere on dragon's wing."

Ana froze with the book hugged to her chest and stared at the woman across from her. "You're not my cousin."

Victoria held her right hand to her heart. "I am too. Do you no longer recognize your blood relations, Anastasia?"

The thing before her spoke like Victoria and certainly favored her physical attributes, but her eyes lacked warmth and emotion. Her dispassionate blue gaze stared through Anastasia without love.

"You look like my cousin, but you are not her. Reveal yourself."

Both women acted at once. Victoria brought a long knife from behind her back and drove the blade toward Ana's heart as the queen thrust her palm against the doppelganger's chest and released a spell. A frigid explosion of magic consumed the creature then spread over its torso in rolling waves of ice.

"Who are you?"

The creature hissed and broke free from the ice binding its limbs. Frozen shards flew out in every direction. What had been Victoria's face shifted and changed. The jaw unhinged and the fair complexion darkened to ashen gray.

Ana raised the book to block the doppelganger's next lunge. The dagger drove through the thick volume and out the other side an inch before it stopped. She twisted the book and ripped it from the creature's grip, denying her foe its only weapon.

It stumbled back and hissed at her again. With every passing second, the similarities to Victoria blurred away and revealed the grotesque being beneath.

A glow surrounded Anastasia's hand then pulsed with power. She flung the changeling assassin into the air and held it in place with her focus. "I won't ask again. Who are you?"

"Doom. You're all doomed." Its cackle made the hairs on her arms stand up.

Although she'd never encountered one before, her half-fae mother had taught her at an early age to beware and never suffer a changeling, as they were creatures of the dark and irredeemable. Closing her hand into a fist, she tightened her magical grip until the choking creature spoke no more. She let it fall limply to the ground.

With the changeling dead, she plucked the fallen tome from the floor. The gleaming knife protruding from it combusted on contact, incinerating the book and all its pages. Startled, Ana cried out and tossed it into the hearth.

The library doors burst open and two guards rushed through with hands on their swords. One jerked back when he saw the corpse on the floor. "Queen Anastasia, are you all right?"

"Where were you both? I was attacked and no one came to my aid!" Not that she'd needed their help.

"The stairwell, Your Grace, on our way to retire for the eve."

Had they been in her home kingdom of Creag Morden, the captain of the guard would have had them whipped and dismissed for dereliction of duty, if her father didn't take action himself for leaving her unprotected and vulnerable. But circumstances differed in Cairn Ocland, and no longer was she treated like a delicate flower.

All the same, she'd also never witnessed two of the guards abandoning their posts.

"What reason do you have for leaving your stations at this hour?" she asked, softening her tone.

The bewildered guards stared at her. "You bid us to leave and dismissed us early to our beds."

"I did no such thing."

The two men exchanged uncertain glances. "Your Grace, you stepped out only moments ago and relayed your request.

We were to the stairs, but turned back when we heard the commotion."

The doppelganger, she realized. The creature had taken her shape before assuming Victoria's.

"We must find my cousin. Quickly! I fear she might have been harmed."

The guardsmen spread out over the castle, but no matter where they looked, they found no sign of Victoria. Like many others across Cairn Ocland, she'd been spirited away.

Chapter 9

"I'M SERIOUS, LASS. The bow may not be my preferred weapon, but I know a good shot when I see one. You're talented."

Pleasure flushed through her, warming Sorcha's cheeks despite the cool night air. They rarely traveled in the dark, but as they closed in on their prey, they'd both decided there wasn't a moment to lose. At any moment, they could be upon the creature.

It couldn't be allowed to recuperate.

"You're only saying that because I caught dinner."

Growing fonder of Conall's company with each passing day, Sorcha had finally become accustomed to his cocksure attitude. She drew parallels between him and Ferghus, deciding he wasn't nearly as smug as her childhood friend.

By now, she would have slapped Ferghus or stormed off to be free of him for a day or two, mission be damned, but Conall's shifter intuition always drew short of pushing her away. He always knew the right thing to say to turn her opinion of him around.

"Have I any need to lie? Perhaps you should be the one to hunt for breakfast each morning too."

"Noooo," Sorcha protested. She had grown accustomed to the wolf rousing first, scrounging up whatever animal he could hunt, and renewing their cold campfire. Few things could beat awakening to a hot meal.

Conall had thoroughly spoiled her.

"Ah, whatever will you do if you're not the last to crawl out from your bedroll." He grinned at her. "Have you ever thought that maybe I want to be pamp—" He quieted and jerked his head to the left, nostrils flaring and eyes wide.

"Conall?" she whispered when he merely stared into the distance.

Without answering her, he lowered to all fours in wolf form and bounded forward to place his nose against the ground. Sniffing furiously, he continued for a few paces before returning to his human body. He crouched there, strong thigh muscles bared beneath his kilt, the fingers of his left hand buried in the soil. "This is fresh blood. He's near."

"How far?"

"Ahead of us," Conall whispered. "I'll go around and try to catch it from the front. Ready your bow and advance with caution. I'll draw the monster's attention to me and allow you to strike from behind."

She nodded and drew an arrow from her quiver while Conall loped away in wolf form. Step after slow step, Sorcha moved forward and sought signs of their quarry. Finding no prints, not even a patch of bent grass blades, she continued with the light of the moon to illuminate her path.

Leaves rustled, and a snapping twig drew her attention immediately right. Her heart leapt into her throat. Prepared for the worst, she drew the string taut and prepared to let her arrow fly.

Into a vacant clearing occupied by a single deer.

"Son of a motherless goat," she swore.

Sorcha lowered her bow and stared into the docile eyes of a doe standing in the middle of the glen. Her fawn lay in the grass nearby while the mother grazed on the lush blanket of clover. Conall was nowhere in sight.

The bastard had tricked her and gone off on his own.

She doubled back and tracked her wolf companion, following his prints through the forest. Having traveled with him for so long, she knew the impressions his paws left behind and the divots his claws tore into the earth when he ran.

Growing more furious by the second, Sorcha ran after him with only the stars to light her path. They glowed with more intensity than ever.

She heard the fight before she came across it, vicious snarls and hair-raising growls. Putting on a burst of speed, she tore through the trees and saw the two locked in battle.

The beast had Conall outsized, superior to him in muscular bulk and height. It was neither a wolf nor a bear, stocky and broad-shouldered like the latter with a narrow muzzle and two upright, pointed ears. Its white and gray fur blended to darker hindquarters, though she couldn't detect all the colors in its pelt at a glance in the moonlight. At night, everything came in shades of gray.

Fangs gleamed from two sets of snapping maws. On the defensive, Conall danced around his opponent, weaving in and out of the larger creature's attacks with remarkable grace.

She drew her bow and waited for a clear shot, determined to help her companion but too cautious to risk striking the werewolf instead. When she loosed the arrow, it flew true. The sharpened point buried deep into the strange creature's flank.

She may as well have been a bee, as little as her strike seemed to bother the thing. Her second shot landed higher, the arrow piercing the creature's side beneath the ribs. Snarling and swinging its enormous limbs, its strike knocked the wolf back and flung him through the air.

When Conall struck the tree, it snapped in half beneath the force of his weight, creating an explosion of splinters. Wooden shards flew in every direction, and he thumped to the ground on his side with a yelp.

After staggering to all four paws again, the wolf shook his head. Two steps later, he stumbled to the side and sustained a blow to the shoulder when the monster crashed into him.

Sorcha drew the next arrow and lined up her shot, praying to the stars above. With Conall and the aberration locked in combat, she couldn't gain a clear shot at its heart. So she went for the next best thing.

She released the arrow, and the whole second of its flight felt like minutes until it reached the monster's throat. She'd never landed a more perfect shot. Spittle flew from its mouth with an earth-quaking roar, and then it reared back onto both hind legs.

Her wolf remained below it, defenseless and dazed. If she didn't act, Conall would die.

With her sword raised to deflect the monster's claw, Sorcha threw herself between the werewolf and the creature. The shrill scrape of claws over metal preceded the rip of flesh. Her flesh. Pain scorched across her nerve endings from her wrist to her elbow. Two of his claws tore through her forearm, splitting the leather vambrace then the skin beneath.

She screamed.

The beast had her at its mercy. It loomed above her, larger than three Conalls. Larger than she anticipated from afar. At that moment, Sorcha's life flashed before her eyes, her body frozen with a combination of fear and memories of her family. Dad carrying her on his shoulders. Egan tickling her at dinner until she surrendered the last meat pie. Her mother tucking her in at night in the wagon.

The cloak blazed around her once more, illuminating her assailant with ruby light. Instead of delivering the killing blow, the beast froze midattack and stared with eerily familiar gray eyes. Then it turned and fled. It had the hind end of a bear, but the short, triangular tail of a deer. Creaking, grotesque noises filled the air as its shifting joints rearranged and it loped away on all fours.

Sorcha tumbled into Conall, lost her footing, and fell in the dirt. Within a second, he was human again and kneeling beside her on the soft soil.

"Red! By the stars, lass. What the hell did you think you were doing?"

"Saving you!" she sobbed. Tears streamed down her face as freely as the blood trickling down her arm. Fat droplets splattered to the ground.

Conall glanced toward the direction of the retreating creature, swore loudly under his breath, then swept Sorcha into his arms. He ran with her faster than she'd thought any man could move while burdened with another being, lacking his wolven speed but possessing an endurance she envied.

When he stopped, the moon had shifted in the sky. Conall's chest glistened with sweat, dampening her clothes and making his tunic cling against his pecs. Tink flit ahead of

VIVIENNE SAVAGE

them, and with her glow, she led the pair inside an abandoned farmhouse.

"Water, Tink. Hot."

The little sprite took off through the house. He set Sorcha down on the water-stained counter and took her arm in his hands. "Foolish woman, look what you've done."

"What I've done? He was going to slaughter you while you laid helpless on the ground. I saved your life."

He grunted. "I had it where I wanted it. I was only pretending to be injured to get it to lower its guard."

"What? No you weren't."

"Do I appear to be joking to you? He rose and bared his belly to me. I planned to shift and gut him with my sword."

Studying his livid expression was the only proof Sorcha needed. She closed her eyes, mortified by her mistake. Because of her, it had escaped.

"I'm sorry," she whispered. "I thought I was helping."

Rather than respond, Conall brooded until the very moment when Tink returned with a pail of clean water. Some sloshed over the edge as the sprite lowered it to the ground. Despite days of traveling alongside Conall and Tink, Sorcha still marveled over the sprite's extraordinary magical ability.

When Tink chimed, he nodded in response. "Aye, prepare the poultice while I bathe the wound." He worked in silence, a muscled healer with a tender touch she hadn't expected of a warrior.

Her werewolf companion surprised her again when he closed the wound with a row of tidy stitches. She refused to cry or utter a sound each time the needle passed through her skin. Afterward, he gazed at her with an expression of admiration.

"It wasn't deep enough to cause permanent damage. You'll heal in time," he muttered while applying a herbal poultice over the injury.

"Thank you," she said in a quiet voice. "Was it a shifter?"

"That was no shifter I've ever seen. There are only the twelve clans, and while the griffins may have the features of an eagle and hindquarters of a feline, they're no abomination. This was *unnatural*."

"Could it be a blend of different clans?" Sorcha asked. "Has there ever been a breeding between both of your kinds?"

Conall cleared his throat. "It does not work that way."

"How *does* it work?"

"During the rare event when we do mate between groups, the child of such a union takes after one parent or the other," Conall explained.

Sorcha frowned. "Then what other possibilities could it be?"

"After seeing the beast with my own eyes, I'm convinced we're dealing with something born of dark magic. Something worse than Rangvald's curse. A skinwalker."

Sorcha leaned forward and studied his face. Conall's features had darkened, lips pressed into a thin line, jaw tense and eyes brooding. "You mentioned the term before but never explained it to me."

"It is an evil thing," he said. "A magic so black it destroys the soul. We only have legends of such a creature, but it's all that fits."

"All right, but what about what happened tonight?" she asked. "It could have killed me, but it didn't. That must mean something, doesn't it?"

"Aye, it proves the thing has a prejudice against shifters and chose to spare you. It wanted *me* dead. Somewhere beneath all that fur, there's a human soul."

"But it could have torn me to shreds then finished you."

Conall frowned. "Which was why I wanted you out of the fight, Red. You nearly got yourself killed. You're damned lucky that magic cloak of yours scared the beast off."

"That was foolish of you, Conall TalWolthe," she chastised. "Partners don't do that to one another. Neither do friends."

"Friends do what they must."

"That isn't friendship, Conall. How can I trust you if you're going to lie and run off?"

He hesitated then glanced away. "Like it or not, you're only human. And if you hadn't interfered, we'd be burning his corpse now." The wolf sighed and ran his fingers through his sweat-dampened hair. "I accept that you're right, and I'm sorry, but it's over and done. We'll rest tonight, set out again in the morning."

"Fine."

"Fine," he repeated before he stomped out of the kitchen.

Sorcha sighed and remained where she was. The slash on her arm stung and itched beneath the poultice, so she ignored it and focused on her surroundings instead. The farmhouse had seen better days, but it was shelter at least, with four walls and a roof. A partial roof. One corner had collapsed and sank inward, and the smell of rotten, damp wood hung in the air.

There were hundreds of homes across Cairn Ocland in the same dilapidated condition. One day, they would thrive again. First, the king's army had to drive out the last of the

Scourge.

Light glimmered from the pail beside her. Sorcha shifted over and cautiously peered over the rim. Worried blue eyes gazed up at her, set within the tired features of their monarch.

"Queen Anastasia?"

"Ah, thank the stars! I've found you at last. I'd grown worried enough to come seek you personally if this night's effort failed."

"We're taking refuge for the night. There's no water here except for this pail."

"I'll have to find a better way to contact you," the queen mused. "But that's another matter altogether. I wanted to let you know that things are far more ominous than they appeared. A changeling was here at the castle, and it's taken my cousin Victoria."

Sorcha's stomach flipped. "If they breached the castle…"

"Yes. They have great power behind them, and during my fight, I lost the book that might have had answers. I'm not giving up, however. I hope you've fared better."

"We were also attacked," Sorcha replied. "Your cloak protected me for the second time."

A deep line creased Anastasia's brow. "It won't be useful much longer. Another attack perhaps, if that much. What attacked you?"

"A creature unlike anything Conall or I have ever seen. It smelled of aberration and at first looked like a wolf, but walked on its hind legs like a bear. It was too dark to see it clearly, but I am almost certain it had antlers as well."

"My husband told me of the twelve clans blessed by stars, but he never mentioned such a shifter."

"Conall told me of them as well. He thinks it could be a skinwalker."

The queen's expression hardened, lips pressing into a thin line. "Then it is no creature to be confused with a shapeshifter. It is a monster, and it is up to us to warn each of the remaining clans. As long as this thing roams free, no shifter is safe. The king and I shall notify the wolves and soon join the hunt."

"How do we fight it if we come across it again?"

"My knowledge of skinwalkers is limited by my ignorance of your nation's legends, but I suppose the tried and true method of slaying any creature will suffice. Behead it. Injure anything seriously enough and it shall fall. If I come across anything to give you an advantage, I will let you know. Until then, do what you do best. Hunt."

Chapter 10

O N THE FOURTH morning after Anastasia's urgent message, they met opposition to their eastbound travel. Sorcha had never strayed so far from Dunrathi lands and knew only rumors about the marsh ahead of them. Rumors claimed it to be a dark place, treacherous long before Rangvald's magic ever kissed the Ocland ground.

Conall stared ahead of them. Wondering what he saw, she followed his gaze to the space beyond the thinning trees. It appeared wonderfully green beneath a serene, cloudless sky, though gentle tendrils of smoke curled from the surface of the water.

"I have something for you," he said.

He drew a leather thong from around his neck then draped the cord over Sorcha's head. She blinked up at him before dropping her gaze to the large tooth that had settled between her breasts.

Scrolling runes—delicate lines patterned in swirls and angular shapes—had been carved into the enamel. The leather thong wrapped around the end, but didn't completely cover up the worn edges where the tooth had been broken off. It stretched across her palm, and she tried to imagine how much longer it would have been whole.

"What's this for?" she asked. "It's lovely."

"It's an enchanted token and will help you pass through the miasma unharmed."

Tink darted from Conall's shoulder and into his face, flashing red and green. The volume of her spritely chimes increased to a frenetic raucous of sound.

"Tink—"

She crashed into his nose, and despite the size disparity, Conall stumbled back a step.

"Is something the matter?" Sorcha stared at the agitated woodkin.

"No," he replied too quickly for Sorcha's liking.

Tink made a sustained, shrill noise then lifted into the heavens and disappeared, a green comet shooting across the gray cosmos.

"What in the name of the stars was that about?" Sorcha asked.

Conall frowned. "Nothing. She didn't want to cross through the bog."

"Aren't woodkin able to withstand that kind of thing? What about you?"

"Aye, she could, but it stinks." He broke eye contact and rubbed the back of his neck. "Anyway, the fumes don't affect me much either. Most shifters are immune to such things, and it troubles me none to walk through it."

"Oh."

A whiff of something awful drifted to her on the wind, the odor of boiled eggs that had been left to rot in the sun. She shuddered, all too aware of Conall beside her. In respect to his finer sense of smell, she didn't complain.

The closer they approached, the greater the stench

became, first tickling her nose and then gagging her. Rapidly blinking her eyes did little to alleviate the stinging, and tears freely ran down her cheeks.

"You can ride me from here."

"Ride you through this?"

"The ground is treacherous. We'll be through in no time if you ride me, Red. Besides, I wouldn't want to make you walk through this muck. Not only is it unbearably cold, but it'll soak straight through your boots."

Lacking a valid argument against his logic, she nodded. The truth was, she was relieved, and the mud squelching beneath her boots had already caked the leather in foul muck.

Conall shifted and lowered to his belly, and with some effort, she climbed onto his back. Being atop him placed her as high as the vantage she'd become accustomed to while riding Eachann, startling her when she realized the wolf shifter was literally as large as a stallion.

He moved at a sedate pace, picking his way along through water of increasing depth. She welcomed the slow walk and used it to get accustomed to his gait, which wasn't completely unlike riding a horse.

No matter how bad the smell became, she refused to voice a complaint. It had to be a hundred times worse to his shifter nose.

"Thank you for this, by the way," she said to break the stifling silence. No birds sang in the skeletal trees stretching up from the slimy water. Even the buzzing of insects was absent.

He made a quiet noise, neither a growl nor a whimper. Once or twice he stopped and snapped his head to the left, only to resume his pace seconds later. Everywhere she looked, red vines covered in thick leaves trailed through the water. The dull russet color reminded her of rust. Or dried blood.

Eventually they reached a mossy swell above the water where moisture didn't squish from the earth and rush above his paws. He moved atop the highest point of the curve and stood for a time, scraping muck off his paws onto the grass. Even as a wolf, she recognized the disgust in his wolfish expression, his lips curled away from his teeth as he growled in frustration.

Would it be wrong of her to offer to bathe him at the first bed and breakfast or inn they encountered? Her father's map claimed they would encounter a settlement along the way to the gorge where the bears dwelled.

"If you want me to dismount, I will. I have to be making you heavier," Sorcha murmured.

He shook his head then stepped forward to follow a sloping descent until his front paws left dry ground. The island lurched as Conall's rear legs lowered into the muck and became submerged above his hocks. At the same time, several vines shot from the water and wrapped around the wolf's long legs, yanking him out from beneath Sorcha.

Without a saddle, she relied only on a handful of the plush fur covering his withers. She lost her balance and fell with a splash into the fetid bog, screaming as something unseen ripped her companion through the water.

Another vine shot out and coiled around her, but her cloak flared, and a sizzling pop filled the air followed by the stench of burning muck. The vine released her and another retreated with her unfortunate companion.

"Conall!"

His assailant didn't remain unseen for long, arising from

the muck as a curtain of water sluiced from its sides. It wasn't a tortoise, nor was it any kind of animal she'd ever seen, but something worse with a circular mouth yawning open in the center of its algae-covered belly. Its appendages were little more than fat, boneless vines, and their brownish-red color blended in with the native flora.

Sorcha scrambled to her feet and drew her sword from the scabbard, sweeping the blade through the air just as the vines launched toward her direction. She sliced through them and pushed herself forward through the mire.

"Conall!" she cried out again. It was so enormous the wolf resembled a toy in its grasp. Shifting forms aided his struggle, and he nearly slipped free until the vines slithered tighter around his legs.

"Sorcha, run!"

She didn't even consider obeying. Her sword flashed through the air and sliced into one rubbery whip. The creature's shriek dropped Sorcha to one knee, her sword planted in the murky water. Slapping both hands over her ears failed to deaden the sound, and it pierced through her skull with the intensity of a cleaver.

It moved, sluicing through the marsh with ease and dragging Conall behind it. Freed from her pain, Sorcha snatched her blade from the water then charged after the retreating creature. For something so large, it moved abnormally fast.

Another head-splitting screech echoed across the marsh, but she pushed through the discomfort and forged ahead. Conall continued to fight. Each time his sword cleaved through one vine, another took its place.

She caught up and hacked at the whipping tendrils flying through the air. The leafy appendages dripped green ichor from every slash. She cut her way through until she reached the bulk of the creature. The stench rolling off it was nauseating. Bile churned in her stomach and burned up her throat. Holding her breath, Sorcha forced her way forward and drove her sword into the algae-covered beast.

It took all her strength to yank the blade free, the weapon stuck at first until she withdrew it with a fount of viscous plant fluid.

The shriek intensified, threatening to deafen her, but she thrust forward again. Without warning, it flung Conall aside, and he landed in a heap not far away from her. Rushing through the water, the bog monster disappeared into the high brush of the swaying grass in the distance, trailing dark green slime behind it.

"Conall?" She waded through the ankle-high water to help him to his feet. He'd landed graceless and limp at first, terrifying her. Each second she waited for him to move stretched into hours. Pressure compressed her ribs and stole her breath. He had to be all right. She had to see him smile one more time. Or even tease her again over supper when they settled down in their makeshift camps.

If he died now, she'd never have the chance to overcome her pride and beg him to kiss her one more time.

Please be alive. Please be well.

"I'm alive," he replied, though he groaned as if he were injured, and soon she saw why.

The water had tinted pink with his blood. A deep gash glistened against his side where the thing had gnawed away a layer of skin. She almost felt queasy looking at it, not because bloody wounds sickened her, but because the injury was on a man she'd begun to view as a friend despite his attempts to baby her.

Groaning, he moved away to retrieve his sword. "Are you injured?"

"Me? You're asking if I'm all right when you were the one it tried to eat?"

He took her by both shoulders. "I'm not concerned about me. Did that thing harm *you*?"

"No," she answered in a softer voice. "My cloak protected me for the last time. But it *did* hurt you."

"I'll survive."

"You're injured. The least you can do is let me care for your wounds." Her gaze raised to his blue eyes and saw him studying her in silence. "Please. Let me return the favor."

Silence hung between them, neither of them speaking or moving, his hands still holding her by the shoulders. He squeezed both before dropping them away.

Conall gave in first. "All right."

Thanks to Sorcha's watertight pack, her belongings had escaped a thorough soaking. Once they were on solid, dry ground, she opened her medicine kit and removed a salve to clean the filth from his wound.

He hissed between his teeth when she blotted his ribs dry, and again when she poured the liquid over the gaping cut.

Sorcha glanced up at his face. The muscles in his neck and shoulders tightened.

"I'm sorry," he apologized, shattering the tense silence between them.

"Why?"

"I should have realized there was danger, lass. Should have noticed it there."

"How could you? That thing was practically part of the marsh."

"I smelled it," he admitted, "and I heard the vines moving in the water more than once. But I didn't realize the size of it. What you fought wasn't part of the marshland. It *was* the marsh, a spirit of the bog corrupted by the curse."

She blinked. In all her years of travel, she had battled many aberrations, but never something like he described. Most had been normal creatures once. Spirits were another thing entirely.

"We need to find someplace to clean up, or the beast we're tracking will smell us miles off."

Bits of the creature were in her hair and the green goop it bled stank. She had never wished for a bath so much in her life.

Luck was with them, and by nightfall, Conall saw the lanterns of a village in the distance. The muck from the marsh had dried on his clothes and skin, leaving a stinking crust that he feared no amount of scrubbing would cleanse.

There were several buildings, but he identified only one as the living quarters by its two smoking chimneys. Another in the early stages of construction appeared to be little more than the bones of a future home.

"Need help, travelers?" a masculine voice called from the distance.

Conall moved closer to Sorcha, prepared to edge in front

of her when he saw the limping farmer approaching them from the field. The man held a loaded crossbow at his side, but not pointed at them.

The farmer stared Conall up and down, then glanced at Sorcha. His eyes eventually returned to Conall and took in his healing injury before he muttered, "Well, aren't you a big son of a bitch? What're you two strangers doing here, and what can we do to help?"

It took Conall a moment to process the man's impressed utterance. Despite his pain, he laughed. "We're on our way to see Clan Ardal."

"You're not one of them? I'd've taken you for a shifter any day."

"Shifter I may be, sir, but I'm no bear."

"You have a name then, lad?"

"Conall TalWolthe. My companion is Sorcha Dunrathi, and we've just had a trying time in the Corpse Bog with one of the angry spirits."

"Ah. You poor pair, it's no wonder you look half-dead then. Still, it's good to make your acquaintances. I'm Havros, keeper of this wee village. You're welcome to what we have, though it isn't much."

"Thank you," Sorcha said. "We won't need much, just some clean water, hot if you can manage."

"And food," Conall said.

Havros chuckled. "You're in the right place for that. This used to be some of the best farming land around. A year ago, a bunch of us decided to venture out, see if we could get it working again now that the curse is lifted."

"You've had some success it seems." Sorcha gestured to

the rows of corn.

"Aye, some, but it's made us a target for bandits. Come along with me."

Five families called the small hamlet home, and they all dwelled in the same communal longhouse. They ventured out from different areas of the farm to offer greetings when Havros led Conall and Sorcha to the cabin. A fire burned at either end of the rectangular structure, heating the space to a comfortable temperature. The cold didn't usually bother Conall, but with the marsh filth still damp in his boots, he welcomed the heat. Beside him, Sorcha perked up and let out a satisfied sigh.

"Damona, love, we've guests. Hunters," Havros called out.

A plump woman with a few streaks of gray in her auburn hair looked over from her work at a loom. Upon seeing the sorry state of their visitors, Havros's wife hurried away to heat water at the stove. The farmer sent his two oldest sons to help.

"You give those boots over to my youngest boy. He works magic with leather, and he'll have those set to rights in no time."

"Thank you," Sorcha said. She sat down to pull off her boots and Conall followed her example. A freckled, sandy-haired boy no older than ten fetched both pairs and left the room.

"Damona, have we anything to fit this one?" Havros asked.

Conall shook his head. "No need to trouble yourself with finding me clothes. I'll wear fur."

Damona set both hands on her hips. "And do you plan to eat that way as well, lad? You'll join us at this table and eat a proper meal with your own two hands. Those are the rules.

Lan…" She sniffled. "Landron always joined us at the table."

"Aye, he did," Havros agreed.

"There were trousers on the line when they came for him and his things. They might be a bit big on you, but nothing a belt won't fix. I'll fetch them." Damona rushed outside, leaving Conall to wonder what happened.

"Landron?" Sorcha asked.

"A fine lad and a fine bear. We found him two days ago out by the north creek, skinned and…missin' his heart. We're all taking it hard. Like losing one of our own." The farmer's shoulders dropped. "It *is* losing one of our own."

Skinned. The word raised goosebumps over Conall's brawny arms as memories of discovering his cousin's corpse flooded back to him. "Wait a moment, Landron was a werebear?"

"Aye. It wounded my soul to find him that way, and my wife's too. We haven't had more than a single encounter with bandits since he took up the spare room on the farm with us."

Conall's brows shot up. A shifter helping a human village.

"I know what you're thinking," Havros said defensively. "He was here because he wanted to be. And a fine help, too, otherwise all these fields you see would be ruined, those livestock in bandit hands. The wild men come from the lowlands to the south to steal and rob from us, too lazy to break their own ground. They form raiding parties instead."

"So the bears gave you aid," Sorcha said.

"Aye. We give them half of our harvest and some of our livestock. They send a bear or two to patrol. It's worked fine for us for the last season until now."

"No one saw or heard anything when Landron was

attacked?" Sorcha asked.

Havros shook his head. "Nae, lass. It's about a three hour walk from here to the creek. We've been digging a trench to bring water into those old fields. All I know is we saw him for dinner, and then he left to patrol as he always does. The next afternoon, we found him. Helluva thing. Too large for any of us to lift into a cart, so we trekked to the Ardal clan and delivered the news to his mum. They came for him at once." The farmer sighed. "If something can kill Landron, what hope is there for the rest of us?"

"It sounds like the beast we've been tracking. So far it seems focused on shifters, not humans."

"But it took my grandmother," Sorcha said.

Conall shot her a warning glance. "Took her. It didn't kill her. Has anyone gone missing around these parts?"

"Couldn't say. We came from Tarling, but that's a good week's ride from here. Since coming back to the farm, the only contact we have is with Clan Ardal and the hunters who pass through," Havros replied.

"Over here, dear," Damona called out to Sorcha. She waved her toward a wooden tub set behind a curtain.

"Go on," Conall encouraged when Sorcha hesitated. He considered offering to join her, but he set the idea aside. Teasing her had its time and place, but never in front of others.

Her smiles and blushes belonged to him.

While the two oldest boys hauled in enough water for Sorcha to take a proper bath, Conall had a chat with Havros about the current state of relations with Clan Ardal.

They didn't blame the humans, or so the farmer claimed. A few of them had attended Landron's memorial the previous evening out in Ardal lands, and then they'd returned to their homestead. The bears had no more spare hands to give them in the meantime, with some of their number away in search of Landron's murderer.

"You'll want to head straight east through the Scarlet Wood," Havros said. "The entrance to their canyon is hard to see, which is the point, but if you keep the marked trees on your left, you'll find it. Of course, more likely they'll find you first."

"Thank you."

"Thank me by destroying the monster that killed Landron. He didn't deserve the indignity done to him in his death."

"I will."

They were low on water by the time Sorcha's bath was done. Enough remained to wash their clothes for the line, and for Conall to scrub the plant muck and mud from his skin. But he didn't receive the long soak she'd taken and looked forward to finding a pond, or even a river with clear-running water.

They joined the families for supper and slept with the oldest children by the hearth wrapped in wool blankets over the hard floor.

Still, Conall couldn't complain about their hosts' generosity. It was better than nothing, because sooner or later, they'd be back to nothing at all.

Chapter 11

SORCHA MADE NO argument when Conall suggested she ride him again. Their quarry had gained ground, so every bit of speed was necessary. The immense gash down his side had healed to a thin, tender line, but it wasn't the swollen and bleeding mess she'd cleaned the previous day.

Wind whipped through her hair as they ran across the valley. Despite her worries, she didn't fall off the moment he sped from a lope to a full-speed bound. Their progress through the bog had been cautious and slow, but now Conall had flat ground and soft grass to race across. She leaned forward over his neck and kept a firm grip in his ruff.

They didn't slow until they reached the Scarlet Wood. Once there, Sorcha stared up with wide eyes at the towering trees. She'd never seen any so large before and wagered it would take at least four people with their arms outstretched to circle a single thick trunk. Heavy clusters of crimson leaves bedecked the branches over their heads, giving the forest its name.

She slid down from Conall's back and stretched out her stiff muscles.

"Am I that uncomfortable to ride?"

"No, but after leaning forward so long, my back gets stiff."

"Perhaps I can…"

Conall stared past her, and the crunch of leaves prompted Sorcha to whirl and come face to face with a mountain of moving, shaggy brown fur towering far above her. It raced over the ground, maneuvering between trunks with grace unexpected for a creature of its immense bulk.

The beast had killed one of *these*?

Trembling, Sorcha stared in petrified awe at the giant bear. It stood taller than the largest draft horse and much bigger than Conall's wolf form. She thought it might even stand as tall as her grandmother's house. With a single swipe of its massive paw, it would reduce her to Sorcha-flavored jelly on the forest floor.

"We come with no intention to harm," Conall said. He placed his body between her and the werebear. "Only to talk."

Growling again, the bear lunged forward with an aggressive feint toward them.

"Stop that right now!" Sorcha called up to it, infusing her voice with steel. "I am a royal messenger, come on behalf of the Queen of Cairn Ocland. You *will* listen to me and hear your queen's words."

Sorcha raised her chin when the bear continued to loom above them, refusing to back away and be cowed, but inside she was shaking. Her stomach churned and her mind screamed for her to run away from danger. She ignored it and stood her ground.

After a moment, the bear shrank down and a giant of a woman faced her.

"You have courage and resolve, messenger. Come, we will hear what words you bring us, though we have our own troubles to worry over without the monarchs adding to them."

  VIVIENNE SAVAGE

That was it? Sorcha's knees were still trembling, but all Conall did was grin at her before he stepped forward and clasped arms with the enormous woman. She stood a full head above him, her skin a ruddy contrast to her flaxen braids.

"Sorcha Dunrathi, meet Heldreth, clan matron of Ardal."

"Pleasure," Sorcha replied.

Heldreth led the way through the forest to a rocky wall, where she disappeared into a narrow, twisting crevice barely wide enough for her broad shoulders. The bears had found a natural fortification, rock walls surrounding a hidden woodland grove with a meadow spreading out on the southern edge.

The breathtaking sight touched Sorcha to the bottom of her soul. She'd never witnessed such an unspoiled oasis. Never crossed wilderness undamaged by Rangvald's curse.

"This is lovely," she said once capable of forming words.

"It is one of the few small pockets to have escaped the worst ravages of the curse," Heldreth told her. "Here is where the bears have made their stand since Rangvald laid his death magic."

"You spoke of troubles. We heard about Landron," Conall said.

Heldreth's gaze lowered. "Yes, his death is a tragic loss, but there have been other things as well. A changeling tried to kill my mate while wearing my father's face. Now we question everything and each member of the clan, but we haven't a clue of where to find him."

"The same happened with my grandmother," Sorcha said. "We rescued her from an unknown werecreature only to discover she was a changeling."

The bear stopped short and swung around. Her gaze shot past Sorcha to Conall.

"What she says is true. I helped dispatch the filthy creature," he said. "Which is part of why we're here."

"You're tracking the ghost beast," Heldreth said.

"I am. I take it you've seen signs of it."

Heldreth grunted and waved her hand. "It moves as a phantom, leaving its scent behind but nothing else. At first we thought it was a wolf, but the smell is… incompatible with your kind."

"You're not entirely wrong," Conall said. "It's a skinwalker, Heldreth. A true skinwalker."

The tall woman sucked in a sharp breath. "That cannot be."

"It is. We've seen it with our own eyes. He had the flanks of a bear, the head of a wolf, and the antlers of a stag. Less than a week ago, we discovered a skinned white hart," Sorcha said.

Heldreth bowed her head and murmured a quiet prayer. When she looked back up, her hazel eyes were solemn. "These are dark times indeed if a skinwalker has made itself known."

"Then it seems to me that Clan Ardal and TalWolthe have reason to benefit from helping each other," Sorcha said. "We should assume the skinwalker and fae are connected. It's killed both of your clansmen, taken my grandmother and your father, and shall continue until stopped."

"She's right," Conall said. "I hoped to suggest such an alliance myself once I came this way in pursuit of the creature."

"As you know, I can't grant such a thing on my own. You'll have to plead your case to all of us. Come with me."

She led them through a winding path paved with river

stones toward the center of the village. To her right, Sorcha saw residents of the haven hanging their clothing on the line. To the left, a pair of knee-high bear cubs streaked down a stone walkway—children playing with their newly acquired gift.

Tanned buckskins painted with dyes made up the large tent where the bear council met. Heldreth stooped to grab a handful of pine cones from a nearby pile, then tossed them onto the fire. The flames flared blue and sent a puff of smoke through the opening in the ceiling of the tent.

"The council was already gathered?" Conall asked.

"We saw you coming. Wolves don't venture this way often, so your appearance seemed a justifiable cause to meet," Heldreth explained.

Two men sat around the fire. One, larger than Heldreth, had a salt and pepper mane of hair that reached past his shoulder. A scar ran across his left eye.

The other man sported a headful of short blond curls. Black and green tattoos covered his chest and arms in zigzagging lines, sprawling over defined muscle that made Conall appear meek and slim by comparison.

"That's Father Bear and Little Bear," Conall whispered against Sorcha's ear, nodding first to the older man then to his companion. "Heldreth is the mother of this clan."

His scruff brushed against her ear lobe, provoking a shiver.

Contrary to his name, Little Bear had to be the biggest bear in all the village, surpassing both Heldrethand the grizzled man beside him. He caught her staring and chuckled.

"Those of my title are usually much younger," Little Bear explained. "I'll be replacing Father Bear when he steps down within the next year or two. Another voice for the lads and wee lasses will take my place. How it's always been and always shall be for us."

"This meeting is now called to order," Heldreth said. She gestured for them to take a seat on the rugs across from her and the other elders.

"What can Clan Ardal do for you?" Father Bear asked. His voice sounded as old as the rest of him appeared, dry as gravel and hard.

Sorcha folded her hands in her lap and looked at each bear in turn without knowing who to address first. "I come on behalf of King and Queen TalDrach. They ask you to commit some of your warriors to their attempt to retake the Shadow Glen."

"Why does a dragon need bears?" Little Bear asked. "Is his fire not enough to rid the forest of the Scourge?"

"It is. He and the queen shall both go into battle."

Little Bear scowled. "Then if they have the queen's sorcery, they have no need of us. Why send you to thin our numbers even further?"

"Because Oclanders," Sorcha said, "and it's time to take back our kingdom together. Rangvald may be dead, but the final vestiges of his magic cling to the distant places, and the Shadow Glen is one of the final infestations. And the largest."

Father Bear narrowed his eyes. "There's too much danger in going. We'll leave this grotto unprotected."

"There's too much danger if we do not," Heldreth said.

The older bear snorted. "The loss of Lorekeeper Darach has weakened our clan. Without his advice, we cannot make this decision."

"The hell you can't," Conall growled. "This skinwalker we're tracking is connected to the troubles in the Shadow Glen, and it's killed a bear, too."

"Two bears," Heldreth corrected him while staring the other elder down. "Neacal was slain in the same manner three months ago, but only skinned."

Conall slammed his left fist into his open palm. "Three wolves, two bears, and one of the last stags dead by this monster. I can't be the only one who sees the link here. That's two lorekeepers missing. Do you not see what's happening?"

"Are you suggesting this beast crept into our homes under our noses and took the lorekeeper?" Little Bear asked. He raised a brow, unconvinced.

"No. I'm suggesting it's got help and is working alongside someone else. Someone with the magic to attack a queen in her own enchanted castle."

Heldreth snapped her attention toward Conall. "You did not mention an attack on the queen. What happened?"

"Another changeling," Conall said. "It came for Queen Anastasia but failed to kill her."

Sorcha nodded. "We believe Maeval has returned."

A hush fell over the group as if a curtain of silence had been drawn over the meetings. After several terrifying heartbeats of being on the wrong end of their aggressive stares, Sorcha cleared her throat.

Father Bear rose from his seat. "We do not speak that name here."

"Well, you had better get used to it," Sorcha retorted. "Because if we ignore the threat she poses, all of Cairn Ocland will suffer. Our queen believes the black fairy has defied death and returned centuries later."

"What is the word of one human sorceress to us?" Father Bear demanded.

"The word of our *queen*," Little Bear pointed out. "She helped end our curse and deserves our respect."

The older bear glowered. "Our king ended the curse. He destroyed the warlock and brought peace to our land."

"With Queen Anastasia's help," Sorcha insisted. "If she wanted, she could order your assistance, but she hasn't. She's *asking*."

"Even if the dark fairy isn't resurrected, there is still the matter of this skinwalker and the Shadow Glen," Heldreth said. "Rangvald is dead and gone, and it is up to us to retake our land now that his spells weaken.

The youngest bear nodded. "Agreed."

"You've been outvoted, Ulrin," Heldreth said. "Your household may remain behind as cowards, but mine will fight alongside our king *and* queen."

"As will mine," Little Bear agreed.

Father Bear bristled but made no further comment.

Sorcha blew out a quiet breath, unclenched her fists from around the hem of her cloak, and shook out her tingling fingers. Some bears were better than none at all.

"Thank you. I've been asked to direct everyone to meet at the base of Mount Kinros. The king and queen have taken their army to scout the remains of Maeval's fortress."

"We will make arrangements and ask for volunteers."

Heldreth dug up a handful of dirt and tossed it on the fire. The other two elders did the same, and then Father stomped away without a backward glance.

  VIVIENNE SAVAGE

"Don't judge him too harshly," Little Bear said. "Neacal was his son, and he'd warned him not to travel far from our home. Same for Landron."

"Thank you, Ramsay," Heldreth said. She brushed her hands together and rose. "As for you two, you must be exhausted. Stay in my home for the night. Rest your aching bones and have a hot bath." Her gaze focused on Conall.

"I don't stink."

"I disagree. You smell like wet fur, lad. Wet fur and other things I won't mention."

Conall glowered at her retreating back and muttered under his breath. It took every ounce of Sorcha's willpower not to laugh at his grumpy expression.

Sorcha had never slept in a bed so soft. In fact, it was so soft she couldn't sleep more than a few hours before she slid from beneath the blankets and slipped into her clothes. Her body left an impression in the fluffy mattress.

Deciding a walk would be a better use of her time, she laced up her boots and stepped from the bedroom into an open hall lit by stone lanterns.

"You should be abed." Heldreth gazed at her across a low burning fire. Cherry red coals burned in the shallow pit, providing warmth more than light.

"Is it strange for me to say that your beds are too comfortable to sleep in?"

The large woman chuckled and gestured to an adjacent log. The long benches had been sanded down smooth at the top and beautiful carvings decorated the sides.

"You are used to the hard ground, I reckon," Heldreth said.

"Most nights, yes, but my grandmother's cottage doesn't have a bed so fine. And, well, even the bed at Benthwaite doesn't compare."

"You humans with your odd frames. They don't let you make the padding thick enough."

"I'll keep that in mind if I ever decide to sleep on a cloud again." Sorcha smiled at her new friend and held her hands out over the coals.

"Conall seems to have taken a fancy to you."

"To me?"

"Aye, lass. He's marked you. Quite a big step there for a wolf or any shifter, but especially a wolf."

Sorcha froze and stared at Heldreth. "Excuse me?" Her mind returned to the morning a week prior when she'd awakened with damp hair and belongings. Conall claimed it had drizzled while she slept.

"He's marked you," Heldreth repeated.

"You mean he's *pissed* on me?"

"What?" The matron blinked then gave a deep belly laugh that almost shook the foundation of the stone cottage. "Marking isn't what you think it to be. We're not animals, not entirely. It means you smell of him, lass. Have you never noticed the way he is never far from you? It's to show other males that you're his."

"We're traveling together and the path is dangerous. Of course he's close by."

"And then there's that." Heldreth pointed to Sorcha's throat.

Sorcha lifted her fingers to the carved fang dangling from her neck. "This allowed me to pass through the marsh without choking on the gases."

Heldreth chuckled. "Are you in the marshland now? I know how to spot an infatuated wolf. And that one is certainly infatuated.

"Forgive me, Heldreth, but you're mistaken. He likes to flirt, it's true, but that's all."

"You'll see."

At a loss for words, she rose from her seat instead. "I should leave you to your own rest. Is it permitted for me to explore?"

"Aye. Perhaps the air and night sky will do you some good."

"Perhaps," Sorcha agreed.

After bidding Mother Bear a restful night, Sorcha stepped from the cottage and onto the stone walking path connecting the various dwellings.

She came across a modest garden and paused. While not flourishing, it looked healthier than the vegetable plots back in Frosweik. She recognized sweet potatoes, bitter greens, and winter squash. Bushes heavy with small red currants grew in a cluster several feet away, and a single tree bore ripening pears.

So much hidden away, all because the humans and shifters had quarreled so long ago.

Without disturbing the growing plants, she continued her ambling path through the quiet village. Rather than clear her mind, her thoughts kept drifting back to Heldreth's words.

Had Conall really marked her? Or was the bear seeing more than what was there?

The path came to an end at a small pond. The still surface, smooth as glass, reflected the moon and stars above like a mirror. Huddling in her cloak, head bowed, she gazed down at her own reflection and considered the matter.

Until meeting Conall, she hadn't known such an attractive man could exist. Their king had certainly been appealing to the eye, but taken and claimed by his loving bride. While Ferghus was handsome, his arrogance often overshadowed his good looks. Conall's confidence felt different; he didn't brag, merely stating the truth instead.

And the fact was, she had enjoyed their kiss, up until his wandering hands revealed deeper intentions. He moved fast—too fast—and that insistent rush put her on edge as much as it thrilled her.

What am I even considering? she asked herself. *He's a clan leader. Strong. Virile. Of course he takes what he wants. Which is exactly why I should stay away.*

A low rumble shook the ground, creating small ripples in the tranquil surface. Seconds later, the source of the disturbance came into view. Four bears and a red wolf bounded down the lane, each carrying the carcass of an elk or some other creature of comparable size. She couldn't identify each prey animal, the shifters out of view within seconds.

Watching him travel alongside the bears had taken her breath away. She'd seen him run before, but never at a distance, allowing her to view the elongation of his wolven body in full gait. He traveled unhindered over the open ground, head high, body as powerful as the magnificent beasts flanking him.

Conall must have joined the morning hunting party. His willingness to assist others and volunteer his time to another clan endeared him to her even more. If Heldreth's words were true—if he did desire her for more than a passing fling—could she ask for a kinder, more generous and selfless man to court her than the leader of Clan TalWolthe?

And did she even want another to try?

Chapter 12

AFTER ANOTHER UNSUCCESSFUL search of the library, Anastasia retired from her evening hunt through the shelves and stepped into the hall.

How could she possibly focus on work with Victoria gone, delivered to an unknown fate? Everything she'd ever learned about changelings told her the beasts kept their prey alive for insidious purposes, draining them slowly of life force to benefit their fairy benefactor.

Tomorrow, she and Alistair were to soar away from their castle and venture south to investigate Kinros, and still, she had her doubts. None of the scouts had returned, and she smelled the magic on the winds.

Maeval would be expecting her, and she'd had nothing but time to create any number of magical fortifications.

"Ana?" Alistair called from the end of the corridor.

Her gaze snapped up to her husband, and she put on a smile. "Yes? What's the matter?"

"Elspeth's asking for you," Alistair said as he crossed the distance to meet her. He pouted like a sulky child. "Apparently, I am not as good at bedtime stories as her mum."

Anastasia chuckled and leaned up to kiss his scruffy cheek. "Don't take it too hard, my love. She much prefers playtime with you, remember?"

Her husband grunted and crossed his arms over his chest, a grumpy dragon who was taking his daughter's rejection to heart. Another kiss against his jaw and then a second on his lips chased his frown away.

"I'll join you in the study when I'm done," she promised, shooing him off.

She ascended to the residential floor then headed down the hall to Elspeth's room. The wooden doorframe had been decorated with preserved flowers from summer and smelled as fragrant as they had when plucked at the height of the season.

With an easier smile on her face, Ana rapped her knuckles lightly on the open door before she stepped inside. Every wall in the room was covered in vibrant color, put there by Elspeth herself. She had drawn a red dragon near her window and ducks beside the bed. Flowers and trees flanked her wardrobe.

"Mummy!" Elspeth grinned from her bed, sitting in a nest of blankets and sheets. Her neatly plaited braid could only be Alistair's work, her husband much better at the task than Ana herself.

"I'm told someone didn't want their daddy to read to them," she teased.

Elspeth leaned forward to whisper in a confidential tone, a serious look on her young face. "He doesn't do the voices the way you do. They sound silly."

A grin spread over Ana's face despite her effort to remain equally stoic. "Ohhh, I see. Well, I won't tell." Alistair would be crushed.

After stroking her fingers through Elspeth's ginger hair, Ana perched on the side of the bed. "Fetch the book you'd like me to read from, then."

Wasting no time, the little girl pointed to a book on the adjacent bedside table. "That one!"

Anastasia frowned. It didn't resemble any of their usual storybooks. "Where did you get this one? I don't recognize it." She ran her fingers over the black leather binding and traced the gold embossed title.

"Sometimes Great Grandmother leaves me little gifts," she confessed.

"Does she now? Like what?"

"Paints, a stuffed dolly, and now a book. I tell her thank you every night in my prayers."

"That's very thoughtful and polite of you. Now lay back and I'll read you a story."

"Two?"

"One tonight." She laughed and pulled the blankets up over Elspeth's tummy.

Opening the book revealed pictures in rich and vivid colors. She ran her fingers over the pages and flipped through them until a single title caught her eye.

A Wish Upon a Fallen Star.

"Yes, that one!" Elspeth cried. "I want to hear that one. I love the stars."

"And the stars love you as well," Ana told her, though she hadn't yet adapted to Cairn Ocland's worship of nature, the skies, and the earth, so used to the gods she knew in her former kingdom. Was it possible for a force of nature to know love? To care about mere mortals?

For Elspeth's sake, she hoped so.

"Once upon a time, many centuries ago, a wicked fairy tricked a kind-hearted lord's son and stole him from the manor's garden. Try as they might to recover the boy, his parents had no success. They hired many knights, and nobles from distant lands made their way into Cairn Ocland, hoping to gain riches from his wealthy parents."

"Why didn't the king and queen help?"

"I imagine they were occupied with other matters, my darling."

"You would have rescued him."

"I would have tried." But with Victoria missing, she'd taken a strike to her confidence. Her own cousin stolen from beneath her nose, the abduction occurring a mere floor below the library. "Devastated by her son's loss, Lady Aoife appealed to the stars for aid. She had only a single child, and she told the heavens she would do anything to have him safely returned. And the stars, moved by her plea, shed a single tear. It fell from the sky and split into three fragments, one to the men of the western lowlands, while two plummeted to the forests south of Calbronnoch. Where they fell, a deep crater formed in the earth, later giving life to Loch Arweg when the rainy season came. But before that, the lord ventured out with his men to investigate this occurrence, and there they found two swords."

"But what of the boy?"

"I'm getting there, my love." She tousled Elspeth's hair again. "The boy's mother and father feared the worst outcome. Dark fairies were known for eating little ones and devouring their souls—"

Elspeth gasped. "Mummy, is that why the bad fairies took Victoria? For food?"

"Oh, my sweet, no. We'll get her back, I promise." Her and everyone else who had been taken.

"With the discovery of the two swords, the people of Calbronnoch realized it was a gift. Lord Brennan prepared to enter the Scarlet Wood, only to encounter his wife before he could depart. 'I cannot allow you to face her alone, even to save our son,' Lady Aoife said. 'I love him as dearly as you, and the stars gave us two. I am meant to accompany you.' Unable to disagree with her logic, the lord relented."

Elspeth's eyelids drooped, only to blink open again in a panic, as eager to hear the remaining story as her body was demanding of rest.

"As the boy's mother and father were the Lord and Lady of Calbronnoch, they each took one of the star shards and journeyed deep into the Scarlet Wood alone. During the fight, the lord was gravely injured, but his sacrifice allowed his wife a chance to plunge her shard deep into the evil fairy's chest. Within moments of her demise, the sword became nothing more than iron flakes and dust in Lady Aoife's hand."

"And the boy?"

"Saved."

"His father?"

"Saved as well, little one, for his mother had the blessing of the heavens and with one kiss and embrace from their son, he was healed and able to rise. Together, the family went home and vowed to protect the second star sword. To this day, it is said the sword resides in a place of honor at their estate in Calbronnoch, treasured until it is needed again."

Elspeth yawned and turned her cheek against her pillow while Anastasia stroked her hair. "That was a good story." Soon, her eyes closed and her breath slowed to an even rhythm. Certain she was asleep, the queen kissed her daughter's brow

VIVIENNE SAVAGE

then tiptoed from the room.

Time with Alistair would have to wait if the story in the book was true. Quick steps carried her through the castle and back to the library. She went from shelf to shelf gathering books she thought might have the information she needed.

"A History of Calbronnoch," she read as she opened the first large tome. She skimmed her finger down the aged paper as she read, flipping through page after page. The name Lord Brennan leapt off the paper and caught her attention.

"Ana?"

She jerked her head up and blinked, wondering how much time had passed as she read. "In here," she called over.

Alistair appeared around a tall bookshelf and frowned at her. "What are you doing now?"

"This appeared on our daughter's bedside table." She held up the story book for his inspection. "I believe it came from Grandmother."

"You said she's not allowed to help."

"She isn't. Technically, she's only given her only great granddaughter a story book."

He grunted and muttered about fairy nonsense. Prepared to help, he pulled a chair from the opposite side of the table and joined her. "What are we looking for, Ana?"

"Any mention of these star weapons. I've managed to locate the original source of the story, I think. It was the Lord of Calbronnoch whose son was taken. See? It's mentioned right here in this passage regarding the city's history." She passed the history book and fairy tale to her husband then returned to her pile of research.

Alistair leaned back in his seat with a thoughtful

expression on his face after he'd finished the story. Five years ago, her husband could barely recall how to read, but had since become as voracious as her when it came to literature.

After all, he'd spent thirteen years trapped in his shifter body until she broke the curse with true love's kiss.

He rubbed his bearded chin with his thumb and gazed out the window. "A third star fell to the western lowlands... that would be near Etherling."

"Then we must go there—"

"Etherling was sacked by Dalborough. If there was anything of value there, then it's in their vaults now," Alistair said. "What's left of the city is a ruin within the Shadow Glen."

"Then we'll have to go and recover it. I will contact Sorcha and have her check the ruins of Calbronnoch. It's in the same direction she's already heading."

"All right. You get that sorted, and at dawn, we'll fly to Dalborough. If I'm going to raze an enemy castle, I need a few hours sleep." His hazel eyes twinkled.

"I'll be up shortly. I mean it this time."

He raised a brow.

"I promise."

His studious gaze didn't end, but he did rise from the table and approached her to cup her face between both of his coarse palms.

"My Ana, I feel as if I've placed undue burden on you over these years."

"Alistair, it's no burden."

His heavy brows drew down, creasing his forehead in consternation. "If only I could do more than fight monsters. Your magic is the true reason we've come so far and restored so much of the kingdom. Even now, others trek across Cairn Ocland to bear my responsibilities in my stead while I remain here in this castle delegating risks to others."

"That isn't true. You've done plenty. You pushed the Scourge back to the Shadow Glen and rallied the hunters. *You* recognized my magic was blind to the darkness festering there."

He stroked across her cheek with his thumb. "Perhaps you're right."

"I *am* right. Cairn Ocland is my home as much as it is yours, and I will fight for it with everything I have. Even the shifters have welcomed me, a human, with open arms. Sure there are some who view me as an outsider..." Her mind went to the reclusive bear clan. "But the vast majority of this kingdom love me. They love us both."

"How could anyone feel anything but love for you? Still… I am sorry about Victoria."

"Shh. We will rescue her. Only one person is to blame for my cousin's abduction, and her name is Maeval." She stood on tiptoe to kiss her husband again, met by him halfway.

After promising to join him in their bedchamber, she sent him away and hurried to her laboratory. Although the room had belonged to her predecessor, Alistair's mother, practicing her arcane arts within the mystical chamber always brought her a sense of peace.

Shelves of books related to alchemical studies, potted plants, and even rows upon rows of magical reagents filled the room with mystery. Even though she'd been its frequent visitor for five years, she uncovered a new secret each time she visited.

A year ago, the crystal ball had been one of those

mysteries. She'd missed her family deeply, and while Alistair was willing to fly her to Creag Morden on a whim, she knew his kingdom needed him too much to bear frequent absences.

One evening, she'd been sitting at the Witch Queen's table in peaceful study when the candlelight glittered off the crystal's orb. It shone like semi-translucent opals and reflected a dozen breathtaking colors. When she'd inspected it out of curiosity, it had responded to her touch, lit with magic, and moments later she was gazing at her mother's face in its polished surface.

She'd stumbled upon a scrying globe, a tool used to spy on others. It could see what her telescope could not and hear conversations from afar with little risk.

It also allowed her to speak across distances, so long as she had something personal to the other person and they had a reflective surface close by.

Clutching the leather hair tie she'd nicked from Sorcha in one hand, she traced the other over the pearlescent sphere. It sang as gentle as a tuned harp, each magical touch from her fingertip releasing another melodic note.

Anastasia's image wavered and faded away, her reflection replaced by the starry, midnight sky.

"Best to sleep now while you have the chance, lass," Conall's voice filtered through the mirror.

"How can I possibly sleep when it's so cold and our fire won't remain lit?"

"Then you'll have to move closer to me. I won't bite."

Recognizing the seductive tone in Conall's voice, Anastasia cleared her throat loudly. "Sorcha?"

The pair quieted. After a pregnant pause, Sorcha leaned into view. "Hello, Anastasia."

"Finding you wasn't so difficult this time."

Sorcha's tired grin filled the image for a moment. "After our talk the last time, I've taken to filling a bowl with water each night when we stop. Of course, it's usually a block of ice when we awaken."

"Clever. Now tell me, how close are you to Calbronnoch?"

"A day or two, no more," Conall said, his voice heard though she couldn't see him in the small image.

"I've discovered a few things and may have a lead to direct your journey," Anastasia said. "Sorcha, I know you're tracking the beast that attacked your grandmother, but I think at this point we can assume Maeval has her, as well as the others who have gone missing."

"What can we do?"

"I've managed to find stories about two weapons forged from cold iron. I have reason to believe one is still in Calbronnoch, likely in the manor house."

"Cold iron?" Sorcha's brows drew together. "I'm not familiar with the term."

"The legends say it falls from the sky and is cool to the touch, even though the earth around where it fell burns."

Sorcha's eyes widened. "When I was a child, Gran told me a tale about a wicked fae who was slaughtered by a sword made from star metal. The fairy had taken a little boy."

"It wasn't a mere story, Sorcha. It was history. Emilia was a lorekeeper, and so was the wolf elder taken from the Misty Woods. Their pack alpha arrived yesterday seeking aid, since the clan leader is with you."

Conall's face appeared beside Sorcha's in the mirror. "Griogair has been taken?"

"Yes. I believe Maeval hoped to remove any threat of discovering her weakness."

"Which is why she attacked you. The library at Benthwaite is massive. Is that where you found this lead?"

Anastasia grinned at the two shimmering faces. "Believe it or not, I found it in a children's storybook in Elspeth's room. A word of advice to you, Sorcha dear. If you should ever decide to have children—read to them every night."

Since Conall knew the way to Calbronnoch, Sorcha opted to let the wolf take the quickest route. Riding him came easier each time, until his loping rhythm was as natural to her as Eachann's galloping stride.

It also became as enjoyable, although she couldn't bring herself to let him know how much she looked forward to climbing astride his back.

They pressed as far as they dared under the rumbling skies, and then Conall led them to the remnants of an abandoned logging camp. Their timing was impeccable. The moment they stepped inside the sawmill, rainfall pounded against the ground. Sorcha pulled her cloak closer around herself and stood in the doorway to watch the lightning streak across the sky.

The weather had taken a turn for the worse over the past few days, nights growing colder and the days shrouded in gray. The wind was the worst. It cut through her clothes no matter how tightly she bundled up.

"How much farther?" she asked over her shoulder.

"A few hours. Calbronnoch was built with lumber from

  VIVIENNE SAVAGE

this mill. As soon as the rain lets up, we can continue onward, but this gives us a chance to rest and eat." His mouth sounded full, so she turned to see him crouched beside her pack, eating from the collection of winter apples the bears had given them from the orchard.

"And stay dry." She grinned. "Tired of smelling like wet fur?"

Conall growled low in his chest then threw his apple core at her. "And hungry. Just remember, if I smell like wet fur, so will you."

"Fair enough."

"I should warn you that the last time I passed through, there were enormous silkstrider spiders in the area, but I thinned their biggest nest. We shouldn't have any issues."

Spiders. She shuddered in revulsion. She'd seen the black silkstriders once or twice over the years. Thepony-sized arachnids spun dark silver silk used in fine garments.

"What do you think will happen once the king and queen reach Dalborough?"

He shrugged and moved to her side, offering bread he'd already slathered with honey. She took it gratefully. "As far as I know, their king has no reason to relinquish any weapon to them. Not that he'll have much of a choice. They could pry it out of the old bastard's hands if they wanted with no one to stop them."

"Did they demolish so much of Dalborough's forces that they can boldly walk inside?" Sorcha asked.

"Aye, they did. Thousands of soldiers gone in a single battle. A cousin of mine served on the castle guard then, and he saw the entire battle when they all reawakened from the fairy Eos's curse. Diarmid says it was spectacular. Like nothing he'd ever seen. The queen is very formidable." He paused. "I guess I was behaving like an ass when I said otherwise weeks ago."

Sorcha grinned. "Well, I'm proud of you for admitting it."

It took three hours for the storm to blow past. During that time, they ate, refilled their water skins, and kept warm with a small fire. Conall rested his arm around her shoulders and she didn't shy away from him, insteadburrowing into the heat his shifter body radiated.

A tremor ran through her. Night after night, they cuddled close, but it never grew old.

"Cold?" he asked.

Too shy to speak the truth, she shook her head. "No." Her cloak provided sufficient warmth and his body heat added to her comfort, but the truth was that she wanted more. She wanted to crawl into his lap,but refrained from the impulsive whim. Instead, she savored every moment of him holding her while warming her face against his throat.

As promised, they reached Calbronnoch in a couple hours. Sorcha slid off his back at the edge of the city ruins, and Conall shifted.

His tensed back and shoulders drew her concern. She touched his arm and gazed up at him. "Worried?"

"Old memories, lass, that's all. I'm fine."

"All right," she said in a gentle voice. She squeezed his hand and smiled up at him. "Where would this weapon be?"

He squeezed her hand in return, a fragile smile on his face. "There was a weapons cache in an old root cellar below Elder Matlock's home, but I don't recall any mystical blade. I'd

VIVIENNE SAVAGE

suggest the lord's manor. He was an arse of the worst kind but had an impressive collection if I recall correctly."

"It's as good a place as any to start."

The abysmal aura of a cemetery hung in the air, a silent and eerie ambience to a dilapidated and crumbling city. Old bones littered the streets, picked clean by buzzards or abominations.

"They say this used to be the shining jewel of the kingdom, next to Benthwaite."

"The stories had it right, Red. It was a beautiful place, but that was long ago."

Sorcha peered into each home they passed, unable to shake the feeling of being watched. Conall appeared equally apprehensive and walked close enough for their shoulders to touch. He gripped his sword hilt in one hand and glowered ahead of them.

"What is it, Conall?"

"It's nothing. I thought..." He shook his head. "I thought I smelled something."

"Spiders?"

He looked down at her and smiled faintly. "Not spiders, no. C'mon, our destination is only a little farther."

The Lord of Calbronnoch had lived in a two-level stone manor surrounded by a high wall, located on a slight elevation overlooking one of three central squares scattered throughout the city. While the home had withstood the test of time, the wooden door hadn't fared as well. The rotting remnants hung loosely in the frame. Conall entered first.

"I can look upstairs while you take the lower level," she suggested.

"I think it's better we stick together, Red. We can start at the top and work our way down."

"Perhaps if we're lucky, the king and queen will find theirs, and we'll have two," she whispered as they ascended the stairs.

"We may need two. If Queen Anastasia's fairy tale is correct, each weapon is only good for one strike, but it's absolutely lethal to fae and their bloodkin."

"What sort of weapon is only good for one hit?" she muttered. The whole idea was ridiculous and made her wonder if it was true—not that she was going to test the theory.

"A magical gift from the heavens," he replied.

Sorcha cut her gaze toward him and sighed, exasperated by his snarky tone.

They continued onto the upper landing and passed a railing overlooking the lower level. The decrepit corpses of the dead lay strewn wherever they had fallen—or wherever the monster left them at the end of the siege. The wolves of Clan TalWolthe had truly left Calbronnoch to its fate. She wondered how many had died, who fled in the night, and how many remained behind to make a final stand.

Dust carpeted tapestries and furnishings, and a dank smell permeated the air where water eroded the leaking roof and mold collected over surfaces.

Conall yanked her back by the wrist. "Something's wrong."

"What?"

He inhaled, expanding his chest with a deep breath. His nose crinkled. "I smell the Scourge. They're here somewhere, so be on your guard."

"Do you think Maeval would have sent her minions to retrieve the sword?"

"At this point, nothing would surprise me."

With each abandoned room they explored, the dread intensified until her pulse raced faster than a herd of galloping horses. A heavy door at the end of the hall led to the last room on the floor. She flexed her sweaty palm over her sword hilt and looked at Conall.

"That would be the master bedroom." His whisper skimmed across her ear, and desire for him warred against the anxiety of a possible battle against the Scourge.

Her cheeks warmed, but her body tensed to prepare for a fight. "As good a place as any to display a weapon."

"Aye. Be ready then. Their stench is heavy there."

Conall moved ahead, counted down from three, and then kicked open the door. Sorcha charged past him with her sword.

Unyielding, agonizing cold hurled her sideways. She struck the wall, head bouncing off a stone block, and she fell to the floor disoriented and covered in snowflakes. Although Conall made it farther into the room with his preternatural speed, he fared no better. The magical attack slammed him into a tall wardrobe.

A ghoul and a changeling in its natural, featureless state, stood in the center of the master bedroom beside the crumbling remains of a four-poster bed. The old animal skins on the bed had rotted, much like the rest of the building. Dusty cobwebs stretched across decaying furnishings, and the smell of mold permeated the air with the underlying odor of death.

The ghoul must have been a former inhabitant of the

city, perhaps even the old lord himself. Dried, leathery flesh the color of old porridge covered the creature's gangly limbs and filthy claws, split from age and wear, tipped each skeletal finger. Its milky white eyes stared at them.

Conall shook off his disorientation first. Shifting midleap, he bounded forward as a wolf and snapped at the changeling, but another ferocious storm of ice chips skidded him backward across the floor. He forged through it with his teeth bared in grim determination, as Sorcha took cover beside a toppled shelf and loaded a bolt into her wristbow.

A shimmer caught her eye, arcane light reflecting off a silver edge. The ghoul retrieved a sword from a case on the wall while the changeling continued to hurl spells to keep Conall at bay. It moved forward with the blade poised to strike.

They weren't there to steal it, she realized with terrifying clarity. They were there to destroy it.

"No!" Sorcha cried. She raised her crossbow and fired, though the bolt did no good. It landed in the throat of the ghoulish creature wielding the cold-iron sword. Undeterred, it sank the weapon to the hilt in the back of the changeling.

The sword broke apart at once, collapsing into tiny pieces of star matter and sparkling dust, glittering motes that blew away on the wind and nothing more.

VIVIENNE SAVAGE

Chapter 13

ANASTASIA HAD HOPED to never set eyes on Darkmoor Castle again, but for Cairn Ocland, she would do anything. With her heart in her throat, she tightened her grip on the horns at the nape of her husband's enormous neck and closed her eyes.

She had to be strong, had to face down the man who fathered her attacker.

It seemed as if a lifetime had passed since she'd been held as a captive princess, betrothed to a spoiled, arrogant prince who saw her as nothing more than a trophy to obtain. She'd escaped by the grace of her own stubborn tenacity, overcoming Prince Edward when he tried to take her by force the eve before their wedding.

This time, however, she'd face his parents as equals, and she'd stare them down knowing they were the monarchs of a broken country, a shattered family without an heir.

Taking strength in her own abilities and the magical power she'd cultivated since her and Alistair's victory over Dalborough's army, she opened her eyes again to see the black spires of the castle rising into the sky. All dark brick and cold stone. Lifeless.

"Are you ready?" Alistair called to her.

"I am."

From atop her king, she had a bird's eye view of the city below. Their descent initiated panic, and men hurried to and from battle stations to man stationary siege weapons designed to defend the city, or rather, the castle against a dragon. There wasn't a single ballista by the gates. And what weapons she did see, they were unmanned. All the defenses of Dalborough had been concentrated around the castle.

Alistair plummeted like a cannonball from the sky, rocketing toward the fortress with his wings tucked against his sides. A lance darted past him, but it missed by an enormous margin, posing no danger to him or Ana. And even if it had been on the right course, her magic would have deflected it.

No amount of time could ever dull the thrill of riding her dragon. With him, she felt truly free, part of the wind itself. It whipped through her red hair without dislodging the tiara tucked amidst her waves, and despite his speed, she felt secure on his back. His wings snapped out at the last second to catch their fall, and he coasted over the open ground.

The landing quaked the ground and threw the small gathering of armored soldiers off balance. The ones who kept their footing rushed from the archways and soldiers drew bows, nocking arrows against taut strings. As the first wave of them flew, Alistair exhaled an effortless arc of flames and incinerated each shaft.

Anastasia gestured with her staff, and the dozen armed knights struck an invisible force. With the next thrust, she flung them back away from them.

Her show of arcane power was all they required. After Rangvald's death, the kingdom had never recovered, its magical defenses annihilated. Men slowed without lowering their arms, eyeing Anastasia and Alistair with uncertainty.

Having their attention at last, Anastasia raised her voice to address them. "We haven't come to play games or tussle with you. We desire an audience with your king. Now this may go easily for you, or we can force our entrance. None here must die today."

"Have you not come to kill the king?" one of the knights called. His shield wavered and his sword arm quaked.

Ana shook her head. "No, though you are a courageous, bold lot to face a dragon for a man undeserving of your loyalty."

"We come to speak with your king, and only that," Alistair agreed.

Another trembling guard, albeit daring enough to face them, lacked the courage to remain in their presence for long. "Ah, please then, allow me to contact the royal emissary and to announce your arrival."

"That is fine," Anastasia assured them. She shifted as her husband gave a low, growling chuckle, exhaling twin plumes of smoke and fire from his scaled nostrils. He flexed his fingers and bided his time, front claws gouging deep furrows in the stone beneath him.

At last, minutes later—not the hours her father had awaited the emissary five years ago when he'd visited to plead for aid—a man arrived in a black and silver uniform bearing the royal crest of Dalborough's monarchy. "The king is not receiving visitors this day. You must come back another time after following the proper decorum."

Alistair snorted, releasing smoke and fire. The man shrank away and fell back a step. "Return another day?"

"The king is not well," the emissary babbled.

Ana scoffed and slid from her husband's back. "When is he ever?"

Without warning, Alistair surged forward, forcing several knights to dive and roll out of the way. His enormous bulk barely fit through, but he cut an entrance way for her to follow. She strode behind him with her magical power engaged, flickers of light dancing upon her fingertips. The men who charged to stop them struck an invisible wall and, again, were thrust back, soaring through the air and landing in broken heaps.

Through the entrance hall, they found more room and no opposition. It was as gloomy as she remembered, bleak and dismal, volcanic glass windows and no light save a small assortment of candles casting shadows over empty corridors that had been manned by guards when she last visited.

Where had everyone gone?

"This way to the throne room. They'll be there," she said to Alistair while pointing forward to the reinforced oak doors.

A blast from her staff blew open the doors. They slammed in and struck the walls. She strode through with Alistair at her side. The large chamber was exactly as she remembered it with one exception—one empty throne occupied the space to Queen Brunhilda's right.

King Frederick sat on the left, an old and shriveled husk of a man scarred by the consequences of his own mistakes. Most of his body had been covered in burns, leaving his skin tight and shiny.

"I'm sorry, my lord, we tried to stop them," the guard cried out from the doorway.

Ana stared up at the King of Dalborough on his dark

throne as she stalked across the room without slowing. The years had not been kind to the old man, nor to his wife, who sat beside him trembling in her resplendent gown.

"You have no right to be here," Frederick said.

"On the contrary," Ana said. "I have every right, King Frederick. You invaded our country. Our home. Now the time has come to pay the blood price owed to us for all the innocent men and women you slaughtered."

"You took my son!" he roared.

"Your son was a monster. Edward was the true beast, and he died because of his choices. Had he left Cairn Ocland alone, he would be with you now. But no, he chose to invade."

"To rescue you, you little bitch," Queen Brunhilda spat.

Alistair growled, and both monarchs flinched back. "Mind your tongues when you address my wife. She is a queen."

"Very well then. What have you come for?" Frederick asked.

"A weapon, made from a fallen star, stolen by you when you sacked Etherling," Anastasia replied. "We found a survivor who saw you take the spear from its place of honor in the fort."

Frederick chuckled, low at first, but then the sound crescendoed into frenzied, maniacal laughter. Ana looked at her husband then back to the mad king, tense as a bowstring.

"You want the star spear? That is why you came?"

"It is. Now give it to us," Alistair demanded, "and we'll leave you in peace to rule your broken kingdom."

"Oh, my dear, foolish, stupid little child-queen. The spear has already been given back to Cairn Ocland."

Anastasia blinked at him. "What?"

He leaned forward, a cruel glint in his eyes. "It was

delivered straight into the heart of King Rua. Slaying a dragon is easy, when one has the right tools."

Alistair's muscles tightened. Ana reached over and touched his arm without taking her eyes from Frederick's scarred face.

"Your days are done. You have no heir. No wizard. No chance to ever regain a speck of glory. The day they bury your rotting corpse cannot come soon enough, and when it does, I will never think on you again. No one will. Dalborough will be finished."

She turned her back to him and started out the way she had come in, Alistair at her side. Rage and fury rolled off her husband in bristling waves, palpable to everyone they passed. People scurried out of their way and no one said a word until they reached the courtyard again.

"Your Highness, a word if I may," a man called from their right.

Ana turned to the knight who had faced them at their arrival. "Be sure to choose that word carefully."

He looked from her to Alistair's scowling face, and while he blanched, he didn't back away. Ana respected that.

"Good queen, what you said before is true. King Frederick isn't an honorable man. He isn't even a good king, and I can no longer serve in good conscience." He ripped his tabard from his chest with a mailed fist, then dropped to one knee and bowed his head. Behind him, six more knights did the same.

"What is this?" Alistair asked.

"We wish to serve you, King Alistair. You and Queen Anastasia."

"You think I would take the men who invaded my home?"

Fury brightened Alistair's eyes as he stepped forward, and he inhaled a breath capable of reducing them to charred bones.

"King Alistair, my men and I went to Cairn Ocland to rescue a princess stolen by a dragon at the behest of her father. We were told nothing more."

"Aye, Your Highness," a second knight spoke up. "The prince claimed you had stolen her and that we would be liberating a young woman. We knew nothing more."

Anastasia drew herself tall. Before her husband could defend himself, she blurted out, "The prince attempted to murder me. In this castle, the night before we were to be wed, he tried to rape me. Is that any way to treat one's future bride? Any woman?"

"No, Your Highness. Though I know of men who would, I personally find no honor in ravaging an unwilling woman. I have served many years in this castle, and I knew Edward's predilection for taking unwilling bed partners. We all did."

"Yet you did nothing."

"We were sworn to obey. What could we do, Queen Anastasia, but follow the decree of our king and his heir?"

As Anastasia quieted, Alistair leaned forward to study the small group of defecting knights. "You would leave your homes? Your families?"

"We have neither. In Dalborough, knights cannot wed nor claim any child. Our lives have been pledged to serving the crown."

What sad and pathetic men. Looking at them all, Anastasia felt nothing but pity, while the rest of the soldiers remaining loyal to the king seemed to look upon them with contempt and disgust.

"You would abandon your duties here?" a loyal soldier demanded. "For this child and her beast?"

"We would abandon a tyrant," the knight snapped back. "What concern has Frederick had for us? For his kingdom? Dalborough is a powerless joke, and the very people to blame for it sit upon the throne right this moment. You would be a fool to remain here."

"What is your name?" Ana asked as she moved to the first knight.

"Lyonas, Your Grace."

"Then rise, Sir Lyonas, and your men with you. How long until you are ready to depart?"

"We could leave now, Your Grace, the moment we saddle our horses. We own no possessions."

"Then let us do so now. We will see you safely out of Ebonwell, but then you must ride to Benthwaite alone."

Word spread like wildfire through the garrison, and by the time Ana and Alistair led the way out the city gates, a column of armed men rode behind them. With magic, Anastasia sped their progress, and soon they'd all put Ebonwell far behind them.

They may not have gotten what they came for, but they had hobbled Dalborough's military without a drop of blood shed, nearly a hundred men newly sworn and bound to Cairn Ocland.

She had to hold on to the hope that Sorcha would have better luck and find the means to their salvation.

Chapter 14

FOR LACK OF a way to contact the queen to inform her of their failure, Conall suggested resuming their original journey east of Calbronnoch to the Floraivel Mountains. There he hoped to find the griffins of Clan Leomlaire.

But if they wanted to meet the elusive thunderbirds, they had to survive the remainder of their sojourn into the mountains. The wind picked up, and while Conall had a shifter's tolerance to the elements, it didn't take long for Red to tremble inside of her cloak. She wrapped the scarlet garment around her and endured without complaint despite the abrupt onset of snow flurries tumbling from the bleak and cloudy sky.

"You're upset with me," Sorcha said as dusk fell, interrupting hours of silence between them.

"What? No."

"If I'd been faster—"

"Don't you blame yourself, Red."

"I let it destroy the weapon."

"I was no quicker than you were. So if the fault lies in anyone, it's me. But I won't blame myself, and neither should you. Maeval is a crafty bitch, and she has eyes throughout the forest to report our whereabouts and actions, lass."

Sorcha nodded.

"We'll have to find another way to destroy her," he said.

"I'm sorry if I seemed upset with you in particular. I'm not. Just my thoughts are heavy with many things."

A familiar scent flit across his senses, the stale smell of rotting flesh, defiled spirit, and evil. And something else. Someone familiar he'd smelled only once.

"The skinwalker is here!" Conall cried as he drew his sword. "Be on your guard, Red."

She loaded a bolt into her wristbow and followed on his heels with her sword in hand. Since their previous argument and the creature's escape, Conall had surrendered any hope of keeping Red out of the fight. A warrior's heart beat in her chest; his huntress was as much of a fighter as him.

And he'd wronged her. Wronged her deeply with his lie.

It wouldn't happen again.

The warmth of her whisper ghosted his shoulder. "Is it up ahead?"

"Aye. Its foul stench isn't far," he warned. "Keep near to my back and be prepared to move. We can't allow it to get away a second time."

Up ahead at the edge of the clearing, he saw the marbled pelt of their quarry stretched beneath a grouping of trees. Conall's blood rushed a furious tempo, pounding in his ears, heart racing as he charged across the ground.

Upon his approach, he encountered a wholly different sight, as if a trick of the waning light had played his senses instead. There was no furry monster, only a man in an olive cloak shivering against the snow-dusted grass.

"Ferghus?" Sorcha stared at the huddled figure beneath the branches of the tree.

A pale face raised, drenched with sweat, and the gray

eyes of the arrogant hunter Ferghus gazed at them both. Terror and sickness clung to him like a foul miasma, a nauseating combination of odors Conall could barely stomach.

"It's my friend!" Sorcha cried. After sheathing her sword, she darted forward and fell to her knees beside the human. She touched his face and jerked her fingers back in surprise. "He's feverish. Conall, help me get him to his feet."

"I'm fine," the huntsman muttered. He waved away Sorcha's hand and climbed to his feet. "I was resting for a moment. It's been a long day of travel and much more to cross."

"You smell strange," Conall said flatly. "Did you encounter the creature?"

Ferghus raised his chin and stared Conall down. "I did. Through fortune and luck of the stars alone did I survive."

"And you're unharmed. Thank the stars for that," Sorcha said as she fussed over the hunter. Conall's frown deepened.

"I think the beast might be hiding in Calbronnoch. I heard strange noises coming from that direction on the wind earlier."

Sorcha shook her head. "That was likely us. Nothing alive remains in that cursed city."

"Ah, a pity. I remember when, some years ago, Calbronnoch was the jewel of eastern Cairn Ocland. When Da' and I would come to trade, you could find any kind of laborer or artisan your heart would fancy. And we'd take home all manner of gifts to Mum. Those were the days." His gaze drifted toward Conall. "A pity some allowed it to fall to ruin."

Conall's spine stiffened, and a livid flush heated his face. "A pity some couldn't be bothered to protect what was theirs and abused those who did."

Sorcha leapt between them and placed her palm over Ferghus's chest. "You look exhausted. We should share camp tonight." She turned her hopeful gaze to Conall, and as much as he wanted to challenge her suggestion, he nodded instead.

"Fine with me, Red."

With help from Ferghus, they scrounged together enough dry wood to make a fire. Conall had never missed Tink more, though it had as much to do with her playful quips and pleasant company as his desire for her to create flameless heat.

Where was his good friend? As he sat on his side of the camp, ignored by Ferghus, his mind drifted to the little sprite he'd saved from a Liangese trap. She'd been young then, barely more than a toddler.

And now she'd reached her rebellious teen years. He worried for her, prayed she'd return soon, then glanced at the cozy pair of hunters opposite him. Sorcha had taken a seat beside her childhood friend. She's been a sullen companion since Calbronnoch, her mood now improved and more animated than ever.

"We've seen so many things since we ventured to the east, Ferghus. The land is beautiful again in many places, but I've never seen anything as gorgeous as the Scarlet Wood. In some areas, the leaves were closer to purple, and they sometimes shone at night."

"I'm glad your travels were fruitful, but even happier you're safe and unharmed."

"And soon we're to see Mount Floraivel. Twenty-two years old and I've never seen our eastern mountain range. It almost shames me to feel so excited, knowing the importance of the mission Queen Anastasia's given us."

"Excited? Have you not considered returning home yet? If your fight with the monster has proven anything, it's that you're not yet ready to be on your own. You were injured."

"I'm not on my own," Sorcha said. "I'm with the most powerful werewolf of Cairn Ocland." Her blue eyes twinkled with delight when her gaze turned to Conall, melting the icy wall he'd wanted to build between them ever since the huntsman had joined their group.

At no point had she ever smiled at Ferghus like that, and in those moments, Conall knew she never would.

She did care for him, and the time had almost come to make his final request to have her hand, to be the mate she deserved.

"It's not safe for you out here," Ferghus insisted.

Sorcha chuckled. "Since when is a hunter's life ever safe?"

"If we are ever to marry—"

"We're not," Sorcha said. She stiffened in her seat and Conall tensed. "We have been over this too many times. I am not going to, nor will I ever, marry you. It would be too strange, no different than wedding Egan."

"That isn't what you told your father. You told him you'd think of it and pay my offer due consideration."

"When did you speak with my father?" Sorcha demanded. "I—well, yes I did say as much, but then I met you on the road and gave you my answer. No."

The back and forth continued, tensions rising between the two until Conall couldn't tolerate another moment. He jumped to his feet. "She's said no multiple times. Be a man and take her answer at its value, or begone from our camp."

Ferghus stared him down, but he said nothing further. Instead, the man pulled his bedroll from his pack and laid down by the fire. Conall offered his hand out to Sorcha, breath held while she glanced at him and her fellow hunter with indecision on her face. After a moment, she stepped toward Conall and took his hand.

"Shouldn't we put out the fire?" she asked.

Conall shook his head. "Not tonight. The cold is a bigger danger than predators, and as there are now three of us, we'll be able to drive off any trouble that comes."

As he took his wolven shape, the smell reached him again. Rot and dried blood. His ears perked and he swung his head around, but the source eluded him. Each time he thought he caught where it was coming from, the smell shifted and vanished.

Behind him, Sorcha stretched out her bedroll, and he lay on the grass nearby. She settled beside him and cuddled against his furry ribs, drawing a blanket over them to conserve heat.

The huntsman stared at them from across the flames. "You lay with beasts now?" His voice dripped with envy and unfettered disdain.

"I sleep where it's warm," Sorcha shot back over her shoulder.

"Do you let him take you as a beast as well?" Ferghus asked, sneering. The yellow light gave his eyes a malicious gleam that raised Conall's hackles.

"What?" The question jerked Sorcha upright.

"You heard me. Is that why you continue to refuse me? Because you've gotten a taste for a wild animal?"

Ferghus rose and Conall growled, following the man's example. He put himself between Sorcha and the hunter.

"You need to go, Ferghus," Sorcha said. "I can hardly believe the filth I'm hearing coming from your mouth."

"I'm not going anywhere." Ferghus ran his fingers over a silver object hanging around his neck. "In fact, I think I'll stay right here and rid you of your new pet. Then I'll drag you home where you belong."

Conall recognized the magic almost too late. As Ferghus jammed his brooch into his upper chest, Conall knocked Sorcha aside and leapt across the campfire. He struck Ferghus in the torso and they went to the ground in a tussle of limbs. Ferghus's human body arched beneath him, defenseless during the brief window of his transformation until claws elongated from his nail beds.

Wild with the desire to slay the skinwalker, Conall returned to his human form. He had only moments, mere seconds to make everything count. He planted his knee in Ferghus's gut and reached for his sword.

"Conall, no!"

Ignoring Red, Conall drove the blade into shifting monster's heart. It roared and tossed its head back, screaming in agony and terror.

Before he could push the broadsword into the soil to pin it, Sorcha tackled him from the side. For so small a girl, she hit hard. He lost his balance and stumbled to the side as the skinwalker arose from the ground and yanked the sword from his chest. Wailing louder than a banshee, it fled into the brush while trailing blood behind it.

"What in the blazes?" Conall snarled. He'd been so close.

Seconds from dealing the fatal blow that would restore safety to the woods and every shifter threatened by its foul existence. And in a split second, she'd ruined that.

He spun to look at the proud huntress he'd traveled alongside for countless weeks. She knelt on the ground with her arms around her body and head bowed.

"I'm… I'm sorry. I just couldn't—" Barely able to utter those words, Sorcha choked on her sobs. "I couldn't watch you kill my friend."

As much as he wanted to swear at her and rage, he couldn't. The heat died in an instant, the fury dissolved, and in its place, he felt only pain for the girl he'd grown to love. His heart ached for what she'd witnessed, suffering as dire as the loss he'd suffered. Because she'd loved Ferghus, not as a lover, but as a friend, and now the friend she'd known was dead.

"He's not your friend anymore." Conall crouched beside her and set a hesitant hand on her head, smoothing his palm over her tangled hair. "We need to move, lass. It won't be safe to camp here. Not anymore. We need to put distance between us."

Silent and withdrawn, she nodded. Helpless to do anything for her, Conall put out their fire while Sorcha gathered up her blanket and packed it away. Together, they pressed on through the night, walking side by side.

At sunrise, they took a short break to eat, but the wildberries settled uneasily in Conall's stomach. Every time he looked at Sorcha, he witnessed her despair. Discovering her friend was the skinwalker had done something to her. Broken her spirit.

"Do you want to talk about it, lass?"

"What's there to talk about?"

He sighed and draped his arm around her shoulder. "I know it's a blow, but you mustn't blame yourself for what happened to your friend."

"I don't blame myself for what happened to him. I blame myself for the rest."

"What do you mean?"

"We had the skinwalker where we wanted it, and I let it go," she whispered. "We could have ended it all, and I foolishly let it go. How can you even bear to look at me now?"

"Not all of it. There's still Maeval to deal with. As for looking at you, I look at you just fine and enjoy doing so."

Sorcha's unamused glower made him sigh again. He'd only hoped to make her laugh, but that had backfired.

"No, Red, it troubles me none to look at you, and I would have done the same in your place." Without waiting for her response, he leaned close enough to kiss her brow, and then he trudged ahead.

The rest of the day continued in much the same manner, passing in silence as they struggled against the harsh terrain and steadily dropping temperatures. By sunset, they took shelter beneath a large pine and huddled together for warmth while catching what few precious hours of sleep they could. Around midnight, when it became too cold to remain asleep, they resumed their journey.

"How far to the mountains?" Sorcha asked, ending her self-imposed silence. She lifted a hand to shade her eyes and gazed toward the distant peaks visible through a break in the trees.

"A few more days. Nothing we can't handle," he assured

her.

"Good, good..." Her voice trailed off and her gaze went distant. "If I had agreed to marry him, do you think he would have become that creature?"

"You're not responsible for the things he's done or the choice he made."

"But I still wonder what drove him to it. If my rejections pushed him."

"You've rejected me, but you don't see me stealing grannies or killing for the fun of it."

"I only wish..." She sighed and rubbed her eyes. "Sorry, I'm tired and cold. I wish Tink was here to help find a safe camping spot, a place with walls, no matter the shape of them."

He hadn't seen Tink since she'd abandoned them at the marsh. Unable to bear the sight of Sorcha's pale skin and ruddy cheeks, he wrapped his arms around her to provide shelter from the frigid wind. "Aye, lass, I miss her too, but I know a place nearby, a safe place where we'll be able to have a proper fire."

She pressed her cheek against his chest without arguing and shivered in his embrace. "How far?"

"Close enough to walk. We need to keep moving, because you'll get frostbite if we stop."

"But I'm so tired," she whispered.

"You can ride me. We'll be there soon, I promise."

Conall rarely visited his childhood home, but for some reason, all his exhaustion flit away at the promise of showing Red the place of his birth. He carried her on four legs up a winding path weaving between the trees. Glacial wind whipped against his muzzle and ruffled his fur. Sorcha's grip

VIVIENNE SAVAGE

on him tightened.

Braeloch, the ancestral home of Conall's forefathers, occupied a vast series of chambers within the mountain range. He had fond memories of looking out over Loch Arweg from the yawning entrance and diving into the pristine water when his mother taught him to swim.

They had carved out a beautiful home fit for over thirty wolves, and they'd all dwelled in Braeloch until the humans made the call for aid. Conall still recalled Elder Matlock's desperate pleas, and Moira TalWolthe had convinced her husband it was the right thing to do.

The door itself had been enchanted by magic, a witch's spell burned into the stone. It reacted only to wolves born and raised within the cavern and would budge for no one else. Somehow, the magic could discern wolves born within the pack from those who struck out on their own.

After becoming a man to touch his palm against the tile bearing his clan's mark, the stone door rumbled and rolled to the side, fragments of rock showering from above.

Beyond the open doorway, darkness awaited with the smell of stale dust in the air and cold stone.

Then a thousand stinging fireflies crashed into him at once, miniature fireballs of doom launched by the hands of one wood sprite. He barely saw the scarlet glow of the infuriated fairy behind her firestorm.

"Ow!" Conall jumped and beat at his arms and chest everywhere the spell singed him. "Tink, stop!"

"Conall?"

"Of course it's me, you fluff-brained mosquito!" he rumbled back. Red welts stood out against his arms from her attack.

Behind him, Red doubled over with laughter. She held herself up against the wall with one hand, her cheeks flushed and tears in her eyes. "Mistaken identity?"

Tink pulsed red, but Conall snatched her out of the air before she could zip toward Sorcha. He recognized that look. The little fae meant business. With Tink cupped between both of his palms, he quickly said, "I can't make any promises about food just yet, but it's a roof above our heads for the night."

Tink's light intensified, flaring brighter than a sunbeam. "Let me out of here!"

"After we've talked," he snapped back at the trapped woodkin. "Sorcha, c'mon, lass, let's get you by a fire."

His huntress lingered at the entrance and traced the glowing sigils carved into the stonework. "Is it safe?"

"The safest place for us to take refuge from the storm."

He coaxed Sorcha inside and secured the door behind them. First things first, he needed to get her beside a fire, but the angry sprite in his hand was determined to make the task difficult. Thankfully, he had set out wood to season and dry the last time he passed through.

Once he guided Sorcha to a seat on an old bench in the main chamber, he hurried to light the hearth. Moonlight shone through the open skylight above the recess bordering the chamber's northern edge. Lake Arweg fed it through a narrow vista in the stone wall on the water.

Conall had missed home, for its beauty as well as the memories. With one hand encumbered, he managed to get a spark to catch. "I'll find us some food. You get warm."

"Th-thank you," Sorcha chattered.

While Sorcha thawed out, Conall considered the issue of filling their bellies with hot food for the evening—and the naughty fae trapped in his fist. He didn't expect them to find anything in the larder, save for old bread and a few cheese wheels. There'd be wine in the cellar.

He took the stairs two at a time, his way lit by magical sconces with cool blue-green flames.

As expected, he found green bread, cheese, shriveled potatoes and root vegetables, stale crackers, and cured meat hanging from hooks, so old the flesh had dried on the bone. Conall chuckled to himself. Wine and cheese, a perfect romantic meal. All he needed were candles, and if he searched deep enough into the cupboards, he'd probably find some from his mother's Liangese collection. She'd loved collecting them in all variety of colors and exotic scents.

"All right, you. Explain why you're here while I seek food."

"Let me go!" Tink demanded.

He opened his hand and the little woodkin shot from his palm like an arrow—a livid, buzzing arrow. Tink's angry light settled on a high shelf.

"Now why are you in my home?" he demanded.

"You said it was *my* home too."

He sighed and softened his voice. "I did, and it is. Surprised is all, after you left as you did."

"There was no room for me."

His brows shot up. "Really? No room for a wee thing like you beside me in this big world?"

She darted down and buzzed around his face. "You don't pay attention to me when Red Cloak is around."

"Ah, lass, I pay plenty of attention to you—"

"Liar!"

"Not as much recently perhaps," he said in a rush. "But you can't do this every time there's another woman in my life."

"You never cared before."

Conall sighed. "You're right. I haven't cared in the past, but I like this one, Tink, and your childish games won't chase her away. You've seen that now, aye?"

She huffed, a green glow bleeding through the red, and returned to the shelf. "But you gave her your mother's fang. You'll have babies with her and forget about me."

"Whoa, lass, take a second here. There's no talk of babies. She hasn't even accepted my interest in courting her yet."

"Yet," Tink said bitterly. "She took the fang readily enough."

Sighing, he reached up and plucked her from the shelf, bringing her close enough to see the fine details of her elfin face. "But she doesn't know what it means to me."

Tink tilted her head. "Why didn't you tell her?"

"I…I don't know," he admitted. "I suppose I'm afraid she'll deny me and that'll be the end of my chance. She's done it twice, you know. I've only got one last try."

"What? She can't deny you."

"Oh really? A moment ago you were angry I even tried."

Her little face scrunched up. "That's different. You're my best friend, and anyone should want you."

What had he ever done to deserve her? Saving her from a trapper's net seemed too small a price for her endless devotion.

Conall sighed and set the fae on his shoulder then removed a cheese wheel from the dusty shelf. Hopefully a tasty meal awaited them once he carved away the outer skin. "Will you rejoin me, Tink? I've missed you. Sorcha is no threat to our friendship, and I'll always be there for you."

"You promise?"

"I give you my word."

"Fine," she said. "I won't tangle her hair anymore. Or leave burrs in her boots."

"Or shield only me from the rain."

"Or shield only you from the rain," she vowed.

"Thank you. I appreciate it, and so will she. Sorcha's had a hard time of it, little one. We discovered the skinwalker is a dear friend of hers. A man she grew up alongside like a brother. She's suffering and needs no pranks or tricks right now."

Tink's little face became solemn, and her color shifted to blue. "No more tricks. Only good things now."

Smiling, he emerged from the larder and made his way into the den where he found Sorcha exactly where he had left her. The fire burned bright and radiated waves of welcome heat.

"It's not much, I'm afraid, but it should be a nice addition to our trail rations." Conall lowered to a seat and set the cheese out on a bench.

"It's fine, really." Sorcha lowered her hood and smiled at him. Color had returned to her cheeks. "Hello, Tink."

"Hi," the sprite said shyly.

"She says hello back to you," Conall translated, relieved.

Sorcha scooted closer to the fire and held her hands out, soaking up the warmth. "What is this place?"

"Not everyone lived in villages, you know. Once, long ago, many of the clans made their homes in caverns like this, open to the air and earth."

As she looked around in a slow circle, her gaze trained on the rocky ceiling above them. Old webs hung from the stalactites, drooping from one stone to the next. He had cleared the spiders out last spring and was confident nothing dangerous remained.

"The wind doesn't howl through it?"

"No, but during a storm, the cenote on the northern edge of this chamber becomes a thing of beauty, and you can watch the water drum against the surface." He gestured to the wide opening in the cavern ceiling above the water. Further away, another opening, no wider than he was broad, revealed the world beyond their cavern. Loch Arweg glittered with the moon's silver shimmer. "I loved to watch it when I was a boy. Sometimes when the sun sets, it paints the surface on fire in shades of ruby and gold."

Red stared at him. "This is *your* home?"

"It used to be, a long time ago before evil besieged Cairn Ocland. The humans asked us to join forces, and it had grown difficult for Mum and Da' to defend our home as well as each of the wolves in our clan."

"Wouldn't you get cold, sleeping without walls around you?"

He shrugged. "There are plenty of walls beyond this particular room. Besides, you'd be surprised how warm this place becomes when we have the need for it. On winter nights, we built large fires. There's space for the smoke to rise while the heat remains trapped."

"It's beautiful," she said, surprising him.

Conall blinked and thought back on happier days when the den had been full of life. He wanted to make it that way again, and he wanted Sorcha to be a part of it.

"All right. We're going to need drink to accompany this fine meal of cheese and rations. Can I trust the two of you to be good girls?"

"I'll be good," Tink promised.

"We'll be fine, Conall," Sorcha replied.

He fetched a bottle of mead from the cellar and returned within minutes. Sorcha had settled on her hands and knees by the hearth as Tink brought additional kindling for the fire. The pines native to northern Cairn Ocland dropped unusual cones capable of burning for hours. With each offering to the flames, the fire flashed purple and blue. While Tink worked, Sorcha stripped colorful leaves and petals from a pile of branches beside her, dropping them into a pot positioned above the flames.

Stars above, he loved watching his two favorite ladies working together for once instead of bickering.

"What are those?" he asked.

"Tink brought them for our supper," Sorcha replied. "There's some turnip as well, but I've tossed it in already."

Conall set the bottle on the low table then glanced at the edge of the grotto.

"Why do the wolves live in the forest when you have all this?" Red asked. She gestured to the space around them.

"When the curse first struck, we went to Calbronnoch to help. More room there, as you can see. We never would have fit a city full of humans in here. With our pack absent, evil water spirits and corrupt silkstrider spiders infested the den. It was too dangerous to reclaim our ancestral home. We tried once, right after we split away from the human communities, but when my father led our clan here, we lost too many."

"I'm sorry. I had no idea."

He shrugged and gestured to the lake. "Care to fish with me?"

"Fish? Now?"

"Aye, unless all you want to eat is cheese and blossom stew. If so, we've got plenty of it."

She rose to his challenge, and soon they had both settled at the lake's edge with a bottle of mead between them, lines cast into the water. Tink hovered over the water, her amber glow the ideal lure to draw fish toward them.

"You haven't spoken much of your family aside to mention your father in the past tense…"

"My father died seven months prior to the king and queen breaking the curse," Conall admitted. "He never saw a free Ocland, so I've been leading ever since. Five long years of doing it all on my own. The responsibilities are endless."

"And your mother?"

The same raw pain arose, creating a churning in his gut and a tightness in his chest. Fourteen years later, and her loss hurt no less.

"She died defending Calbronnoch from an ettin rampaging through the village square. The humans all watched from behind their windows and doors, even their so-called hunters. No one lifted a hand. That was the day we left them all behind."

Sorcha was quiet for a time, her brows furrowed and her lips pursed. She stared out at the water, so Conall continued.

"After us, the other clans followed. I don't know what tales they told the villagers once we were gone, but that's the truth as we know it. Because we lived it. Because it was my mum left to die. Father and I returned on the tail end of the attack, but it was too late to save her."

"I can't even imagine what that must have been like. I've seen my mother and father fight before, and I've known the fear of losing them, but they've always pulled through at the end." She stretched her legs out in front of her and wiggled her line.

"You're lucky to have them."

"Yeah, Egan and I both think so. That's my twin brother. It's always been the four of us working together, until this adventure. I can't imagine what my father would do if he lost any of us. Yours must have felt great pain."

"I think Da' died of a broken heart more than anything. He was never the same after that. Blamed himself, you know? We'd all gone hunting and Mum stayed behind." His line tugged, going taut, so he pulled it in and hauled a protesting, flopping bass from the water. After catching it by the gills, he dropped it aside in a bucket. "There you have it. I don't have a mate and wasn't eager to change that before."

"I'd always wondered the truth about what happened in Calbronnoch. The stories I heard, well, they were always in favor of the humans, made to sound like the shifters had abandoned them for no good reason."

"Now you have our side of the story." He paused to consider his words, then twisted to look at her face to face. "Your friend came from there?"

"He had some family there, yes, but mostly they were traders at the time. But he's always been bitter about what happened."

"It was something we had to do," he replied stiffly. Sorcha leaned over and touched his shoulder.

"I'm not blaming you, or the shifters. Just as I'm done blaming myself for what happened with Ferghus. You were right, he made his own mistakes and choices."

"I'm glad to hear it, Red."

Her eyes glistened, and after a few blinks, the moisture was gone. "The best I can do for him—the *kindest* thing—is put him out of his misery. The old Ferghus of my memories would want that. Before his heart was twisted by Maeval's influence, he was another man. He never... he never pushed me that way."

"Maeval's end will come. You have faith in that. We'll get vengeance for your friend and all others she's wronged."

"I hope so."

"We will," he insisted, "and then we'll have a grand celebration. Or maybe we'll just sleep. Stars know we've earned a long and proper rest." He winked.

Red's quiet laughter and bittersweet smile loosened the tightness in his chest. Ferghus's reprehensible behavior hadn't broken her after all. "Are there even any fish in this lake?"

"Of course there are, as you've seen." He picked up his catch and waggled it in front of her. "You're a poor fisherman, it seems."

Tink tittered and dipped down closer to the water. A minute later, Sorcha's line pulled. She dragged the large specimen close enough to sweep from the water with a net. "Mine's bigger."

"It's not the size of it that counts."

Sorcha grinned. "What does then?"

"Yours is all bone, lass." Smugly, he grinned back at her. "You want meat. Something to really fill your mouth."

The innuendo flew over her head. "I think you're just jealous my fish is bigger. And for that, I'm not going to share."

"Hopeless," Tink muttered, though he wondered if the sprite was referring to him or Sorcha.

Side by side, they scaled and cleaned their catch for the fire, and soon the cavern was filled with the aromatic scents of cooking meat. He'd discovered the dried herbs from the pantry, while old, still imparted enough flavor to be pleasant.

While the fish roasted and Tink's soup bubbled, he guided Sorcha deeper into his home. "I want to show you the real secret of this place."

"What's that?"

"You'll see." He led the way to the eastern wall of the cavern, where the rocky awning stretched out over a section of the lake. The rock had been carved away, creating a little pool that curved into the living area. A gentle bubbling disturbed the surface, and thin curls of steam rose into the cooler air.

"A hot spring?"

"Aye, lass. With the water from the lake cycling through, it's always a comfortable temperature. You can swim out into the lake if you're too warm, or return here if too cold. Not many can claim to have access to such a natural bath."

Sorcha dipped down and trailed her fingers through the warm water. "How did you make this?"

"Clan Ardal fashioned it for us. Feel free to use it, if you wish," he said. "Come, I'll show you where you can sleep."

The state of the bedchambers hadn't changed, frozen in time aside from a thin layer of dust. Each room had been hewn from the rock to create walls of polished stone. Another example of Clan Ardal's work.

"You weren't lying about it being cozy."

"Wolves like comfort as much as anyone. We can search around for blankets after we eat dinner."

"It's going to burn," Tinkerbell warned.

"Which we should get back to," he quickly told Sorcha. "Tink says we're about to lose our dinner."

They returned in time to rescue their fish from becoming charred. Between the flavorful bites, fragrant soup, and ripe cheese, they filled their bellies. Sorcha yawned, stretched, and practically fell asleep where she sat, so Conall ushered her to bed. Blankets stored in cedar chests had survived the passage of time, assuring them a warm and restful sleep.

Sorcha murmured a sleepy "goodnight" and passed out the moment her head touched the pillow. Resisting the urge to crawl into bed beside her in his wolven form, Conall watched his huntress until exhaustion finally drove him to seek his own bed.

Contrary to Conall's worries about the uncomfortable beds, Sorcha slept well. Refreshed after a mere handful of hours on a comfortable mattress without shivering, she crawled from the bed and set out barefoot through the cavern. The view of a night sky greeted her, stars twinkling in the great distance through the narrow opening feeding into Lake Arweg.

Sorcha tiptoed to the edge of the water and dipped her toes in the black surface. She hadn't had more than a quick wash in days, and the idea of soaking in a hot bath delighted her. With only a glance behind her toward the torchlit walking path, she unfastened the laces of her pants and pushed them down. Then she started on her blouse.

From the darkness, a low cough drew her attention. She tensed and reached automatically for a weapon, but came up empty. A few feet away, a shape moved in the water. She made out the dim shape of broad shoulders.

"Conall?"

"Aye, it's me."

"What're you doing here?"

"The same thing you're doing here, I suppose. Tinker Bell told me I stink."

"Do you always do what Tink tells you to?"

"Only when she's right."

"Then I imagine there are few times when you're not doing her will."

At Conall's height, the water splashed his midsection, but it was too dark to reveal anything more. Sorcha didn't need to see the rest of him to know every inch of his body was hard muscle.

It was the kind of awkward meeting she'd read about in one of her tattered romance novels, a small but cherished collection of books from the neighboring country of Creag Morden she'd discovered on a bookshelf in an abandoned house.

In those books, however, the couples always made love. And she had no intention of giving her body to Conall TalWolthe, no matter how delicious the cocky werewolf appeared. Or how well he kissed her.

That kiss outside of Granny's home would be the first,

last, and only kiss between them if he couldn't give truth to Heldreth's speculations and admit he'd marked her.

Sorcha hesitated and eyed him.

"Shy?" Conall asked.

"No."

Would he turn if she asked? Did she care if he looked?

The weight of his interested gaze sent tingles zipping across her skin. She unfastened the remaining laces securing her linen top and pulled the garment off over her head, dropping it to the floor at her feet with her discarded pants.

Conall didn't look away, and part of her was thrilled to have held his attention so long. Surely a man who lived among shapeshifters saw naked women at all times.

Without breaking eye contact, she raised her chin and proudly stepped into the water. Warmth surrounded her, lapping gently against her calves, rising to her thighs then her lower belly. It rose as high as the top of her breasts once her feet touched the bottom. She wiggled her toes into the sand and sighed in contentment.

Year-round access to a hot spring was a sinful delight, and one she envied. She couldn't recall the last time her family had come across one on the trail that wasn't infested or ruined. While she'd enjoyed the bathtub at Benthwaite, there was nothing like floating in a pool.

She sank beneath the surface and ran her fingers through her hair, loosening all the dirt and debris that came with living on the road for days and weeks at a time. Coming back up for air, she smoothed the wet strands back and wished she had soap. Something sweetly scented, with an oil to unknot the tangles until every inch became sleek and smooth.

When she looked up, Conall was standing right beside her. Sorcha jumped.

"What do you want, Conall?"

"Want? I don't *want* anything in particular…but what I *have* is soap." He dangled a bar from a long twine of rope tied around his wrist, its textured surface glistening in the muted light. "I could wash your back."

"Or you could pass it over, and I'll wash my own."

His smug grin widened. "Are you secretly an abomination, lass, with arms able to bend in unnatural ways?"

"You don't have to be an abomination to be flexible," she muttered. To her chagrin, her words only stoked his amusement.

"Turn around anyway, then maybe you'd return the favor?"

"Too many muscles in your way?"

Despite her best intentions to resist her flirtatious companion, she turned and pulled her wet hair over her shoulder. Nothing sensual about a shared bath. *It's practical,* she told herself.

His rough palms smoothed the soap up and down her back. He rubbed the bar across her shoulders then moved lower, beneath the water, following her spine to the upper curve of her bottom.

"Need help with the rest?" he asked, breath a warm caress against her ear.

"No," she whispered, hating the tremor in her voice. His hands slid over her hips and lingered.

"Too bad."

He abandoned her hips and turned his attention to her

hair, as if he'd read her thoughts about wanting to scrub it clean. He lathered soap thickly into the dark mass, putting his strong fingers to work against her scalp.

She loved every second of it. Despite the warmth of the water, goosebumps pebbled over her skin, and she imagined his hands touching her in inappropriate places. Cupping between her thighs. Molding against her breasts.

"Do you truly loathe my company so much, Red?"

"I've never said that."

"You've given no reason to think you enjoy it, either."

She huffed and shifted her weight from one foot to the other. "I find your company perfectly acceptable, and I appreciate it as well. I don't think I would have made it this far without you."

"Maybe not. Maybe you would have done fine on your own. Regardless, we're goin' to rescue your gran. It didn't kill her, so I can only assume it wanted her alive for some reason. It needs her."

"Strange beasts and fairy magic." She sighed and closed her eyes.

"Duck down now, lass."

Rinsing her hair took less time than usual with Conall assisting. When his touch fell away, she experienced an odd sense of regret, a quickening of her pulse, and an emptiness in her gut.

"Turn around. I'll get your back," she said.

"*My* hair, too?"

She chuckled and flicked water at his eager smile. "Yes, your hair as well. I won't have Tink saying I did a poor job."

She took a guilty sort of pleasure in washing him, sliding

her soapy fingers over brawny shoulders and a chiseled back. Colorful ink covered his arms from the elbows up to his shoulders. She traced her fingers over the scarlet tartan pattern depicted in the angular shapes amidst the accents of silver glittering over his flesh.

After getting him to crouch down, she delivered the same attention to his hair that he had paid hers. She had daydreamed about running her fingers through his auburn locks, so she took her time, enjoying the opportunity.

It's practical, she told herself again. *We'll both appreciate not smelling the stink of the other.*

But touching his shoulders had nothing to do with her sensory comfort and everything to do with her own selfish desires.

"Red?"

"Yeah?"

"I'm glad to be traveling with you. I hate what's happening and the lives that have been lost, but I'm not sorry about meeting you."

Her heart swelled and seemed to rise into her throat. She swallowed back the sudden thickness and whispered, "Nor I."

Conall turned, took the soap, and set it aside on the rocky ledge. Then he looked down at her, his intense gaze bringing a rapid beat to her pulse. No man had ever looked at her with such attention, as if nothing else in the world existed save for her.

"This belonged to my mother." He touched the tooth resting between the swell of her breasts. "It is one of my most precious belongings."

Her throat clenched. He must have wanted it back. "Then

why did you give it to me?"

"Because when we wolves court someone we care about, we give them whatever is most valuable to us to show them they've now taken its place."

"Conall…"

"No, don't say anything now. Listen. Please."

Sorcha swallowed. Words waited on the tip of her tongue, but she swallowed them back in favor of letting him talk. For all their time together, she'd grown accustomed to a brash and confident werewolf alpha, not a man who spoke his heart.

"We wolves have another tradition. When we court, we only have three chances. Once denied three times, we abandon the chase. If you don't want me, Red, I'll respect your wishes, and you won't have to worry about me approaching you this way again."

"And if I do?"

"Then you become mine. My mate."

His. The thought alone made her quiver and tingle.

"And if I say no, will you leave?"

"Leave you to recover your granny alone? No. But I won't touch you like this anymore." He trailed his fingers over her hip, tracing slow circles. "I'll stand by your side and face any danger we come up against, as a friend alone."

The tightness in her throat became unbearable, and tears pricked behind her eyes. She looked away and swallowed, touched to her soul by his honest confession and stalwart loyalty.

Sorcha had never considered marriage for more than a few fleeting moments, though part of her had always imagined she'd one day marry Ferghus out of convenience or friendship.

"Must I answer now?" she asked.

"No. Is that what you need? More time?"

"It's not an easy decision. My whole life would change. Everything I've ever known would be different, wouldn't it? How can I travel with the hunters if I'm...mated to the alpha of another clan? Would the other wolves respect me?"

"Aye," he said, turning her around until her naked back was to his chest. His arm curved around her waist. "Respect is earned, and you wouldn't be the first human to ever join us, rare as it may be."

She leaned into him. "And in the meantime?"

"Until you deny me, I'll continue to court you." His fingers crawled over her hip bone and drifted down over the curls between her thighs. "To show my admiration and respect for you. My desire."

Her heart thumped in her chest with the force of a hammer, and desire throbbed in her core. She sank back against him and closed her eyes, eager for more, until his touch withdrew and his palm glided over her lower belly.

"Do you have to stop?"

"Aye, Red. Until you're mine, I won't do anything more."

He was a tease. An awful, horrible tease. Sorcha made a restless shift against him, aware of the hard length trapped between their bodies. How would it feel to join her body to his? To know him in the most intimate way possible.

"That's not fair," she whispered.

He stroked her tummy again and kissed the curve of her ear. "It's wolven tradition, lass. When we mate, it's for life."

"Wait, you mean…?"

"That I've never taken another woman to my bed."

"But you seem so, um, knowledgeable."

Conall laughed. "What have I done besides kiss you?"

And touch her in ways that should be illegal if he wasn't going to continue. A ragged breath shuddered from her lungs.

Without waiting for her response, Conall pushed back from her. "I'll leave you to the rest of your soak and hunt up whatever I can find for our breakfast."

Sorcha wet her mouth and took a step after him. "Not even a kiss?"

"Not even a kiss. I'm a man of my word, and as I said, there'll be no more kisses between us until you beg me for it, Red."

Before she could protest, he cut through the water to the shoreline. Her eyes grew large. Clear rivulets trickled over his tanned skin and the sculpted perfection of his torso when he climbed to the rock and strode away.

Damn him for making her want to follow.

Eventually the heat dimmed, allowing Sorcha to consider the realistic possibility of leaving her clan and no longer hunting abominations.

But wasn't that the future they all strove to create? They all desired a free Cairn Ocland without the taint of Rangvald, and if Anastasia's hunch was right, their kingdom wouldn't be free in its entirely until Maeval was slain for good. In a world free of aberrations, hunters would no longer be needed.

Sorcha sighed and sprawled back into the water's embrace.

Though there were heavy concerns on her mind, floating beneath the moonlight delivered a sense of peace she'd craved—a quiet lull before the figurative storm. Her mind roamed in a hundred directions, from Conall to her family. Were her parents all right? Her brother? Queen Anastasia hadn't mentioned them, and she didn't know where to send a bird to find them—one of the pitfalls of living on the road.

Then there was Maeval.

"We need help," she whispered up at the night sky. "I'm not good at this prayer thing. I'm used to relying on myself—on my family—but we need a little more than sword and bow. We need more than the queen's magic. We need a miracle. Conall and I failed to retrieve the weapon needed to kill her, and if Anastasia meets the same misfortune, we'll be without any hope."

The stars twinkled beautifully, though a warm touch of golden-orange bordered the horizon. Soon, Conall would return with their breakfast and they'd embark on their journey to find the griffins.

"Without a way to kill Maeval, the shifters will always be in danger, and so will we. If Conall's right, she'll want our first-born daughters. And whatever monster she's set upon them will continue seeking their skins. I...don't want to lose him. I've never met anyone like him before. I want… I want him. I want to know where our lives will take us."

The more she thought about it, the more she desired to know if they were compatible after all. If her family would approve of him. If his clan would welcome her into their number despite her inability to shift.

"Please help us one more time."

Floating for a while longer in the tranquil little oasis confined within the wolf den, her mind quieted at last. Above her, through the opening in the grotto's wall, she watched the pre-dawn sky dance with colors. Rainbow light in shades of turquoise, rose, and teal streaked across it, brighter than any comet she'd ever witnessed. The bolt skimmed one of the white peaks atop the distant Mount Floraivel and landed in the lively green range beneath it. Radiant waves shimmered out from the point of impact.

She swam to the pool's edge and pulled herself out, sloshing water over the floor. Before she could wring out her hair, Conall burst inside. His chest heaved and he clutched a fat pair of rabbits in his hand.

"Red! Red, did you see it? A star fell!"

"I did." She pulled on her tunic, modesty forgotten. "How long to reach those peaks?"

"Three days on foot if we're walking." Conall glanced at the mountains framed behind her. A fine line creased his brow before he added, "Less if you ride me and we run."

"Then we'll run."

Conall had only climbed the formidable Mount Floraivel twice in his life, and each time, he wondered if he had been struck by selective amnesia.

Not that he had much of a choice about scaling it to the top. Over the years, the griffins had grown increasingly antisocial and turned away all seeking their help, including the childish dragon heir of Benthwaite who plunged his own castle into a sleeping curse.

But King Alistair had changed. He was no longer the same impulsive child.

Conall had to hope that counted for something.

Vivienne Savage

"Tink, I need you more than ever now, lass."

The sprite poked out of his shirt collar where she'd huddled from the cold.

"Go to Clan Leomlaire and speak with their elder. Tell them what we're after and that we need their aid. Beg them if you must."

"And if that fails?"

"Do what you do best. Annoy them all until they're ready to help or hurl themselves from the aerie to escape you."

"Will do!"

At first, they made their way up the green slope at the base of the mountain where the occasional tufts of grass poked amidst the rocks and thickening layer of snow. The steep incline made it too dangerous for her to ride him, so they picked their way up using whatever handholds they could find.

The falling snow added to their troubles, creating slippery grips. The wind intensified, but Conall protected Red from the powerful gusts by placing his body between her and the onslaught.

He reached the first ledge ahead of her and tugged Sorcha to safety. Her chest heaved from exertion.

"Here," he said to her. "Come warm yourself beside me."

"I can barely feel my fingers."

Conall took both of her hands between his palms and chafed. "We can do this, Red. If we saw the star fall, then so has Maeval, but we've got the upper hand. We're closer than ever to reaching our goal, and her minions can't be here ahead of us yet."

"Follow the smoke. Move fast. Beat Maeval's minions. No sweat." Sorcha managed a grin and set her sights on the distant, gray tendrils curling up into the sky. Anyone around for miles would be able to see it.

"Aye. No sweat at all. Does this help?"

She turned her face against his throat and lingered with her cheek against his pulse before she answered. Too much time had been wasted denying her attraction to him. "Yes, thank you. I'm good to go on now."

A level plateau provided a break from the treacherous climb. As if sensing their progress, the snow fell heavier, coming down in fat flakes that clung to their clothes and hair.

Conall turned his face toward the sky and frowned. The air smelled of magic and wickedness. "It's Maeval trying to slow us down. It must be. She knows we're after the shard."

Appearing torn between cuddling longer or resuming the climb, Sorcha withdrew from him. "We have to keep pushing through. If she's trying this hard, it means she's scared."

They continued onward, leaving their small shelter and leaning into the wind. Conall moved into the front again to create a windbreak, but a forceful gust knocked Sorcha off to the side. She stumbled and came close to losing her footing.

"Red, are you all right?"

"Yeah, just tripped over something is a—" Sorcha shrieked and disappeared, as if the ground had swallowed her whole. Conall scrambled back down the rocky incline, bits of loose shale slipping beneath his boots.

"Red!"

He skidded to a halt, dropped down to his hands and knees, and peered down the sinkhole.

"Red! Speak to me."

No answer echoed from the darkness. He swore and

pulled at the edges of the small hole, but the stone resisted his efforts to widen the opening. Without Tink, he had no idea how far down Sorcha had fallen.

"If you can hear me, stay where you are. I know a way into the caverns further up the mountain. Stay where you are!"

In his worst fears, he could only imagine her crumpled body at the bottom of a rocky cavern. Conall forced the vision from his mind and pushed his body to make the steep climb.

She had to survive the fall. He wouldn't accept anything less, refusing to believe so bright a star and talented a warrior could be snuffed from the world by a pile of weak rocks.

Bits of rock crumbled beneath his fingertips during the desperate ascent until he finally scrambled over the ledge, chest heaving and perspiration running into his eyes. His fingertips bled, hands raw from the frantic effort.

Each moment that passed increased the tension coiling in his gut, and worries for what might happen if he didn't reach her in time added speed to his steps until he ran on all fours.

Sorcha deserved an honorable warrior's death in battle, or at the very least, one surrounded by her beloved grandchildren—*their* grandchildren if he had his way.

The twisting caverns through Floraivel were said to be unpassable, a maze to confuse even a shifter's keen senses. Even the griffins avoided them. For Sorcha, he risked becoming lost.

Her scent guided him through the dark tunnels and narrow crevices. Time ticked away to the beat of his pulse until the trail intensified. A pale hint of light ahead turned the murky blackness to a dismal gray.

He shifted and called out her name, but only his voice bounced across the stone walls. Conall tilted his head up to see a pin light circle of sky. Pebbles and crumbled shale crunched beneath his booted feet. A bloody smear glistened against the rocks beneath the opening.

He may have located where she plummeted into the mountain, but Red was nowhere to be found.

Chapter 15

FERGHUS AWAKENED CONFUSED and disoriented. He'd found a hollow beneath the roots of a large tree and crawled into it the previous night, still wearing the skins of the deceased shifters.

How long had passed since he'd stripped it away and walked like a man? Without his close friend Brute, he'd been forced to rely on the wild shape to travel with any speed, and when the cold snap arrived, he'd needed the furs even more.

Stealing power from the shifters made him strong, a stark contrast against his fragile human body. With endless stamina, he'd been unstoppable.

And then he'd seen Sorcha with the werewolf. The memory of his fury came crashing down around him, twisting his insides until he doubled over and retched.

How could he have said such awful things to her? For one terrifying moment, he'd wanted to rip his closest friend into small pieces for the simple act of speaking her mind to him.

Ferghus pulled at the metal clasp embedded in the center of his flesh. It tugged, and while a droplet of blood welled from beneath it, the silver trinket never budged.

If he couldn't unfasten the cloak, the enchantment wouldn't unravel and return him to a human form. He could feel the magic twisting his limbs. Bones cracked, sending excruciating pulses of pain throughout his body, but the transformation stalled halfway. He stared down at his clawed arms in horror, his limbs misshapen and covered with sporadic patches of fur and thick hide.

"Puck!"

The imp appeared in a puff of sulfurous smoke. "What? What?"

"I want to talk to the fairy again."

Puck's bright green eyes narrowed, and he rubbed his long-fingered hands together. "A favor is what you ask."

"I'm not asking. I'm telling. Take me to her now, or I'll wring the life from you."

Cackling, the imp leapt backward into its own shadow and disappeared. He seared the grass, leaving his outline in the ground.

"Coward!" Ferghus cried. He should have expected as much from a devilish creature, but he'd been desperate. Again, he fumbled at the metal brooch embedded in his skin until his fingers became slick with blood.

"You dare to order my servant?"

Startled, Ferghus spun around. A cloud of frost crystals and the falling snow drifted together into a voluptuous, feminine silhouette. "I saved you, fairy. You'd be a husk lying on the bloody forest floor in the glen if not for me. I pulled the dragon's claw from your feeble body at your behest. You owe me!"

Had it been a year since the day he'd entered the Shadow Glen with the other hunters. They'd traveled as far as the edge of Mount Kinros, when he found the fairy.

All men and women of Cairn Ocland knew the fair ones

gifted those who were kind to them. And he'd never had a fairy godmother of his own—not like their undeserving King Alistair.

Upon discovering her, he'd seen a glimpse of the beautiful fairy queen she would become, heard her whisper caressing his ears, and he knew without a doubt he couldn't leave her to suffer.

"Look at him, Mistress. The hunter is stuck." Puck squealed in amusement as he reappeared. "I can help him, yes? Shove the brooch deep in his chest."

Maeval chuckled. "Perhaps, but not just yet."

Upon shaking off his stupor, Ferghus growled. The noise rumbled deep in his chest, resonating with inhuman volume. "What have you done to me?"

"Only what you asked for, sweetling." Maeval smiled, and her icy visage shifted, flecks of snow and swirling ice chips recreating her form.

"I didn't ask for this," he spat.

"Didn't you?" she mocked. "'I want revenge on them all,' you said. 'I want the power to make them pay,' you said. Haven't I given you that and more? How many shifters have you slain when another hunter would have fallen?"

"Why can't I remove this damnable thing?"

She sneered. "Do you truly want to remove it?"

"Look at me!" he roared. Blood filled his mouth as his tongue slid against a sharp, serrated fang. "I'm a monstrosity. An aberration. You promised me power in exchange for saving you, but you infected me with the Scourge!"

"Such is what happens when one spurns a gift from the fae. Didn't you realize that?" Her smile broadened.

"This is no gift. It's a curse, and I want no more of it. Because of this, I nearly hurt my dearest and oldest friend."

"You mean the friend enamored with a wolf? One of the beasts you abhor so much? Do you know what they are doing right now? Oh, it's so delicious, dear human. If only your feeble brain could imagine it. At this moment, she lies beneath him as he calls her name with desperate urgency."

"No."

Her crystalline ice smile widened. "You know the trueborn fae cannot tell lies. She will never be yours."

At first, the fairy's words split his heart into two pieces, wounding sharper than an icepick to the chest. Then the rage overtook him again. A snarl bubbled from his throat, and before he could reign it in, he leapt forward. His left claw swung down toward the icy construct, only to pass through a harmless apparition.

Puck sprang from the ground and struck Ferghus in the chest with unexpected strength for a creature so small. Razor-sharp claws dug into his right shoulder, and then the imp shoved at the brooch with his other hand.

Ferghus screamed. He tried to throw the dark sprite off, but the tenacious creature clung like a burr and drove the brooch through his flesh.

Cold so intense it burned wracked his body and sent fire raging through his veins. The brooch struck his ribs, seared into his bone, and became a part of him. Puck's maniacal laughter was drowned out by the pounding pulse blaring in his head.

Ferghus dropped to his knees in the snow, collapsed to the forest floor, and could do nothing as the cloak consumed him. Pain sizzled throughout every inch of his body, a bone-deep eruption of unrelenting sensations.

He lay face down for the longest time, gasping for breath and certain each would be his last. When the agony vanished, so did his fears. They drowned beneath a tumult of violent whispers echoing through his mind.

"Go, my pet," Maeval crooned. "Go kill the red rider and her wolf."

Ferghus crawled to his feet and loped away as bidden.

His thoughts were of simple things. Hunger. Anger. And the color red.

Chapter 16

THE ENTIRE AREA smelled of Red, the scent of her blood permeating the air entwined with the pungent odor of goblin. He searched for her with his nose to the ground, claws tearing at the stone and earth beneath him. Because the dirty creatures lived beneath the ground in squalid, subterranean settlements, they had avoided the devastating impact of the curse above them.

And he almost envied them.

Of the most recent, freshest scents on the ground, he easily identified one as Red. A single drop of blood against stone.

If one of those miserable creatures had harmed her, he'd personally gut them all. With his heart pounding a wild drumbeat in his chest, he hurried into a downward sloping tunnel leading into the heart of the mountain. He passed a boulder larger than his head, its smooth surface covered in a layer of luminescent moss. More glowing markers led him deeper into the goblin's territory, each one emitting a subtle blue-green light.

Hollows carved into the cavern walls made up the bulk of the underground city. Painted skins and woven spider silk hung across many of the entrances, little spots of color in an otherwise dark and dismal setting. Delicate mushrooms in shimmering shades of yellow and green sprouted from carefully cultivated plots across from the homes.

Not a single goblin peered out and no sentinels challenged him. At first he thought perhaps the city was abandoned, but the scents were too fresh and the faint din of voices echoed from deeper in the mountain. Abandoning his wild shape, he continued forward on two legs.

Following the path, he emerged in a massive cavern. He weaved his way through a forest of stalagmite pillars covered in the same glowing moss then came to an abrupt stop. Over a hundred goblins stood in the center of the chamber, circled around a dark shape so large Conall couldn't make out most of it.

His gaze snapped to Sorcha, finding her easily among the crowd. Her red cloak stood out, a beacon in the dim light. She knelt on the cavern floor, head bowed, the dark shape rising tall above her. The scrawny creature's scarlet skin stretched taut over its bones.

Terror laced with astonished disbelief shot through him as he recognized the creature. His pulse leapt as adrenaline shot through his veins.

A dragon. And Sorcha looked as if she were about to be its meal.

Fueled by desperation, he drew his sword and charged.

Sorcha twisted around at the sound of Conall's battle cry. Like her own personal knight in shining armor, or perhaps in his case, an alpha in patterned tartan, he crossed the ground with his sword raised to come down in a mighty arc.

"Conall, wait!" Sorcha cried as she leapt to her feet. The sudden movement spun the world around her out of focus. One step was enough to lose her balance, and then the ground rapidly flew up to meet her.

Metal clattered against stone then muscled arms surrounded her. Conall crushed her against his chest before she could collapse to the rocks.

"Red? Have they hurt you?"

A worried, frantic gaze met hers when she peered up into his handsome face.

"Red? Are you hurt?" he repeated.

"No," she said quickly. "I'm fine, see? The goblins brought me here to *help* me."

He didn't believe her. His gaze shot wildly over the interior of the cavern from the dragon above them to the small contingent of guards. A dozen spears pointed at them, the goblins wearing makeshift armor scavenged from human warriors long ago fallen in battle. They'd even fashioned crude clubs and blunt axes.

Sorcha cupped his cheeks between both of her hands. "No one's harmed me. We're safe here. I'm safe," she repeated in a softer voice. Her words got through to him that time, and the tension faded from his shoulders. His tightly coiled muscles relaxed, and then he touched his fingers against her hairline. They came away sticky with drying blood.

"Magic may heal the body, but rest is still needed," the dragon said, pulling their attention from one another and back to their surroundings.

Around them, the goblins lowered their weapons and backed away, though they remained on guard. Most of them

  VIVIENNE SAVAGE

had fled when Conall charged to her unnecessary rescue.

The dragon's snout lowered, and Conall stiffened as she sniffed him. "You did not mention your companion is a werewolf. Strange to find one of you so far from the forests."

"Strange to find a dragon in a goblin hovel," Conall countered.

The dragon huffed, her chuckle a comely contrast to her malnourished appearance.

"Conall, this is Princess Teagan. I was telling her about our kingdom and what's happened since the Great War."

Conall's eyes widened. "Teagan? Sister to Dragon King Rua? We were told she had been vanquished."

"Almost," Teagan said. "When my brother and I fell in battle, we both plummeted from the sky. He perished on the peaks of our mountain, but I crashed through a goblin mine shaft."

"How did you get here?" Conall asked. "We're leagues from Benthwaite."

"The goblins brought me through the deepways connecting each mountain. They are kind, if skittish creatures, and largely misunderstood by many." Her green eyes stared into Conall until he yielded first and turned away.

"Teagan has been asleep here ever since her fall. She only woke up recently and hasn't wandered farther than the mountain," Sorcha said to cover the awkward lull. "I was telling her that Dalborough is ruined, their wizard and prince dead."

"And their king?" Teagan hissed.

"Rumors say the king is a sickly man on a broken throne with death looming on his doorstep. Cairn Ocland and Creag Morden have banded together against them, united through marriage," Sorcha replied.

"Good. And Alistair? He is a good king? A good man? When last I saw him, he was a hotheaded youth too eager to leap into a fight."

Sorcha dipped her head. "I've only met him once, but he seemed like a good man, yes. His wife and children adore him. He's been active in restoring our lands, but war is coming to Ocland again."

"Aye, war and worse," Conall said. "Maeval the Black has returned. If we're to have any hope of defeating her, Sorcha and I must fetch the fallen star in the middle peaks. That's where we were headed when she crashed through the tunnels."

"The goblins can lead you back to the surface, but you should wait until dawn. These mountains would be treacherous in the dark. I would fly you myself if I had the strength."

"What then?" Conall asked. "Surely you don't plan to remain here in hiding when King Alistair can use your help."

Teagan blew two hot plumes of smoke from her narrow nostrils. "My body remains too weak to endure the flight to Benthwaite. What magical power I had amassed during these past weeks was spent to heal your Sorcha."

Sorcha jerked her eyes away from Conall and stared at Teagan. *His Sorcha?* Did even the dragon princess see the developing bond between them?

"The Shadow Glen is closer than Benthwaite," Conall pressed. "Even if you didn't fight, I'm certain your wisdom and experience would be invaluable."

Teagan turned her gaze on him and blew out another warm breath that ruffled through his hair. "If only it were so easy, young wolf. What use will I be if my power is depleted before I reach Mount Kinros? However, I will give your words the consideration they deserve. Until then, eat. Rest. The goblins will lend you a nook to sleep in."

Conall frowned. "But the shard—"

"Will remain when you awaken. Neither of you would survive the blizzard currently underway."

Sorcha elbowed Conall in the ribs before he had the chance to argue and bowed her head. "Thank you, Princess. We will speak again in the morning."

A goblin in a brown tunic led them to an empty hollow on the edge of the community. Sorcha crawled through the small opening, surprised to find a larger space within. Tall enough to sit up in, at least. The stone walls had been smoothed and painted with a colorful mural depicting a subterranean river. She leaned closer and noticed tiny sparkles in the blue pigment reflecting in the pale lichen glow. Patches grew on the walls in a way that complemented the imagery beneath them.

Conall crawled in beside her and drew the curtain across the entrance. The top of his head came within an inch of the low roof.

"Were you really going to challenge a dragon to save me?" Sorcha asked.

"I was."

Overwhelmed by a surge of emotion, she grabbed a fistful of his tartan and kissed him. Conall made a single sound of surprise then wrapped his arms around her waist. He dragged her close, their surroundings spun, and then soft furs were suddenly beneath her and Conall's hard body stretched above her.

He didn't settle for a simple kiss—he plundered her

mouth, and she loved every minute of it. She arched beneath his touch, loathing her leather corset and wishing it was his fingers against her bare skin. He kneaded one breast and followed the outline of her curves with eager fingers. When his hand reached her thigh, he coaxed her leg over his hip.

"I knew you'd break down sooner or later," Conall said against her throat. His warm breath feathered across her skin.

"But I didn't beg."

"No, lass, you didn't. But I prefer you throwing yourself at me for now. The begging can come later."

Goose bumps arose over her skin, inspired by the veiled promise in his husky words. She searched for his mouth to continue where they'd left off, while his hands crept over her chest and tugged on the cords to her studded leather bodice.

"Blasted laces. Do you knot them on purpose?"

His grumbles earned her quiet laughter. With tentative fingers, Sorcha reached between their bodies and felt the heat of him, the lively pulse of his arousal separated from her touch by only red tartan. One adjustment was all it would take to bare him, and the thought of it sent desire coursing through her.

He pressed his hips forward into her touch, as if sensing the direction of her thoughts, and groaned against her throat.

"I've dreamed of you touching me like this," he whispered. "Don't be shy."

"I'm not shy."

His breath feathered against her skin. "I want your touch, so if it's permission you're waiting for, you have it."

A yank of the kilt pulled it up toward his waist. His bare lower body settled against her leather-clothed thighs. Hot, smooth skin filled her palm, as hard and firm as a sword hilt. She wrapped her fingers around his length, and he rewarded her with a satisfied growl.

"As much as I love your legs in these pants you favor, you should consider a kilt."

"Why?"

He thrust his hips forward, nudging his exposed erection between her thighs. "The easier to claim you with, Red. To have my wicked way with you without the hassle of removing all of this."

She swallowed back the thick lump his words evoked, pressure building between her legs and desire coiling in her gut. She wriggled against him without shame, seeking to find relief. Conall rocked against her, subjecting her to a sweet torture. Her eyes rolled back and she moaned, whispering his name.

The patter of bare feet against stone jolted Sorcha out of the mood. She froze beneath him, a handful of his tartan wrapped around her fingers, his hand beneath her loosened corset and calloused palm abrading her nipple. One glance to the side revealed two pairs of green feet, visible through the gap between the curtains and the floor.

"Looks like we have an audience," Conall muttered against her ear.

"Or a guard."

"Do you care?"

Did she care? She hesitated to speak, but their presence was as damaging to the mood as a splash of ice water. She sighed.

"It's all right to be truthful." He nipped her ear, but the

weight of his body raised and shifted to the side of her.

"I'm sorry."

"Nae, lass, there's naught to apologize for." His voice, rough with need, sent shivers coursing through her spine. She stroked the iron length of him in her hand before releasing it.

"How are you so patient?" she whispered.

"Because I must be. When I take you to bed, it'll be without others around to ruin the moment. When you're all mine and there are no distractions." He stole possession of her mouth again, dominating her lips with every kiss. She sighed against him.

"Sleep now."

"How can I possibly sleep?' she protested.

Conall laughed and stroked his fingers over her hair. "Sleep, and let pleasant dreams finish what we could not."

"You're impossible."

"Perhaps so, but you like me this way. Admit it.

"I do."

Conall tucked her against him, his chest to her back and his arm around her waist. Warm and secure in his arms, she closed her eyes and surrendered to the call for sleep. Tomorrow would bring them one step closer to their goal.

One step closer to rescuing her grandmother and all of Cairn Ocland.

When Sorcha woke, she took a moment to enjoy the feel of Conall's arms around her. He'd held her all night, her head pillowed on his shoulder and his heartbeat her lullaby.

Feeling bold, she raised her head and awakened him with

  VIVIENNE SAVAGE

nibbles to the edge of his jaw. He hadn't shaved in weeks, since before they'd first embarked on their adventure together, and the golden-red fuzz on his face suited him.

In the near dark, their room lit only by the subtle glow of the lichens and fungi, she stroked his cheeks and studied his face. Learned every curve and angle. Envied his long lashes.

"Are you going to paint a picture, lass?" Conall peeked open one eye and grinned at her.

"No. I'm admiring what's mine. I was beginning to wonder if you'd miraculously become a heavy sleeper."

"Far from it, I was merely wondering what you'd do with my defenseless sleeping body."

"Not as much as I'd like," she admitted, blushing.

Outside their cozy abode, the goblins were stirring. She could hear their guttural language echoing through the cavern and see many feet passing outside their curtained door.

"I don't want to get up," she whispered.

"I know, but this is all almost over. Soon we'll be able to laze about as long as we like. We'll have the nights to ourselves," he said, stroking his thumb over her cheek, "and the mornings too."

She smiled and hoped he was right, not wanting to think about the battle to come or the endless possible outcomes. One after the other, they crawled from their room and made their way back to the chamber where Teagan awaited them.

"I will make my way toward Mount Kinros," she told them. "Though I cannot guarantee I will arrive in a timely manner. It may take me many days." The older dragon adjusted her frail wings and sighed.

"No one would fault you for staying here where it's safe,

Princess. I'm certain the king will be happy enough to have a member of his family returned to him, whether it's after the battle or not," Sorcha said.

Teagan's enormous green eyes glistened in the pale glow of the goblin lights. "No. I will go. Many years have passed since I last saw my nephew, and I couldn't live with myself if I didn't try when he needs me most."

Sorcha stepped forward and laid her hand against Teagan's snout. "I won't forget your help or your bravery. Goodbye, Princess Teagan."

Surprising her with his sudden sense of etiquette, Conall stepped forward and bowed low at the waist. "Neither will I, Princess Teagan. Go with honor and strength."

"Goodbye, Sorcha and Conall. May the sun light your path and the stars shine in darkness."

A pair of scrawny goblins led them from the vast chamber into a wide passage broad enough to fit even a dragon. Before them, a pair of minecarts faced opposite directions, each straddling a single steel rail.

Sorcha had never seen anything of the like, and she studied it in confusion.

"I think he wants us to hold onto the bar," Conall said, though he sounded uncertain himself.

"Why do I need to—"

The cart pitched forward and flew down the shaft. Wind whipped through her hair and blew her cloak about her shoulders. Sorcha shrieked and squeezed Conall's thigh with one hand.

"Hold the damned rail!" Conall yelled. "Not me!"

As they flew through the tunnels, Sorcha appreciated the

darkness, grateful she couldn't see the path ahead of them. Every now and again, the wheels threw sparks from the tracks and the screeching sound of metal scraping metal filled her with dread.

At one point, she glanced to the side and saw the narrow track high above a bottomless chasm. A few alchemical orbs hung suspended in the air, lighting the tracks with green light. Certain they were going to crash or plummet to their doom, she screamed as they careened around a curve in the tracks.

Just when she began to question her sanity, they soared to the bottom and broke into daylight on a track parallel to the ground with the open sky above them. One of the goblins threw a lever, bringing the cart to an abrupt stop. Sorcha jerked forward in the seat, half afraid her neck would snap. Pleased with themselves, the goblins snickered and released the mine cart's doors.

After a valiant struggle to find her dignity, Sorcha climbed from the cart.

Conall wavered on his feet beside her. "For the love of the stars. I will never climb inside a goblin contraption again."

To conceal her own fading terror, she twisted to face her partner and poked his arm. "Is the big bad wolf afraid of traveling too quickly?"

"We're not meant to travel so fast and not be on our own feet. Besides, you were just as scared, lass, admit it. I wasn't the one screaming."

She glanced up at his smug but impossibly handsome face now that he was no longer green from motion sickness and grinned. "Fine. No more wild cart rides. Are you ready for a run, though?"

"I'll have to be."

He shifted and shook out his russet coat, then nuzzled her neck. Sorcha stroked his throat and kissed his damp nose before she moved around and swung up onto his back. The goblins had brought them out on the southern side of the mountain, closer to their destination than they had been before.

Miles away, past the next low rise, Sorcha saw the shimmering waves of steam rippling through the air, marking their destination.

They had one hell of a ride ahead of them, racing against the clock and Maeval's underlings.

Chapter 17

THEY REACHED THE crater at high noon, renewing Sorcha's sense of hope. By her reckoning, the final leg of the journey hadn't quite taken them four hours. Conall paused at the edge of the wide depression, and she slid off his back, boots sinking into the slush.

She shielded her eyes against the glare of the sun. Faint wisps of smoke curled up from the ground, creating a dusty haze, but the metallic spear jutting from the center of the crater stood out as bright as the stars that made it.

Conall paused and touched a hand to her shoulder. "Take care."

"Afraid of skinned knees from tumbling to the bottom?" Sorcha teased.

"Afraid it'll burn your delicate human fingers." He snorted and proceeded ahead of her.

Rocks and loose shale slid beneath their feet as they made their way down the steep slope. Heat remained from the force of the celestial object's collision with the ground, and each time Sorcha steadied her balance on the smoking earth, the lingering warmth awed her. By the time they arrived at the bottom, she had to unfasten her cloak. The air around them shimmered.

Conall hung back a step. "I can't believe it. The stars truly did answer."

"After your story about receiving your shifter gifts from the stars, did you doubt?"

He rubbed his chin, his smile rueful. "Stories have a way of becoming exaggerated with the passage of years, as you know. And some stories are merely that, fables to inspire and impart hope."

"Do you think it's safe to touch? Do we just pull it out?"

The metal was like nothing she had ever seen before, shifting between silver and dark purple depending on which angle she viewed it from.

Her wolf studied the jutting spear then stepped forward. "Better for me to risk a burn than you while drawing a hot sword from the ground."

"Conall—"

Before she could protest, the alpha closed his hand around the hilt. Both of his brows flew up. "It isn't even a little warm," he said.

"It isn't called cold iron for nothing."

"You had the same worry, Red."

"Maybe—"

An unrecognizable, dark shape blurred across the edge of her vision then slammed into Conall. The creature roared, and flecks of spittle flew from its monstrous mouth. The heat of it blasted Sorcha in the face, its breath like carrion, its eyes wild and frenzied. But human.

Her dearest friend. Her childhood playmate.

Forbidden magic had perverted Ferghus's body into a hideous shape resembling no shapeshifter in existence. He hunched over in a feral posture, long arms dangling inches

VIVIENNE SAVAGE

shy of the ground and armed with a bear's black claws. Thick and coarse fur covered him in patches of gray, black, white, and every other shifter he had slain.

At first, her mind didn't want to acknowledge the identity of the murderer stalking Cairn Ocland's shifters, but there was no mistaking the beauty of the beast's gray eyes. She'd seen those eyes a thousand times before.

As Ferghus and the werewolf tumbled across the pit, the weapon fell from Conall's hand and clattered to the rocks. Sorcha dashed for it, but the moment her fingers closed around the cold hilt, she paused.

If she used it now, then they'd be defenseless against Maeval.

Conall shared her thoughts. "Don't use it, Red! That's what she wants!"

Could she have even used such a thing against Ferghus? Her heart screamed for her to beg Conall not to hurt him, but her senses and every ounce of her intellect knew he couldn't be saved. It came down to the man she loved or a friend who had willfully defiled his own soul.

Sorcha dropped the sword and whipped her bow from her back. The first arrow flew true, the sharpened point burying in the creature's shoulder, buying Conall precious moments to shift. He rolled to the left as Ferghus brought his claws down and came to his feet again on all four paws. Twisting in the air, Conall launched his own offensive, though it did little good. The beast batted him aside like a pup.

Bigger than Conall, Ferghus had the bulk of a bear but the speed and agility of a wolf, with fangs longer than her hand and a whiplike tail. But it was his eyes that scared her the most.

His familiar human eyes burned with hatred.

Back and forth the aberration and shifter struck, feinting, biting, snapping and snarling, their growls reverberating across the skies. Blood and spittle flew, their teeth flashing white.

Each time Sorcha saw an opening, she released another arrow at her mark, though they did little good. The skinwalker may as well have been invulnerable to all attacks, including Conall's fangs. The wolf's teeth gleamed red with blood.

Conall darted out of reach then lunged in, snapping his jaws at his opponent's leg. He pulled the corrupted huntsman to the ground, but the creature kicked outward with his other foot and raked his claws across Conall's muzzle.

Sorcha's next shot troubled her target no more than its predecessors. He swatted most away, each arrow a mere nuisance and nothing more. Over a dozen protruded from his back and chest, his torso bristled with gray-fletched shafts.

Conall shifted. "Take the weapon and run!" he cried while drawing his sword. His human form revealed the extent of his wounds, spiking Sorcha's pulse in terror. Her wolf had taken enough damage to kill a normal man.

"I can't leave you behind!"

"You must!"

Ducking another swing, Conall came up with his blade in a powerful, underhanded stroke. It cleaved through the monster's ribs, laying open the tissue to the bone.

And still Maeval's pawn didn't die.

Ferghus yanked the sword from Conall's hand and tossed it aside. Rendered defenseless, Conall transformed into his werewolf body. The two titans clashed again, her shifter's impressive bulk outsized by the skinwalker's corrupted body.

For a while, he ran circles around his enemy and played the role of the distraction, even tearing through the tendons supporting his opponent's heel.

Before the wolf could hobble his enemy, Ferghus thrust his massive left claw into Conall's chest. The blow hurled him through the air, and Sorcha held her breath when he collapsed limply to the ground.

At that moment, she knew exactly how Conall had felt when she disappeared into the mountain. Her chest ached as if her heart had been torn from it. The pulse pounded in her ears, rising in a frantic roar to drown out all other sound.

"Conall!" she cried.

She couldn't leave him. She couldn't run away and save her own skin.

And she couldn't leave Ferghus to suffer another day in that body.

Step by slow step, Ferghus advanced on Conall, drooling thick ropes of saliva from a maw filled with oversized teeth. There was nothing human left of him, only the twisted creature.

Something wild overtook Sorcha. She pulled a small dagger from her belt and tested its weight in her hands. It gleamed in the bleak light of the winter sun, a golden-pink spark shining over its flawless edge.

Charging forward, she leapt onto a blasted chunk of rock and propelled herself through the air toward her target.

The beast threw his head back and roared when she landed on his back with a dull thump. One of the bone spurs jutting from his spine pressed against her chestplate, threatening to penetrate the leather armor with its sharp tip. She gritted her teeth through it and clung tenaciously to his back by a handful of fur.

He shook and thrashed, roaring his outrage. Her fingers bled, cut from maintaining a determined grip of his wiry fur.

You couldn't have me, and you won't take Conall. With her final act of defiance against her former friend, she drove the knife home into the base of his skull.

The blade sank into his flesh and struck bone. She pressed with the heel of her palm and put her muscle into it, severing his spinal column. Ferghus collapsed to the ground with a thud.

Sorcha left the blade jutting from his neck and rolled to the ground. On her hands and knees, she scrambled to her werewolf's side then placed her palms over his still body.

"Conall?" she whispered at first. "Please say something."

Leaning over him placed her face close enough to his muzzle to feel the warmth of his slow breaths. He stirred, but only barely, making a pitiful whining noise. She took one of his enormous paws between her hands and sobbed in relief.

"I'm here..."

Sorcha glanced over her shoulder at Ferghus's corpse, the mangled human body beneath a macabre quilt of shifter furs stained in his own blood.

Killing him had fulfilled her only duty to the man who was once her friend, and now Conall deserved her attention.

With tears stinging her eyes, she barely saw the rise and fall of his chest, her own sobs drowning out the low whistle of air cycled through his lungs. She tried to quiet, but the emotion overcame her again.

And then his soft head touched her lap. She blinked down through the blurry haze to see Conall gazing up at her.

Tink shot down through the sky, a bright blue ball pulsating with swirls of red. She buzzed around Conall's face, tugged at his ears, and jingled in alarm.

King Alistair landed a few seconds behind her, flanked by a pair of stately griffins. All three transformed into their human shapes and hurried over.

"Y-your Majesty?" She had to be dreaming. "How did you know where to find us?"

"I didn't. After we saw the star shoot across the sky, my wife lost all ability to contact you. Not knowing whether you were close or had even seen it, I took it upon myself to fly here," he explained, crouching beside her. He laid a hand on Conall's flank and pursed his lips. "What's happened?"

"The black fairy sent her beast to stop us from getting a weapon. And Conall—" A sob bubbled up from her throat. She bowed her head and squeezed her eyes shut.

"Yorick, secure the weapon. Gerta, please see to our brave friend. I'll handle this abomination."

"Let me tend to him, lassie." Gerta, a steel-haired matron with kind green eyes, kneeled beside Conall. Sorcha tightened her grip on the wolf's scruff until she saw the woman pulling bandages from her pack.

Numb, she watched as Alistair's fiery breath incinerated Ferghus until nothing remained but ashes. With Conall still and limp in her lap there was no sense of triumph. No satisfaction in the death of their foe. None of it would matter if the man she loved didn't live to see another day.

Yorick fetched the starmetal sword and gazed at it in wonder. "A gift from the heavens itself." He then returned to his griffin form and took the weapon into both talons.

Greta glanced up from her examination of Conall's injuries, deep lines furrowing her brow. "He'll need magical healing if he's to live, my lord."

"Then I will fly him to my wife." Alistair moved over and laid his hand on Sorcha's shoulder. She lifted her gaze to his face, struck by the admiration and gratitude she saw in his hazel eyes. "You have done more than I can ever thank you for, Sorcha, more than was asked of you."

"I still want to help. I want to fight."

He studied her face then gave a nod. "Then come. I will carry your Conall."

Her Conall. The words felt right in her heart, and she only hoped she would be given the opportunity to share them with the wolf she had fallen so desperately in love with.

She forced her fingers to loosen, allowing Alistair to lift the broken wolf into his claw.

"Come, dear," Gerta coaxed. "You ride on me."

Throughout the flight, Sorcha found herself watching her wolf as he dangled between the king's claws. Alistair carried him tenderly, with respect to his injuries, but her heart shattered each time she heard a hint of a whimper on the wind.

Be strong, she told herself. *Each sound is a sign that he still lives.*

The moon rose high above them by the time they reached the camp at the base of Mount Kinros. Dozens of campfires shone orange beneath them, highlighting a hundred tents and over a thousand warriors.

The culmination of sweat, tears, and weeks of effort came together as the clans reunited. Humans and shifters gathered below, and when Alistair and the griffins came in for the

VIVIENNE SAVAGE

landing, they all cleared ground to make room.

"Anastasia!" Alistair called. His voice boomed across the snow-kissed valley. "This one needs healing!"

Queen Anastasia emerged from the largest tent and rushed to them as her husband lowered Conall to the ground. The werewolf hadn't yet reverted to his human body, listless form still and pale. A hush fell over the camp, the valley silent save for the low murmur of voices carrying the news from tent to tent.

Tink hovered nearby after an unsuccessful attempt to awaken Conall by tugging his ear. Zipping from her wolven friend to land on Sorcha's shoulder, her jingling became increasingly frantic and terrified by the second until the tiny voice, filled with desperation wept, "Please don't die."

For the first time since their initial meeting, Sorcha comprehended the little sprite's delicate speech.

"He won't die, Tink." She blinked away the tears stinging her eyes, too determined to maintain the illusion of strength for her friend.

"I'll need help. Fetch clean water and bring my salves!" Anastasia called.

With a barrel of the water collected for their enormous war band, the queen bathed Conall's wounds and applied healing tinctures. Sorcha had no knowledge of the arcane but remained by his side throughout each spell, watching the awe-inspiring sorceress each time she touched him with magic-infused fingers. Before her eyes, the bleeding stopped and the most debilitating injuries began closing.

With the next pass of the sorceress's hands, the smaller wounds regressed and became smooth, unblemished flesh.

The once gaping wounds remained pink, but no longer raw.

"Can he be saved?" Sorcha asked, voice barely above a choked whisper. "Will this be enough?"

"I believe so," Anastasia said. "He has a strong will to survive so long with such injuries." Her fingers brushed over Conall's auburn pelt.

"What happens now?"

"For now, he must rest. My love, if you could carry him to the wolves, I'm certain they'll wish to tend to their alpha."

The king nodded. "Of course."

Sorcha rose to follow when Alistair took Conall into his claws, but Anastasia stilled her with a touch to her wrist.

"It's your turn, my brave rider."

"I'm not—"

"Lying will help no one, especially your beloved," Anastasia advised her in a gentle voice. "Come with me to my tent. No one will trouble us there."

"I'm going with Conall!" Tink declared before flitting away.

Numbed by the weight of the events she'd endured, Sorcha trailed after her queen. At some point, the benevolent monarch had taken her by the hand as a friend—an equal—lacing their fingers together.

The royal tent was more modest than Sorcha expected. A single table occupied the center of the space with a map rolled out across it. She barely had a chance to glance at the depiction of the Shadow Glen before Anastasia guided her through the partition curtain into the private side of the tent. Fallen logs served as seats and the bed looked to be a thick pile of furs and blankets. The king and queen hadn't brought in furniture from

VIVIENNE SAVAGE

the castle, camping like everyone else.

"You sit right here and drink this." Ana passed her a full wine skin and waited until Sorcha had taken a long swallow. With water and a cloth, she dabbed the gash on Sorcha's brow.

Anastasia's magic warmed her from head to toe, spreading through her limbs with the same comfort as a nap in the spring sunshine. Her aches dulled until they were gone altogether, and her tightly wound muscles relaxed.

"Better?"

"Yes, thank you."

"I know you've been through an ordeal, but are you willing to tell me what happened? I feel a weight on your heart, Sorcha. You don't have to carry your burdens alone."

The queen's concerned expression and genuine care were too much to withstand, though Sorcha tried with all her might to stay in control. When she failed to blink back her tears, the fragile facade of strength cracked, and the pain erupted to the surface. The moment Sorcha's shoulders shook, Anastasia hugged her close.

"This isn't about Conall, is it? You killed the skinwalker?" Anastasia asked in a soft voice while stroking Sorcha's back.

"I did," she whispered. "It was Ferghus, a fellow hunter and a friend. Or he was, once upon a time. I know it was for the best, I do, but…"

"But this wasn't a nameless beast." Anastasia hugged her tighter. "Was he given a proper funeral?"

"Aye, King Alistair cremated his body. Now there's nothing to return to his family. How could someone change so much and become something completely opposite of all they believed in?"

"A black fae like Maeval can take even the best man and find the most minute crumb of darkness in them. No human is perfect, my friend. Not even I. It resides within all of us. Remember your friend Ferghus for the good man he once was, not the beast you both slew."

Although nothing eased her worries for Conall, the weight lifted from Sorcha's shoulders. "What do I say to his family? And why does it hurt so much despite everything he did?"

"The truth," Anastasia said. "That the hunter once known as Ferghus of Clan Corwell was yet another of Maeval's victims."

Anastasia's wise counsel eased her heart and helped her come to terms with her friend's death. While she had freed Ferghus from servitude, it was time to avenge him and all others Maeval had hurt.

An hour passed before the queen shooed her from the tent to rest. Thanks to Anastasia, Sorcha's body felt revived and her stomach was full of good food and warm wine. No sooner had she stepped outside the tent did a familiar voice call out her name.

"Sorcha!" Her twin brother rushed over and swept her into a tight embrace.

"Egan? No one told me you were here! Where are Mum and Da'?"

"In a tent of their own asleep. When we heard Gran had been taken by the fairy, we feared the worst. Are you all right?" Egan asked. He looked her over, searching for injuries.

VIVIENNE SAVAGE

"I'm—" Fine, she wanted to say, but the lie refused to pass her lips. Instead, she shook her head and hugged her twin close. "I've been better."

"How did you do it?"

"Do what?"

"Gather all the shifters. You should have seen the way Da's eyes bulged when the bears showed up invoking your name."

"They all came?"

Egan pressed an exaggerated kiss on her cheek. "They did, and fifty strong at that. Then the wolves arrived with nearly twice the number. But enough about that, what about the starlight sword? Is it true? Did you truly find a weapon to kill the fairy?"

"We did." But at what cost? Her thoughts turned to Conall, but as she sought an excuse to part from her brother, her mother and father's voices rang out.

"Sorcha!" her mother called.

When Egan released her, she ran to her parents. She'd never needed her mother's embrace as much as she did then, although Anastasia had been a marvelous substitute.

"I missed you both so much!" she said when she finally had the breath. "Granny… They took Granny. And Ferghus was—he's dead. I killed him."

Over the course of the next hour, she told her family everything, from the moment she arrived at her grandmother's vandalized home to the epic battle with Ferghus. They heard her out with patience, though her mother touched her hands often and her father tensed each time he bit back a question. At the end, all three of them stared at her in varying degrees of wonder.

"We are proud of you, lass," her mother said. "Proud of everything you've done."

"Aye," her father agreed. "You've accomplished the impossible, Sorcha. Look at all the people you've brought together. Somehow, against the odds, you even found a weapon to use against our foe. I was wrong to have doubted in you. Wrong to question your wanting to separate to embark on your own adventure. I see that now."

Tears misted Sorcha's eyes by the end of her father's heartfelt speech. Aengus Dunrathi wasn't a man who often admitted his wrongs, concealing his mistakes as if they were badges of shame. "Da'..."

"I mean every word. Twenty-five years your mother's battled beside me as my other half—my better half—and I know her to be a true warrior. I should have known the same of you."

Sorcha swallowed the hard lump in her throat. Her tongue was as dry as sanding paper. "If not for Conall, I wouldn't have managed any of it. I... I love him, Da'. I chose him, and now he may not even survive."

Uncomfortable with the subject change, Egan dropped his gaze to his scarred hands. Her mother and father exchanged glances, and then her father moved closer to embrace her. Her mother held her from the other side.

"If you want to help him, then you need to rest," her father said. "The sun will be up soon."

"I can't rest. Not while he's—"

"You can and you will," her mother insisted. "I'm sure Conall would tell you the same. Rest so you can give him the care and attention he'll need once he's on his feet."

He would.

Giving in, Sorcha allowed her mother to guide her through the camp with an arm around her waist to their familiar wagon and tent. Sorcha recognized many of the faces around them, fellow hunters and villagers who had aided them in the past.

"How secure is this camp?" she asked.

"As well as can be this close to the Shadow Glen," her father replied. "The queen has put up all manner of protection spells, but we have sentries as well. The shifters have added their own members to the watch teams, which has helped immensely."

Humans and weres, working together once again. Sorcha looked up to the stars above them and wondered if that was why they'd decided to answer her prayers after so much time.

Please don't take him away from me, she wished, praying the stars would answer one more time.

Chapter 18

"SORCHA! SORCHA! YOU missed it!" Egan cried as he ducked into her tent.

She jerked awake, torn from the sweet embrace of dreams, and blearily stared at her brother.

"Missed what? Has the battle started?"

"I know you've been on the road a long while, but it's no reason to be sleeping in the middle of the afternoon."

"Wait, what?"

"Aye, sleepyhead, you've slept like the dead all day, but I thought you'd want to see this. A hundred or so goblins appeared. The wee blighters poured out of the old mine shafts in dozens of carts, and then a dragon crawled out behind them. They're saying it's Princess Teagan!"

"Princess Teagan is here? She arrived?"

"Aye, she—wait, you don't seem surprised."

"I met her in the heart of Mount Floraivel. She healed me after I fell through a weak spot. Saved my life, Egan. I thought for sure I was a goner and these goblins were taking me away to meet our makers, then suddenly there was this dragon above me."

Her brother's mouth fell open, then he twisted around to stare at the field beyond her tent. "Of all the things to forget to tell us, you leave out the part about meeting a dragon princess."

Once Egan bowed out of the tent, Sorcha crawled from beneath the blankets and pulled on her clothes. Tink flit up from the unfamiliar pile of wolf furs, startling Sorcha so greatly she nearly tumbled through one of the canvas walls.

"Where did you come from?" she asked, holding a hand to her heart.

"Your blankets," Tink replied.

"But when?"

"Umm, an hour ago. Conall asked me to look after you."

Her heart lurched again. "Is he awake?"

Tink wriggled through the air. "No. He went back to sleep. I put dust in his soup. And I brought those!" She zipped down to the gray and white mountain of wolf skins littering the ground, certainly not among the woolen blankets when Sorcha first drowsed to sleep.

"Are those… is that wolf skin?"

"They're from normal wolves, silly. Not *werewolves*. Conall wanted you to be warm and sent them."

"How did you…? You know what? Nevermind. I'll chalk it up to pixie magic." She didn't want to imagine some stranger sneaking into her tent with the enormous pile.

While Tinker Bell hadn't appeared to be anything more than a glittering speck, she picked out the finer details of her features when she flew close. A small, heart-shaped face and a shock of sunflower-gold hair. Her dress could have been woven from grass blades, little more than a green wrap around her miniature body.

"Tink, I need a favor of you."

"Yes, yes?"

"I want you to tell me once Conall is awake again. Right

away."

"Should I go watch him?"

"Like a hawk."

Busywork occupied the remainder of Sorcha's day. She worked alongside the fletchers, making arrows and gathering feathers from the geese a few hunters had shot down during their travel to the glen. As was tradition for a warband, they'd feast well the night before the battle.

Later, she sharpened her sword and enjoyed supper with her family. Not once did Conall stir from his tent. According to Anastasia, he'd awakened once in the early afternoon and vowed he would sooner die than miss the siege planned for the morning.

"He's awake, he's awake!" Tink reported.

Anxiety dampened her palms and sent a stutter to Sorcha's heart. She stared toward the cluster of tents constructed from thick animal skins where the wolves had claimed their stake. Conall's had been marked with red paint identifying him as their leader. A pair of wolves stood guard, flawless beasts with ebony coats flanking the entrance.

They'd stood watch all day, moving only once to swap with another pair and take dinner.

Tink zipped down and grasped Sorcha by her index finger. "Come on, slowpoke. Let's go to him!"

"No, Tink, not this time," she said in a gentle voice. "I need to see Conall alone to… to tell him what's in my heart."

The tugging ceased, and Tink raised to Sorcha's eye level. "Ohhh. You're going to make pups. Why didn't you say so, silly human?"

The little sprite's observation nearly made her choke. "I,

um, no. No pups. Not right now."

Tink swooped down and patted her face. "I'm glad he has you. Conall loves you very much. I was afraid you would take him away from me, but you make him happy."

"Is that why you knotted my hair?"

"Maybe."

"Well then, I'm glad you've come to realize I can never replace you. You'll always be welcome with us."

A pink flush overtook Tink's yellow glow, preceding a kiss to Sorcha's cheek. Without another word, she darted away.

Alone at last, Sorcha gathered her courage and strode forward. It was now or never. She could accept where her heart and affection belonged or risk a future where she forever regretted failing to share her love with him.

The bitter mountain cold cut through Sorcha's cloak, tunic, and leggings, a fraction of the intolerable weather they would face while scaling the rocks come dawn.

Conall's tent beckoned her, the flap drawn shut against the biting wind.

Now or never, she reminded herself.

The wolven pair nodded, and she returned the courteous sentiment before lingering outside in the frigid cold. Whether or not they understood her intentions, both wandered away into the heart of their camp without a second glance, leaving Sorcha as the sole caretaker of their alpha.

After parting the heavy animal skin, she ducked inside the tent. Conall sat on a pile of furs, bare from the waist up, and anything below concealed by thickly knitted blankets. A fresh set of scars stretched across his chest, healed but pink and shiny, and he was rubbing herbal-scented ointment into them.

Without a word, Sorcha knelt beside him and took the jar of salve to apply it in his stead.

"You should be resting, Red. You'll need all your strength tomorrow," he said.

"I've had enough rest, and I couldn't sleep if I wanted to." She dipped her fingers into the jar again then tucked her chin, avoiding eye contact while massaging the cream into his newly healed injuries. "I nearly lost you."

"That blighted fairy will have to do more to kill me." Conall caught her wrist then set the jar aside. "But why are you really here now? You didn't come to baby me."

She answered him with a kiss filled with all her passion and longing. Conall's strong arms wrapped around her and crushed her to his scarred chest. The herbaceous fragrance surrounded her, astringent and floral at once, calming notes of lavender blended with the healing properties of moon lily root.

Her grandmother would have been proud of her for recognizing it. And for her grandmother, for all victims spirited away by the dark fae, she'd storm Mount Kinros in the morrow.

But tonight was hers. If Conall's near death at Ferghus's hands was any indication, tomorrow wasn't promised to them.

Stroking her fingers through his cinnamon-hued hair, she set her brow against his forehead and whispered, "I love you, Conall, and I want to go into this battle at your side. Not as your companion, but as your mate. I won't waste another day without consummating our union."

"My mate."

"Yours. Body, heart, and soul."

The lacings of her simple bodice stood no chance against the strength of an eager werewolf. His fingers tugged, a leather strap snapped, and he pulled the garment from her body. Her tunic swiftly followed.

"Co—"

Before she could protest his reckless conduct with her garments, the world spun and she landed on her back amidst the furs. With one yank, he drew her leggings down from around her waist. After exposing her flesh, he nibbled her hipbone then drew her clothes down her thighs.

Stripping before him at the spring had been different, a necessity to enjoy her bath despite his roving eyes. Now he was watching her, devouring her with a lust-starved gaze, his eyes lingering upon the slick treasure he had unveiled.

He tossed the leggings aside to join her tunic and sat back on his heels, her own virile and naked warrior. The length of him jutted up stiff and proud, as arousing a sight as she'd hoped for.

"Gods you're beautiful," Sorcha whispered in awe.

Conall chuckled and leaned forward. He dragged his nose across her inner thigh and nibbled the sensitive skin, moving higher until his lips skimmed across the dark curls between her legs. "Not as beautiful as you."

"Conall, what…?"

"I want to know the taste of you," he whispered. His tongue parted her flesh and teased across the tight pearl hidden beneath. Sorcha's back lifted from the furs and her hips bucked.

His whiskered jaw tickled against her thighs, and his

kisses trailed up higher, lingering at her hip, then her navel, until his mouth reached her breasts and each nipple learned the heat of his mouth. She writhed beneath his attentions, scorching heat following the path his mouth made.

Warmth surged to her face. "I don't know what to…what to do." How could any man be as talented with his tongue without having an ounce of experience? It wasn't fair. Beneath him, she felt awkward, her sexual innocence surfacing when she least desired.

Conall leaned up on one strong arm and cupped her chin. "We'll learn together. There's no wrong thing to do, lass. Remember that. As long as it's the two of us, and you're loving the way I touch you and hungry for how I make you feel."

No wrong thing to do.

With that in mind, she let her fingers wander over the curves and planes of his body, exploring each unique angle.

"I want to touch you," she whispered.

Allowing her the chance to admire him in full, Conall rolled to his back to reverse their positions. From his scarred chest to the flat plane of his abdomen, she found every inch sculpted to masterwork perfection. Every inch worthy of her kisses.

And still, she hadn't reached the part of him she craved the most. Her core ached with desire, and her fingers longed to touch. Her palms traveled over strong thighs corded with muscle then reached his hips, both carved with definition.

Gaining confidence, her hand wrapped around his arousal then slid up and down from the root of him to the tip. Mesmerized, her eyes raised to his face. He'd become as hard as a steel sword hilt, and just as dangerous, because once she

VIVIENNE SAVAGE

began to stroke him she didn't want to stop—couldn't stop.

Now, for the first time since their unusual relationship began, she was the one with absolute power. His breaths quickened, and his hips rose with each pump. Her thumb circled over the ridged edge of his crown, and she dipped her head to taste the single salty drop at the tip. Conall's body drew taut and his head fell back.

"Sweet stars above, Red."

In a moment of sheer impulse, she leaned forward and nipped his exposed throat.

A subtle growl rumbled in his chest, reverberating notes of approval and pleasure.

For an alpha to bare his throat to her, it could mean only one thing. He truly did see her as his equal.

"I love you," she whispered. "My wolf." How had it taken her so long to realize she'd been falling in love with him?

"Yours always, Red," he said, his voice raw with emotion. "Ride me, lass. Take what belongs to you, for I surely plan to do the same. I can't wait another moment to have you as my wife."

With Conall holding her hips, she angled his thick length to her aching body. Her cheeks warmed when one of his strong hands guided their union, sweeping up and down her glistening folds in a teasing path until she trembled with desire.

"Conall… Conall that's not fair."

"Feels good?"

"Yes," she murmured with emphasis as his thumb brushed over the tender button nestled within her cleft. "But now I need… I need more."

"This?" He found her entrance, and when she lowered herself upon him, Sorcha knew she couldn't tolerate it if he claimed her slow and gentle.

She slammed her body down and claimed him whole— every single inch. He slid home in a perfectly snug fit that left her shuddering in pleasure, and as one, they both groaned.

It hadn't hurt. Not like she'd expected. A brief and fleeting snap of tension was all she'd felt when her body adjusted to his generous girth.

His hands slid around to her bottom, squeezing her soft flesh. His touch guided her into the first rolling movement, a single undulation bringing her backward until he nearly slipped from her body's embrace, then forward again in a swift glide. The satisfied moan he made bolstered her confidence, and she moved again, slower, finding a rhythm that pleased but didn't rush.

"Say it again," Conall urged.

"Say what? That I'm yours? That I love you with all that I am?"

A low groan rumbled in his chest. "Aye, that and more."

"I mean every word," she panted.

"Mine," he repeated. "My wife. My love."

The word rung through her heart and filled her with joy.

"I love you, Red."

She leaned forward and Conall wrapped an arm around her. With one hand propped on the furs by his head to support her weight, she cupped his face with the other and directed his mouth to hers. Conall shifted beneath her, the hand on her buttocks kneading and tugging, bringing her in tight against him after each backstroke.

VIVIENNE SAVAGE

Tension coiled through her body, a blissful warmth that started at her toes and spread upward. Conall dipped his head and drew one rosy nipple into his mouth, the light skate of his teeth over the sensitive bud pushing her toward the edge. She cried his name, tipped her head back, and closed her eyes as everything came undone.

Beneath her, Conall sped his pace and pistoned with inexhaustible strokes. He anchored her hips with his strong hands and thrust a final time, burying himself deep within her body, and called out her name.

For a long while they rocked together, unable to do anything more than breathe and sing intimate, whispered praises by lantern light. She collapsed against him and pressed her flushed cheek against the hollow of his throat.

"Worth every day of waiting," he murmured after a contented sigh, breaking the silence.

She could only mumble in response, too relaxed to frame proper words in her head, let alone speak. Conall chuckled at her and spent the next few minutes smoothing his fingers up and down her back. Eventually, her heart settled into a normal pace, and the hazy fog of passion cleared from her head.

"I thought… I thought wolves took their mates another way."

"Mm? What way is that?"

Heat surged to her face. "I thought I'd be on my knees."

He kissed the upper curve of her breast. "Would you like to be made love to that way? As a werewolf female is taken by her husband?"

While Conall had fulfilled her desires and left her sexually sated, the thought of him taking the lead and guiding their lovemaking enticed her. "Yes."

"I didn't think you'd like it." His lips closed around her swollen nipple and playfully tugged the tip.

"I don't know if I would or not, but… I'd like to find out."

He kissed his way down to her bellybutton before he moved, coming up to his knees. One strong tug flipped her onto her belly, and then he was behind her, between her spread legs, his warm palms smoothing over her bottom.

He showed her how it was to be loved like a werewolf, tireless and passionate, until Sorcha knew nothing else in the world but the pleasure of his touch. They found their bliss together and slumped to the furs in a sweaty heap, bodies still joined as one. Conall held her, delivering soft and gentle kisses to her nape and shoulders until her body cooled and her racing pulse slackened to a calmer beat.

He stroked her hair and nuzzled her throat, abrading her skin with the golden-red stubble covering his jaw and chin. "You're the best thing to come into my life, Red, and tomorrow, we're going to retake our kingdom."

In the privacy of their tent, Red and her wolf sprawled nude among the furs with their limbs entwined. And then she knew nothing more than dreams of a free Cairn Ocland with her werewolf at her side.

VIVIENNE SAVAGE

Chapter 19

CONALL ROUSED BEFORE dawn, but it was difficult to part from Red's side and face the battle ahead of them. On the one hand, he had his people to protect, but on the other, he wanted to stand by her side until the final seconds of combat, whether they emerged victorious or not.

For a while, despite the pressing obligation to exit the tent and rally the werewolves, he remained sprawled beside his slumbering mate. In sleep, the tense lines of her face smoothed and all signs of stress melted away.

After walking his fingers down her bare arm, his touch skimmed her hip and smoothed over to her abdomen. He'd never taken the time to truly appreciate her beauty before, lacking the chance prior to their intimate moment in the hot spring.

As for the previous night, that had been different—her pleasure had taken precedence, his unyielding shapeshifter stamina used to bring her to absolute fulfillment in every way. He'd sacrificed the opportunity to learn every inch of her body in favor of bringing her to the brink of orgasm time and time again.

How could one woman be so right and perfect?

"Red," he whispered before kissing the back of her shoulder. His lips skimmed over her skin until he reached the sweet pulse at her neck. There he delivered a succinct kiss. "Time to be up, lass."

Sorcha's lashes fluttered and her limbs straightened in a languid stretch. Her sigh—a sweet exhale of sated pleasure—was music to his ears.

Loathing the circumstances for awakening her, he suppressed the urge to stake his claim a third time before they emerged to fight the difficult battle ahead.

"We have to dress."

She yawned. "Must we?"

"We must. We have a fairy to kill."

Exercising willpower he didn't know he had, Conall slipped from his place beside her in the makeshift bed. Donning clothes didn't help. To distract himself, he fastened his kilt and laced his boots, the occasional glimpse of her bare body a temptation to shirk his duties for a moment longer, to worship at her feet and take the sweet core of her into his mouth again.

He would soon. Once Maeval was dead, making love to his new mate would be his celebration dance.

Although they had slept the previous night, Sorcha had also stirred more than once, eager and ready for him. Then at some point between their feverish rounds of lovemaking, she'd crept from the tent and retrieved her belongings. They'd even washed with what water he'd been afforded in a nearby basin, while longing for the chance to soak in the spring at Braeloch again.

"I'm ready."

"Together then, Red?"

Her dark eyes raised to his face. "Why do you still call me

Red even when I'm not wearing my cloak?"

"You'll always be Red to me, regardless of what you're wearing. It's more than the color of your attire—it's who you are. Passion and courage."

Conall tilted his head down to claim her mouth, daring to steal another kiss before they emerged from their honeymoon den to face the brutal reality of war. His mate rose to tiptoe and met him halfway for a kiss sweeter than each of its predecessors.

"I love you," she whispered against his lips.

Hand in hand, they stepped from the tent to find the war council gathered around the central fire. As one of the alphas, Conall's tent hadn't been far from the center of the gathering. He joined Heldreth and the other shifter leaders.

Father Bear's remaining eye narrowed. "Well. We wondered if you ever planned to show your face, lad."

Conall grunted. "You said to be present at sunrise." On the distant, western horizon, the twinkling stars glittered their blessing, still visible against the ever-brightening sky to the east behind the mountains.

"So we did." Heldreth's lips turned up at the corners in a knowing smile, but her levity only lasted a moment. "We're ready to join the king and queen, as well as the human leaders. This ends today."

He accompanied his fellow shifters through the camp to the king's tent. The crimson silk banner blazed beneath the dawning sunlight, a bold declaration against their dreary surroundings. Two guards admitted them inside.

"Welcome, friends," Alistair greeted. Like Conall and Father Bear, he wore no armor, clad in only his clan tartan.

Standing at his side, Queen Anastasia wore a golden-brown cuirass of molded leather over dark silver robes spun from tough spidersilk.

"We lost one of the griffins in the wee hours of the morning. Testing Maeval's boundary, he flew too closely to her fortress and was shot from the sky," Anastasia announced.

"Shot by what?" Egan asked. Sorcha's brother had volunteered to ride with the griffins.

The king sighed. "We don't know."

"We must all exercise caution. Any number of traps or enchanted pitfalls may await you once we reach her stronghold," the queen continued.

"Three griffins will remain apart from the battle to bring the wounded back to Princess Teagan. She'll tend to those within her power to mend," Alistair said.

Conall swept his gaze to the tall, willow thin princess. If pressed to give a number to her age, he would describe her as timeless. Although silver strands glittered amidst through her waist-length black hair, her face remained unlined until she smiled. She stood to the side, calm and regal with Tink perched on her shoulder. It had taken him a long while to convince the sprite that a battle was no place for her and that her talents would be better suited helping whoever remained in the camp.

"Clan Arval will make a path to the fortress," Heldreth promised.

"As for the honors of wielding this sword, we've decided one of you should be the one to bear it," Alistair said. He held the weapon over both of his palms in offering toward Sorcha and Conall.

"Not me," Sorcha said. "It should be him. I may have helped to find it, but he risked his life to protect it from Ferghus." Her gaze lifted to Conall. "Besides, it's only fitting if a shifter's the one to hold it."

"Me?"

"Aye, lad. I had a feeling she'd refuse it, but just the same, I wanted to hear the words from her lips." Alistair grinned at them both. "Will you stand alongside me as I address the troops."

Conall bowed. "Aye, my king."

"No more of that. Today, I am Alistair. Your friend."

Alistair stepped from the tent and moved toward the center of the camp. A procession of clan leaders and able-bodied elders followed him, and Anastasia took her place at his side. The king and queen joined hands.

Years ago, Bradoc TalWolthe had called Alistair a brat prince, a truly spoiled child who failed to lead when his nation needed him most. A man stood before them now, and Conall had never been more proud of his country.

"Eighteen years have passed since I failed as your king. When King Rua and Queen Liadh fell in battle, I did not lead in their place. When you needed me most, I was not strong. When Dalborough ravaged Cairn Ocland, I did not defend you. Today, I will do everything within my power to right those wrongs, and we will persevere through whatever dark sorcery this fairy unleashes to defend her fortress. The Scourge will end today, or the stars will take us."

Cheers erupted from the camp and weapons raised in the air.

With a warhammer resting over his shoulder, Father

Bear made his way toward the base of the mountain where the steep, impassable rise prevented them from climbing higher on foot. Clutching a variety of massive, blunt weapons in their enormous hands, Heldreth and Little Bear led the other bears to join him.

The first hammer blow initiated an instant chain reaction. Stone flew and ice-glossed rocks crumbled to dust with a thunderous boom. With each strike, the mountain trembled, the ground shook, and dust cleared to reveal chiseled stairs in the mountain face.

Within the hour, or perhaps even minutes, the bears would have the way cleared. Hundreds of feet of stairs carved with powerful magic, after all, each of the twelve clans had their own gift—dragons' fire, bears' stoneshaping, and wolves' wind.

As a child, witnessing the power of the bears had always filled Conall with awe. It impressed him no less as an adult. He watched while Red stood beside him. Her fingers hovered above the hilt of her sword.

"Are you ready?" he asked.

She glanced up at him and nodded. "Absolutely."

With their king and queen in the lead, and a thousand men and women all around them, they charged the mountain.

An explosion threw Sorcha off balance before they reached the stone stairway. Conall tried to catch her but staggered the other direction as a great geyser of soil and frost rocketed in the air. Another blast shuddered the ground, then another, each one popping in rapid succession. Through the clouds of dirt and raining snow, skeletal figures burst from the soil.

"She's raised our own dead against us! This must be… these must be our ancestors!" Conall cried.

Sorcha gasped. "They've been beneath us all of this time, waiting!"

"She's preserved them with magic," Anastasia said grimly. "Remove the heads from their bodies. It's the only way."

Fighting against the bones of their forebears dealt a blow to their morale. The undead felt no pain and walked away from wounds that would have cut down a living creature.

The two armies clashed, the living against the undead and creatures wrought of dark magic. Imps threw fire, changelings blasted them with ice, and the skeleton warriors surged forward in eerie silence.

Everything around them was chaos. In his wolf form, Conall pounced a ghoul to the ground and tore it to pieces. Behind him, Sorcha held her own against a pair of imps, making quick work of them with her blade.

With waves of creatures at Maeval's beck and call, it became a battle of endurance over skill. Despite their combined fighting prowess, the true challenge came in outlasting a never-ending flood of aberrations from the Shadow Glen.

"Behind us!"

Conall spun around and his stomach dropped. Men in Dalborovian armor flooded through the pass, though the banners they carried bore the TalDrach colors.

TalDrach colors?

With undead ancestors still clawing their way from the rocky soil, Conall struggled to prepare for the opportunistic assault from the Dalborovians. It surprised him none to see them joining forces with a dark fairy.

Despite his fears, the attack never came. The small army slammed into the undead ranks.

"What in the blazes is happening?" Conall demanded.

"Sir Lyonas has arrived!" Anastasia called out. "Take heart men, we are not alone! They've come to aid us! Press forward and leave the undead to our new friends!"

With their spirits bolstered, the clans surged forward and pushed back the rising tide of reanimated corpses.

"Hurry, Anastasia! To my back!" Alistair called. "Now that our allies are here, we must go for the citadel."

Upon taking his dragon form, he exhaled a hot stream of fire at the ghouls closing in on them. He cleared their immediate surroundings, only for Yorick and the human leader of one of the hunter clans to race toward him. The former bowed in his human form.

"Allow us to escort you, my king," Yorick said. "The way is treacherous. As I reported to you this morn, something dangerous awaits in the heart of Kinros."

The huge dragon paused. His heavy brows drew close, and his jaw clenched with apparent indecision on his scaled face. Conall glanced over the flock of griffins prepared to guard their king with their lives. One by one they shifted then a hunter armed with a bow leapt astride them.

"Then fly quickly. We haven't a moment to lose." Alistair scooped Sorcha and Conall into his front claws and lifted into the air.

The griffins flew as one in a defensive formation, thirteen in all, both old and young. In their beast forms, they ranged a wide variety of patterns, from leopard spotted hind quarters to stripes. And they were so beautiful. Conall hadn't seen them since he was a child taken up the mountain during a meeting between his father and Yorick.

A javelin of ice hurtled through the air but missed its intended target—Alistair—by a narrow margin. Conall whipped his head toward the source of the assault in time to see Gerta dart into the next projectile's path.

The griffiness plummeted from the air with her rider, but the rest of her kin never broke ranks.

"No!" Sorcha cried.

A third spear followed close behind the first. Alistair made a dizzying roll out of the way, leaving Conall clutching at the claws around him while his stomach lurched. Sorcha shrieked from the dragon's other fist.

Their flight became a frantic race. The mountainside trembled and shook, thick walls of ice cleaving away, and soon the source made its appearance.

An ice giant.

Thunder echoed across the sky as the griffins tapped into their power. Two veered off from position in unison, and when they screamed, lightning streaked from the heavens. The giant flinched away from their attacks and swung his massive club through the air. Jagged shards flew from the magical weapon, forcing the griffins to scatter and Alistair to veer sharply toward the citadel's lower courtyard.

"Prepare to drop," Alistair warned. He glided low then released Conall and Sorcha. They hit the cold ground and rolled clear before a volley of arrows rained down from the bow-wielding ghouls on the upper terrace.

Conall channeled his magic and released a sharp howl. The resulting gale blew the next flurry aside as easily as leaves in the wind. Broken arrows clattered to the ground far off their determined path.

Alistair landed on the next pass, and Anastasia leapt down from his back with her staff. Invoking a spell in her own native tongue, the tip of the staff glowed brightly with arcane energy, and a semi-translucent shield materialized around them, a large dome able to protect even her husband.

"I'll come with you," Alistair said.

"No," Anastasia said. "Stay with your people!"

Alistair balked, divided between remaining by his wife and helping his people. "Don't ask me to send you alone."

A stray lance from the giant's club struck Anastasia's shields. She flinched as if struck, and a line creased her brow. "I won't be alone. I'll be with Conall and Sorcha. If the griffins face the giant alone, it'll decimate them."

Behind the dragon king, the courageous griffins swooped low and dragged the giant's attention back to them, but two more fell beneath the behemoth creature's attacks.

"We'll protect her with our lives," Sorcha vowed.

"Come back to me," Alistair said with a fierceness Conall knew all too well. Their king took off into the sky and soared toward the giant, a crimson streak bent on protecting his people.

While the citadel forces were thinner, they still met opposition. Guards flanked the stairs to the upper terrace, creatures that seemed carved from black ice melded with the flesh of ghouls. Conall brought up his great sword to block their attacks while Sorcha ducked beneath and stabbed outward with her sword. Behind them, Anastasia made a swirling inferno around her staff and released a focused jet of flames on the nearest aberration.

With each attack, they gained ground until at last they reached the doorway. Inside, dark walls and blue flamed chandeliers gave the citadel an oppressive and gloomy air. With no clear direction on which way to go, they turned to the left and followed the passageway deeper into the castle.

"How do we find her?" Sorcha asked.

"Like any magic-user, she'll be at the highest vantage point."

Around the next corner, they discovered a steep and narrow stairwell. The higher they ascended, the colder the temperatures plummeted until ice layered the walls and their breath fogged the air. The stairs ended in a large corridor that ran the length of the obsidian keep. Statues carved from black stone lined the walls on either side of them.

Conall half expected them to spring to life, but the ominous sentries remained inert.

An archway at the end of the hall led to an upward sloping corridor. Conall stepped through first with Sorcha right behind him, then the queen.

Anastasia bounced off an invisible barrier. The blast threw her back amid a shower of ice shards.

Sorcha skidded on the frost-rimmed floor and doubled back. "What happened?"

A shimmer lingered in the air, more visible when Anastasia raised her open palm toward the empty space in the passage. When she touched it, power stirred and forced her fingers back.

"Are you unable to pass?" Conall asked.

"I feared this may happen, but it appears Maeval has

warded herself against interference. I cannot follow. My fae blood won't allow it," Anastasia said. Bearing her staff in a white-knuckled grip, the queen straightened her spine and turned to face the path behind them. The sound of approaching monsters grew closer, the scrape of claws dragging over stone joined by the groan of the hungry dead. "I'll defend you here. Go without me."

"Alone?" Sorcha asked.

"Yes."

As dubious as his mate, Conall stared at her. How could he live with himself if their queen made her final stand alone? Better yet, how could he ever look their king in the eye? "We can't—"

"You must," Anastasia said in a firm voice. "Worry not for me and go. Every second you delay is more time for Maeval to shore up her defenses, and then all of this shall be for naught. She draws her power from the life force of her prisoners. Our loved ones."

"As you wish," Sorcha murmured.

The stench of the moldering ghouls grew closer, and the pale blue lanterns threw ominous shadows down the curving hallway.

He swallowed the lump in his throat, hating the choice ahead of them. "Stars keep you safe, my queen." Conall curled his fingers around Sorcha's wrist and tugged her back.

"And you."

He loathed the idea of leaving their queen as much as his mate, but he respected and understood her choice to make a stand at the outer doors. On their own, it was up to them to bring an end to the battle outside, before they lost everything.

The twisting narrow corridor ended in a large circular chamber deep within the mountain stronghold. Five pillars fashioned from black onyx flowed upward from the stone floor to the diamond ceiling. Four archways sealed with bars made of ice were spaced around the circumference of the room.

Both beautiful and terrifying, the fairy queen Maeval sat upon an ebony throne in the center. Her skin glowed pale as winter frost, contrasted by midnight hair floating around her in an inky cloud. Her bright eyes burned with an inner fire, shifting colors like a crackling flame, blue then purple then gold. A small imp glowered at them from his perch on her shoulder. His skin reminded Sorcha of soot and embers.

"I've been expecting you, little red. You and your mangy wolf. How bold of you to visit my domain after killing my favorite pet." She tsked, clucking her tongue at them.

"You turned Ferghus into a monster," Sorcha said, training her bow on the woman.

"Oh no, dear, he did that to himself. I merely helped him along." Maeval's cold smile revealed sharp teeth behind her red lips. "All I did was give him the means to take the power he desired from the shifters. He took their skins all on his own, but he didn't factor in the price of such magic."

"You beast!"

Sorcha released the arrow on a perfect course for Maeval's heart. The black fae stood unflinching in its path. Inches away from striking its target, the arrow broke on an invisible barrier. Cracks seemed to splinter across the air, a glowing fracture that faded away within seconds.

"My turn."

The dark fae lifted her hands over her head then threw them out toward the pair. Wind howled from her palms, blasting them with cold and ice, pushing them back across the slickening floor. Conall knocked Sorcha to the side and dove after her, bringing them both behind the shelter of a pillar.

"Now, now, are we to play hide and seek?" Maeval crooned. "What if you have no place to hide?"

The pillar exploded over their heads. Stone chunks blasted outward and rained down on them. Sorcha cried out and dropped the arrow she'd clutched in her hand. She drew another from her quiver, leaned around the broken shelter, and fired.

The black fae batted the projectile aside. "Is this the best they could send against me? Is this paltry assault all the stars could deliver? Let me show you true power."

A bulky shape smashed through the bars behind the fairy queen and flew across the room into her waiting grip. The griffin hardly resembled its proud people. Patches of fur were gone from its scarred hide and the feathers had been plucked from its wings.

It slumped to the ground, held upright by the fairy queen framing its beak between her hands. Black threads of energy flowed from the thrashing creature until she'd depleted it entirely. Its feeble resistance ended when it became nothing more than a limp, desiccated husk.

Flush with energy, Maeval gestured with her hands and spoke in a language that hurt Sorcha's ears. Each word dripped with foul magic and stabbed like a knife. The temperature in the room dropped and the air moved, swirling around the chamber and picking up speed with each second.

"I am a force of nature! I am the indomitable winter!" Maeval shouted. "You are only a mortal girl and a mongrel."

Excruciating. Nothing else could describe the flurry of ice shards and cold mist whirling around them. At the epicenter of the storm, Maeval raised her arms and the magical presence intensified.

Flecks of ice cut past Sorcha's cheeks and sliced the leather armor protecting her. Defenseless and without a shield, she cried out and raised one arm to fend off the relentless assault.

They hunkered down behind a pillar, but the maelstrom still battered at them. Although Conall shielded her with his larger bulk, she flinched whenever an ice chip whistled past his brawny arm or shoulder and left a line of blood.

"She's tearing us apart," Sorcha said. "We have to do something. The queen and king won't be able to hold off the armies for long."

Conall tightened his grip on the sword hilt and shifted to the left, peering from behind the icy column. "I'll put an end to this."

"You can't just run in there. She'll rip you to shreds!"

"If I don't, then who will?"

"Conall—"

"I love you, Red. Whatever happens after this, I want you to know I love you more than the sun and the stars. You're my world, everything I've ever wanted and needed. You proved to me humans can be good."

He spoke the words to her desperately, urgency in his voice as if he'd never have the chance to utter them again.

Sorcha wiped her tears with one wrist. "I love you. Be one

Red & the Wolf

with the wind."

Conall shifted and they both abandoned their cover, pushing toward their target from different directions. Sorcha ignored the pain, willing herself to push through the frigid maelstrom. Shards of ice as sharp as thorns sliced past her cheeks then jagged spears erupted from the icy floor. Fist-sized hail pounded down from above.

"Foolish girl, you're no match for me."

Sorcha blocked the first strike from Maeval's staff. The fairy moved swift as a snake, sweeping her weapon first at Sorcha then jabbing it back at Conall. She caught him in the snout and knocked the wolf to the side where he struck the stone column and fell to the ground, unmoving. Conall's pained grunt drew her attention away for a split second.

Droplets of crimson blood froze on the unforgiving current. Her mate's blood.

Maeval used her distraction and slammed her across the room with a dark blast that seemed to suck the very warmth and life from her bones.

Whether from sheer arrogance or apathy, the black fairy turned her attention on Sorcha and laughed, ignoring Conall as if he were already dead. She clenched her fist, and the dark spell anchored to Sorcha's heart stabbed deeper, drawing out a tortured scream. Agony racked her body, scorching through every fiber of her soul. She'd never experienced anything as painful, nothing so awful as Maeval's cruel magic.

"You have been a thorn for too long, little red cape, but no longer. First, I'll drain you to a husk. Then I'll skin your wolf. And then, then I will bring down the high and mighty dragon who dares to think he is above me. Even his ancestor

VIVIENNE SAVAGE

had no chance of defeating me. I have returned stronger than ever!"

Through the tears blurring her vision, Sorcha made out Conall's furred shape rising from the floor. As the wolf leapt through the air, Conall shifted to his human form. He held the star sword with both hands, raised and angled to deliver the killing stroke. Inaudible above the storm winds, it sank into Maeval's back and emerged from her chest. Upon making contact, the cold iron blade erupted in black flames.

The fairy queen's mouth froze in a wide circle, eyes enlarged in shock. The howling winds died.

"No… You can't. Can't."

A spiderweb network of black veins surrounded the entry point of the sword then crawled outward over the rest of her body.

Freed from the spell but frozen in place, Sorcha stared across the room. Maeval's skin dusted over and her body shriveled. Seconds later, she cracked and fell apart into so many pieces of frost and ice shards. The blade disintegrated in Conall's hands, and he fell to one knee as motes of starlight glittered to the ground.

Sorcha crawled to his side and knelt in front of him, afraid to risk physical contact when he bled from so many wounds. His chest heaved and his eyes watered.

"Conall, sweet gods, you're bleeding."

"I'll recover," he breathed out once he snapped out of his daze. "They aren't deep."

True to his words, the most superficial of his injuries sealed as they spoke. She wiped her thumb across a red line on his chest, revealing undamaged skin beneath.

"Thank the stars," she whispered. Then she threw herself into his arms and sobbed in relief.

"Go see to those she took," he said after kissing her brow. "I'll join you in a moment."

In her fear for him, she had briefly forgotten about Maeval's captives. With the dark fae slain for good, the room warmed, and the frosted bars on the cells glistened with trickling water as they melted away.

Shoving aside her fatigue, Sorcha rose and discovered endurance she hadn't known she possessed. She pushed through the exhaustion, the pain, and the horror to rush to the nearest barrier. She smashed through the weakening ice wall to discover a huddled figure by the wall. Frost glittered against the grizzled man's unkempt hair and long beard, but he shook off the icy flecks and blinked his eyes as if waking up from a long sleep. His large, brawny frame made her think he was the missing bear, rather than wolf.

"Lorekeeper Darach?" Sorcha asked. She helped the man to his feet and shivered at his ice-cold touch. Had they all been frozen?

"Aye. What's happened?"

"Maeval is gone, for good this time. You're free."

"Sorcha, your grandmother is over here!" Conall called from the other side of the chamber.

"Go on, lassie, I can make it from this cell on my own," Darach said.

Excusing herself, she rushed from the cell to find her grandmother. Conall carried her from her prison to the center of the room.

"Granny? Granny, it's me, Sorcha."

"I'll get the others," Conall said in a quiet voice, giving her shoulder a squeeze.

Sorcha shrugged out of her red cloak and settled it around her shivering grandmother. Emilia Dunrathi looked at her with wariness at first, but then the distrust faded away and she sagged in relief.

"Is it over?" she croaked in a dry, brittle voice.

"Yes, Granny, it's over. The beast who took you is dead, as is Maeval. They can't hurt us anymore."

"Bless the stars for that, child. I thought I'd never see you again."

Conall returned with the other prisoners. The two shifter men seemed well enough, considering all they'd endured, but the queen's cousin trembled on the verge of tears, until at last, her composure shattered. She huddled into a tight little ball and wept against her knees. Griogair, the wolven lorekeeper, sat beside her and curved an arm around her waist, lending her what comfort and warmth he could.

"I've got you, lass. It's all right. We're all safe now."

"Sorcha! Conall!" The queen burst into the room and looked around with wild eyes. The moment her gaze fell upon her cousin, she sped across the chamber and fell to her knees beside Victoria and Griogair. Ignoring the wolf, Anastasia pulled her cousin into her arms.

"I felt Maeval's death, though it took a moment for her wards to fall," Anastasia said. She looked over Victoria's shoulder toward Sorcha and gave her a grateful smile.

The chamber shuddered around them.

"We shouldn't tarry here," Darach said. The bear stood and sniffed the air. "With the black fae gone, her fortifications will crumble around us.

"What about the red and black imp?" Sorcha asked. "Did anyone else not see the wee blighter?"

"I did," Conall said. "He ran during the heat of battle."

Griogair scooped Victoria up in his arms without further comment and started across the room, Anastasia close behind him.

"I can carry you, Emilia," Conall offered.

"I'm quite capable of walking out."

"Of course, you are," he agreed, "but after your burdens, I think you deserve to rest rather than run."

Emilia stared at him a moment before she snorted and gave a sharp nod. "I like him, Sorcha. Very well, this once I'll allow it."

Sorcha and her mate exchanged grins, then Conall lifted her grandmother and followed the others. As the rumbling increased, their steps hastened, until their entire group was running through the twisting halls. The walls around them cracked and splintered, icy chandeliers crashed to the floor, and it seemed as if the ground itself would give way beneath them.

The moment they broke free from the fortress into the night air, griffins swooped down and plucked them up. Sorcha gazed back at the fortress below her and watched as the entire structure collapsed in on itself.

Epilogue

D AYS OF CELEBRATION ended with the clans splitting to go their own ways as friends. The shifters retreated into the forests and flew away to their aeries, but Sorcha watched her fellow hunters struggle to find purpose.

With no abominations, what were they to do?

For a time, she and Conall had no choice but to separate. Standing beside the clan alpha as his mate would have to wait when she owed loyalty to her people as well. And if he'd abandoned his pack when they needed him most, he wouldn't have been the strong alpha she adored with all her heart.

He traveled with her as far as Frosweik, where they parted ways with promises to be back in one another's arms as soon as possible. Afterward, she reclaimed Eachann from the town stables and joined her family at her grandmother's cabin. While it lacked the space to house the five of them in comfort, it was better than no home at all.

They spent the remainder of the day restoring Emilia's home. Then Sorcha claimed a space on the floor near the hearth and fell asleep the moment she lay down.

Her eyes closed for two seconds, and then it was morning.

"Sorcha," Egan hissed, nudging her awake. "The king is here."

"So?" she mumbled up at him.

"He's plowing the fields. With his claws."

"He's what?" Did royalty never rest?

Sleep-rumpled hair fell into her face as she sat up and crawled from beneath the blankets on the floor. With Maeval gone, the unnatural winter released its hold over the land, allowing spring warmth to return. Snow ceased falling, the ice melted, and the trees budded with new green leaves.

Egan left her alone to dress. After pulling her hair into a quick braid, she rushed through a morning scrub, tugged on leggings and a tunic, then dashed outside to saddle Eachann.

As her brother had said, their dragon king stood in the middle of the field with freshly turned over soil all around him. Alongside him, Anastasia passed baskets of seedlings to a group of local farmers.

Leaving Eachann to graze, she joined the others and was greeted with a warm hug from Anastasia. The king shifted to his human shape and offered the same once his wife released her.

"I'd hoped we'd see you, Sorcha," Alistair said.

"As did I, though with all due respect, I didn't expect to see you farming."

Alistair's handsome grin widened. "These are my people. My lands. Nothing I may do to help restore them is too menial."

"We're flying to each town and homestead, passing out baskets of seeds and doing what we can," Anastasia explained. "But we also wanted to check on our friends. How is your grandmother?"

"Already recovered from her ordeal and full of frightening tales to scare the little ones," Sorcha replied. She smiled and rubbed the back of her neck. "You should see her when she

VIVIENNE SAVAGE

recounts the story to the townsfolk."

Alistair laughed, a deep belly rumble. "I can imagine. The tales have spread far and wide, and we've told a fair share ourselves when asked."

She believed it. All the kingdom would have felt the end of Maeval's magical hold on the land.

"How is your cousin, Anastasia?" she asked. "I didn't have much of a chance to see her after we escaped the tower."

"She's doing well, thank you," the queen said. "Griogair of the wolves has remained with us during his recovery as well, sharing his knowledge of the shifter clans' history with me. I think it comforts her to have him near as they both endured their imprisonment together. He's even nicknamed her Goldilocks."

"I'm glad to hear it. And Teagan?"

"A joy to have around the castle," Alistair answered. "She credits returning home and family as the motivation behind her growing strength. Elspeth adores her great-aunt, and I take comfort in knowing not all my family was lost. That the dragons will not end with my line."

"Perhaps one day the TalDrach line will be as plentiful again as the wolves," Sorcha said.

"Perhaps." His wife placed a hand on his arm, and the great king cleared his throat before blinking away the moisture in his eyes. "To be truthful, we had another reason for our visit today."

Sorcha swung her curious gaze between the two monarchs. "Oh?"

Anastasia's benevolent smile broadened. "We did, yes. An opportunity we wished to offer your family and the other hunters."

The queen spoke no more on the matter until that afternoon when they met with her whole family. Emilia welcomed them into her humble home and offered sweet tea.

"I apologize for the close quarters," Emilia said for at least the fifth time. "This place was never meant for more than myself and my husband, stars watch over his soul."

"We mean to add to it," Aengus said, "but getting the farms set up in town has been our biggest priority. Your aid saved us much work."

"We're happy to help," Anastasia said. "And we have an offer for you."

"So Sorcha said," Margaret said, eyeing her daughter.

"We know how hard it has been for hunters like yourselves to find a place," Alistair began. "We've crossed paths with several others over the past few days."

"Not all of them have even this much to go back to." Anastasia gestured to the room around them. "The towns are already packed with people; that's been a problem from the beginning."

Aengus nodded. "Aye, and why some of us left to become hunters on the road."

"Exactly. But what if there were a place for you? For all of you."

Sorcha perked up. "You're referring to the old cities, aren't you? Like Calbronnoch and Etherling."

"Exactly," Anastasia said, "though Etherling will take a longer while to reclaim from nature, and memories of the war with Dalborough may be too raw. But Calbronnoch is another matter."

"I'd like to see it restored," Alistair told them. "The hunters will have their own city, should they choose to go."

Sorcha turned and looked at her family. "We should do it. We should make Calbronnoch our home. Braeloch is only a day or two away from the city. We'd still be close then when I leave to rejoin Conall."

"But, Sorcha, your gran's life is here," her mother said.

"Aye, my life *was* here," Emilia spoke up, "but recent events have given me the understanding that home is where your family is. I don't need this cabin to remember what I've lost. Calbronnoch seems like a good place to me if it means keeping my family close."

Sorcha abandoned her seat and hugged her grandmother tight.

"It will take weeks to get there with everything we need," Aengus said. "Perhaps even months."

Alistair looked at his wife then back to them and grinned. "Not if you fly."

With the aid of their winged friends, relocating the hunters took as little as two weeks. Alistair flew entire wagons in his claws, and the griffins carried blindfolded livestock. Entire families moved, dazzled by the promise of beginning anew in the historic city.

"It figures the most ostentatious house would be the one to stand all these years," her father grumbled as they stood in the deserted street. He set his fisted hands on his hips and glared balefully at the manor house where she and Conall had lost the star sword.

"We'll make it something new," Margaret told him. "It'd be a shame to waste the building itself."

"Make it the town center," Egan suggested. "A tavern as a common gathering place downstairs. Upstairs we'll have plenty of room for those who need it until homes are built."

Taking Egan's idea to heart, they began with the old manor. A half dozen of the other hunter clans reached the city over the course of several days, and with their arrival came eager laborers and master artisans seeking a new home.

By day, the volunteers cleared debris and the remains of the dead. By night, they all gathered to share meals and tales around the hearth.

Two weeks after their labors began, Sorcha awakened to a piercing howl in the air. She jolted up in bed as several other wolven voices joined the initial cry, and she rushed to the window as dozens of wolves trotted into the square. One of them stood apart from all the others, his auburn coat shimmering like copper beneath the rising sun.

Conall led his pack to the center of town. One by one, wolves became humans who claimed wheelbarrows, shovels, and tools. They dispersed throughout Calbronnoch and joined the restoration efforts.

He'd come for her after all, neither abandoning her or his pack. Conall had done the next best thing and brought them all together. Eager to reunite with him, Sorcha hurried into her clothes. Her bare soles slapped against the wooden floor as she rushed through the cottage. At the door, she came face to face with her mate when he walked up the stepping stone path to the two-story home her mother and father had claimed.

She froze in the doorway, taking in the sight of him in

his red and silver tartan, bare chest scarred from the near-fatal blow dealt by Ferghus's claws. He paused midstride, appearing to be under the same spell.

"Missed you, Red."

Willing her legs to cooperate, she sprinted toward him. They met in the middle. Strong arms surrounded her as the hoots and hollers of spectating wolves cheered from various points around the square.

Unconcerned with their audience, Sorcha rose to tiptoe and kissed her mate. She kissed him for each day they were apart and every moment missed.

"I didn't think I'd see you for months."

Conall grinned down at her. "Did you think I could go that long without seeing you?"

While more wolves arrived and donned their clothing to help, Sorcha led Conall inside and to their kitchen table. Then she crawled into his lap and buried her face against his neck. Hugging him, she breathed in the smell of the woods and the wild scent that lingered against his skin. Her wolf. She remained pressed against him and listening to his powerful heartbeat until he broke the silence.

"We're going to relocate to Braeloch," Conall said. "But first, we're going to help you rebuild Calbronnoch. My father abandoned these people. Maybe he was right to do it, but there were innocents who died here who had no fault in Mum's death. She died doing what she believed was right, and I think... helping here is what she'd want us to do."

Sorcha squeezed his fingers. "Thank you."

"We're glad to do it. Let there be no more enmity between wolves and men. Fighting against Maeval with the lot of you has taught me something valuable, lass. We all bleed red."

"Where's Tink?"

"Outside with the wolves. I asked her for some alone time with you, and she seemed happy enough to give it. Besides, she brought a few friends to help out with things."

When she could finally bear to part from his lap, she hurried around the kitchen to throw together a breakfast for him and her family. Everyone still slept, and they only appeared when the fragrant aroma of cooking eggs and ham summoned them from their beds.

"Conall, you've returned."

Her father clasped his arm and welcomed him with a grin. Then her mother kissed both his cheeks. Emilia repeated the kisses, much to Conall's bashful embarrassment. Even Egan embraced him as a brother. They all sat around the table and dug in to the meal she had prepared.

"We never had the chance to welcome you properly to the family," her father said. "I hope you'll allow us to do so now."

"I've been made to feel more than welcome," Conall assured them. "I know you expected a different son—"

"Ferghus was an arsehole," Egan muttered with a mouthful of eggs. "Her falling in love with you is a bit of a godsend from the stars. Thank the heavens you beat him out. Honest."

"Egan!" Sorcha kicked him beneath the table.

"What? It's true. Didn't I tell you all he was a rotten egg?"

"You stay out of my love life and worry about your own." Egan snorted.

Their father only laughed at them and pushed back from

his seat. "You behave, all of you. Tonight we'll have a celebratory dinner, but for now, I'm off to the farmhouse. We're raising the walls today, if your wolves haven't beaten me to it."

"I'll come help."

"No, you finish breakfast and stay with your wife. She's worked hard but moped without you by her side." Her father winked and headed outside.

"I believe all of us have some work to be doing," Granny said. She collected the plates from the table, leaving dishes in front of Conall and Sorcha only.

"Too right," her mother agreed. "We should get going too, Egan. You and I have to plow the south field."

"But I'm still hungry. Gran took my plate from me before I finished," he protested.

Her mother stuffed a thick cut of bacon into a biscuit then shoved it into Egan's hands. Without a word, she pulled him from the room. Her grandmother departed seconds later, clutching a basket in her wrinkled hands.

Conall's brows dipped together. "Your family is nice."

"I believe they're trying to give us the house to ourselves for a time."

His deep chuckle and the caress of his hand against her breast brought a curling heat to her gut and an ache between her thighs. Conall tipped her head back and took possession of her mouth, delivering a slow kiss that made her heart skip a beat.

She'd missed him. Missed his smiles and his laughter, missed the way he made her body sing with only a touch or a look. Despite all the work needing to be done, she wanted nothing more than to take him to her room, curl up in his arms, and remain there forever.

Conall slipped his arm under her legs and scooped her up, making her wonder if he sensed her thoughts, as if something magical had happened during their bonding in the tent, when they'd made love and declared their hearts eternal to one another.

"Which room is yours, Red?"

"I'm sharing with Egan, upstairs on the left," she mumbled against his mouth. She'd never minded bunking with her twin until now,and was thankful for her grandmother's interference in guiding everyone away.

In the privacy of her temporary bedroom, Conall stripped away her leathers and tunic. She unraveled his kilt, and he loved her with all the tenderness she'd longed to experience anew. Afterward, she dozed in his arms, cheek against his throat while his fingers traced idle gestures across her back.

"As much as I'd like to laze the day away with you, I should show my face." Conall leaned up on one arm and gazed down at her. "Not very good of me to lie about while my pack works."

Sorcha sighed. Regrettable but understandable. She'd have kept him for the entire day if she could. "Yes, I suppose we should."

"Don't worry, Red. Soon we'll have a room of our own and all the time we like."

"I'll hold you to that promise."

They cleaned up and dressed, but she took every opportunity she could to touch and kiss him as they did, until Conall playfully growled and threatened to put her back in bed. She almost took him up on the offer, until cries of wonder from the townsfolk alerted them to a new arrival. Hand in hand, they hurried outside to see a red dragon circling overhead.

Sorcha raised her hand to shade her eyes and smiled.

Conall squinted against the sun. "Is it Teagan? She and Alistair look alike to me from afar."

"No, it's the king. Look, you can see his horns."

They wove through the city streets and joined others on the outskirts where the dragon had lowered. Sorcha spotted her father and tugged Conall over with her as she joined him. A huge pile of stone wrapped in a net too flimsy to carry such a heavy load sat in the center of the field. Enchanted, surely. Their king landed a few feet away and folded his wings in against his body.

How did the shifters appear so stately and regal even in their animal forms?

"The nearby quarry is still rich with material," Alistair announced. "Have your masons tell me how much they need and I will bring more."

"Thank you," Aengus said as he pulled away the netting. He ran his hands over the cut stone then turned his startled gaze on Alistair. "Did you claw this out of the mines?"

The dragon grinned, large fangs glistening in the sunlight. "Maybe. Why? Did I ruin it?"

A grizzled woman with a limp to her step examined the rock and shook her head. "On the contrary, Your Highness, these are the cleanest cuts I've seen. Thank you."

Alistair bowed his horned head. "I've other news as well. I saw over a dozen bears approaching as I flew over. They should be here by sunset to assist with their magical gifts."

"With their assistance, we'll have Calbronnoch restored

to livable conditions again in no time. No one shapes wood or stone better than Clan Arval," Conall said. "They built our wolf den."

A week later, soldiers from Benthwaite—including the desertees from Dalbarough—hauled in carts of lumber. Alistair returned with his wife astride him, and the mesmerized, future citizens of the city watched their queen work her spellcraft, imbuing stone with magical protection.

Proud of her accomplishment and the role she'd played in bringing together the kingdom, Sorcha watched the cooperation of over a dozen clans. When she left, it would all remain in good hands.

Two months after the death of Maeval, the humans completed restoration of Cairn Ocland's most beloved city.

The sight of humans and shifters working alongside one another in peace and cooperation never failed to bring a smile to Sorcha's face. With each day, old alliances revived and new friendships flourished.

What had once been a dismal ruin, a ghost city filled with the skeletal remnants of five hundred unfortunate Oclanders, became a beautiful marvel of art. Calbronnoch transformed as their coalition of shifters and humans erected new buildings to replace the fallen and cleared the streets of debris.

Crops grew in the fields beyond the walls and flowers bloomed in every garden. They had the fae to thank for that. Tink and her woodkin friends, eager to thank them for destroying Maeval, blessed the fields with magic. Orchards sprang up overnight while rows of summer vegetables thrived

VIVIENNE SAVAGE

despite the spring season. And with the completion of the city came the time for Sorcha to leave. It was upon her before she could prepare herself for parting from her parents for the last time. Standing on the edge of the upper floor balcony, she leaned with her arms on the rail and gazed over the city.

They'd accomplished so much in so little time.

Conall moved up beside her and wrapped his arm around her waist. "Your parents will lead this city well."

"I'll never forget Father's face when they all chose him." She laughed at the memory. "But yes, I think you're right. And us?"

"Clan TalWolthe will honor the peace. What's more, we'll uphold and defend it, as we did in the past."

"Last time I left my family, it was to embark on an adventure for our queen. I'd never parted from them before, but I knew I'd return to our wagon. Now I'm leaving for another adventure."

"The greatest adventure of all," Conall agreed. "As my wife, my equal, and the mother alpha of our clan. No one could deserve it more than you, Red." He buried his face in her dark hair. "Your loved ones won't be far, lass. They'll always be welcome in Braeloch."

"I know." She leaned into him. "It's different, is all. Knowing I'm leaving our home together and walking away to build my own."

"Are you happy?"

"I am." She had never been happier, and she looked forward to the coming days, knowing Conall would be at her side.

Overhead, rainbow streaks shot across the evening sky,

a sparkling shower that seemed to encompass all of Cairn Ocland, as if the stars themselves were celebrating with them.

The End

VIVIENNE SAVAGE

About the Author

Vivienne Savage is a resident of a small town in rural Texas. Over a cup of tea, she concocts sexy ways for shapeshifters and humans to find their match.

To get on Vivienne's mailing list for news and upates, go online and visit http://viviennesavage.com/newsletter

Made in the USA
Coppell, TX
05 March 2020

16521781R00164